W9-CFG-459

The House
by the Lake

Center Point
Large Print

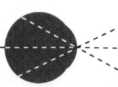

The House by the Lake

ELLA CAREY

CENTER POINT LARGE PRINT
THORNDIKE, MAINE

This Center Point Large Print edition
is published in the year 2017 by arrangement with
Amazon Publishing, www.apub.com.

This is a work of fiction.
Names, characters, organizations, places,
events, and incidents are either products of the
author's imagination or are used fictitiously.

The text of this Large Print edition is unabridged.
In other aspects, this book may vary
from the original edition.
Printed in the United States of America
on permanent paper.
Set in 16-point Times New Roman type.

ISBN: 978-1-68324-604-6

Library of Congress Cataloging-in-Publication Data

Names: Carey, Ella, author.
Title: The house by the lake / Ella Carey.
Description: Center Point Large Print edition. | Thorndike, Maine :
    Center Point Large Print, 2017.
Identifiers: LCCN 2017041313 | ISBN 9781683246046
    (hardcover : alk. paper)
Subjects: LCSH: Germany—Fiction. | Inheritance and succession—
    Fiction. | Large type books. | GSAFD: Mystery fiction.
Classification: LCC PR9619.4.C367 H68 2017 | DDC 823.920151—dc23
LC record available at https://lccn.loc.gov/2017041313

CHAPTER ONE

San Francisco, 2010

The decision was made in the Italian Café on Chestnut Street. Afterward, Anna wondered if she had any say in it at all. Everything beyond the table in the window had become one inextricable whirl. There was only one thing Anna was sure of: change was coming, and fast.

Her mind bounded with questions, but one stood out among the others. Why today? Why this morning?

Anna had woken at the usual time, thrown on her standard black work outfit and one of her mother's favorite scarves, hand watered her garden, removed dead leaves from her roses, even paid a few bills before heading out the door. There was nothing unusual in that.

Now shoppers with wicker baskets over their arms strolled up and down the sidewalk outside the window. Saturday morning traffic sat at a standstill in the busy street. Anna could only stare and stare at her ninety-four-year-old grandfather, Max. It was impossible to know what to say.

If anyone had asked Anna whether she thought her grandfather was capable of the revelation he had just made, she would have told them that they were mad. He had been the greatest source of consistency and love in all her twenty-nine years. She was devoted to him—and always had been.

She had tried countless times to get him to talk about the past. And countless times he had refused. It was a no-go zone. Now Anna knew not to touch it. Anna knew not to ask. She had no idea what had happened to make him never, ever want to talk about it.

One day she had found him in his apartment, snipping up photographs that he said were from his childhood. He was going to burn them all up. Anna had not known that he owned any photos at all until then.

And then Max had looked up and asked about Anna's day. As usual. Diversion. Away from him. And definitely away from his childhood, his youth, in the former East Germany. All she knew was that his family had been forced to escape at the time of the Soviet invasion, that Max had never returned, and that he never, ever wanted to talk about it. His past had always loomed in Anna's imagination, and yet it repelled her too— she found it too confusing so left it, out of respect and love for Max.

This morning, Anna had left the glass counter

that ran the length of one wall of the café as soon as she saw Max walking up the street. She had made her way past all her customers, who were lined up for her thirty-four varieties of sandwiches, her Parma hams, and her Italian cheese selections—Rocca Reggiano, Parmigiano, Locatelli Pecorinos, and Dry Jacks—all of which had garnered her something of a reputation in Pacific Heights, indeed, throughout the whole of San Francisco. She continued past the second line that had formed for her artisan breads and delectable cakes.

Anna had amassed a loyal following that came back again and again for the magical blend of coffee that she had perfected. Her Italian Café was scented with it, along with spices, garlic, and hints of red wine. Anna's customers often told her that if they closed their eyes, they could imagine they were in Rome.

Anna had placed one of her small black reserved signs on her grandfather's table an hour before he was due to arrive. If she did not reserve his seat, someone would settle down to read the Saturday newspapers and not budge for hours.

When Anna held the door wide to allow him to enter, every other table was full. The counter staff were in nonstop motion and the café was abuzz with refreshing weekend chatter. Anna led Max through the melee, one hand guiding his thin arm. Then she settled him into place and made sure his chair was in exactly the right position before going to prepare his coffee.

Cass, Anna's business partner, appeared at her side. "Mind if I join you today? I am so in need of some Max time."

"Well." Anna pulled off her black apron. She grinned at Cass. "Perhaps you need a 1930s man. Now that's an idea. You could always go back in time."

"If only," Cass said. Several curls had escaped from her attempt to confine them in a bun. Today her hair was red. The following week it could be purple. Whatever week it was, Cass hoped to meet a man.

Anna was grateful for every week that she did not.

She took Max's soft almond-meal biscuit out of a glass jar and placed it on a plate. She sensed Cass watching her. A drop-dead gorgeous man had just walked into the café. He looked as if he worked out at the gym full-time, and his white T-shirt showed off the loveliest of biceps.

"Forget it," Anna muttered, swiping a look at her friend.

"It is becoming a bit ridiculous, Anna," Cass said in a whisper. "Six years? It's a very long time."

"Watch me." Anna smiled at the woman standing at the front of the line.

Ten minutes later, Anna kissed her grandfather

on the cheek, sat down with him and Cass, leaned back in her chair, and stretched her tired legs out in front of her. She inspected the black pumps that she wore every day. They were polished; they looked fine. She tugged at the pencil skirt that she wore under her black apron; it had risen a little under her black top. Her long dark hair was pulled back into a ponytail, highlighting her almond-shaped brown eyes.

"I brought this." Max pushed a newspaper article across the table toward her.

Cass leaned in toward Anna, reading over her shoulder. "A Belle Époque apartment in Paris that was abandoned for seventy years? How intriguing. Imagine the ghosts!"

Anna frowned at the photographs before her. A faded Mickey Mouse plush toy was propped up against a stuffed ostrich with a patterned shawl draped over its poor stiff back. There was a photograph of a sitting room, wallpaper peeling off in long strips. Yet another showed an antique dressing table complete with cut-glass bottles containing the remnants of some ancient perfume.

But Anna couldn't take her eyes off the very last photo. It was a painting of a woman. Her dark hair was tousled and her face turned to the side. Though elegant and beautiful, she also had a touch of the erotic about her. Her dress had been painted with such feather-like brushstrokes that she seemed ethereal and not of this world.

"The apartment was . . . ," Max began, then paused. "Full of beauty once." There was an old Hollywood quality to his voice that blended with his slight European accent. It lent gravitas to almost everything he said.

Max meant, of course, that the apartment *must* have been beautiful once. Anna smiled at him, adopting the sort of expression that she often took these days with her grandfather. Inside, she felt a twinge of sadness at his advancing age.

"You see, this is why I want to go to Paris," Cass said. "This sort of thing never happens here. If I could get Anna there, maybe I could find her a man. It's exactly what she needs. Don't you think so, Max?"

"A vacation could be wonderful," Max said. "If Anna would ever allow herself to let go of the past."

Anna almost choked on her coffee. "Excuse me—I am in the room!" But she was laughing.

Max appeared to be thinking.

The only thing to do was wait.

"Anna, darling. I haven't asked you to do anything for me in a while."

"If, by that, you mean *never* . . ."

"Don't speak too soon," he said, his voice softer now. It was easy to picture him as he had once been—glamorous, young, his fair hair swept back, showing off his sparkling blue eyes. Anna's grandmother had kept her wedding photograph on the chest of drawers in her home. Anna had often picked it up as a child, turning it over in her hands.

Cass scrutinized him. "What is it, Max?"

"Anna, you have never been to Berlin," he said.

"No." A knot formed in her stomach.

Max leaned down and pulled a piece of paper out of the leather bag on the floor by his feet. Even Cass stayed silent as he opened what was clearly an old map and laid it across the table, spreading it carefully with his gnarled fingers. Anna stacked the empty coffee cups and plates to one side; she hardly noticed when a staff member appeared and took them all away.

A neat interior plan of a building covered the yellowing paper. Anna ran her eyes over the rows of rooms, all lined up in sepia ink. A faded drawing of what was clearly the building featured on the map was sketched into the background. Elegant turrets and pretty French windows hinted at beauty beneath the more prosaic diagram.

Anna stared at Max.

"Schloss Siegel," Max said, his eyes meeting hers.

"Oh, my." Cass leaned in toward the old paper, smoothing the parchment with her fingertips. "Did you pick this up in an antique shop, Max?"

"Not exactly."

Anna stayed silent.

Max inclined his head and pushed the paper toward her, inviting her to have a proper look. Anna studied the drawing: there was an enormous entrance hall on the ground floor. A set of double doors gave way to a room labeled "music salon," which, in turn, led out to a terrace overlooking a park with its own lake.

The rooms leading out from the entrance hall were all labeled in the same handwriting: smoking room, billiard room, library, ladies' room, guest bedrooms, small and large dining rooms, estate offices, footmen's rooms, individual rooms for the valets, even one for the silverware. The second floor housed several large bedrooms above the salon and corridors that led to smaller rooms labeled "maids."

"I left something there, you see," Max said.

Anna looked up. Her eyes caught Max's.

"Something valuable," he went on.

"Sorry?" Anna whispered.

"You heard me, darling. It was . . . another life."

Max had always been open about his life in the States—how he had wound up in San Francisco in the 1950s, earned a degree in economics, worked hard to build up an investment company of his own. He had married Anna's American grandmother, Jean, and they had had what looked like a tolerable marriage. Max had not spoken of her since she died. But it was what Anna had seen growing up—and it was the last thing she wanted for herself.

"Anna." Max sounded like his gentle self, but there was something firm in his voice.

Anna wanted to stand up. She pushed her chair back to do so, then pulled it forward again. Everything in her life was going so smoothly these days. The unsettled feeling that had coiled into her system became more pronounced.

"It's your family too, Anna."

Anna inhaled deeply.

"Two hours northeast of Berlin. The old Brandenburg—Prussia. Forests, lakes." He paused. "So beautiful—my old home."

Anna's gaze returned to the map, her eyes roaming faster now: twenty-six rooms on the first floor; twenty-four on the second; stairs leading down to another floor, with an arrow marked kitchens and scullery—no basement, but several attic spaces. So. Four floors. Anna's brain always retreated into numbers when she was overwhelmed. Logic never let her down—and most importantly, it was always, always there.

"I want you to go back there for me, Anna. I want you to find what I left behind."

He wanted her to go there? To this house by the lake, this—Schloss, he had called it?

"Oh, my." Cass sat back in her chair and let out one of her customary whistles. "I told you I needed a dose of Max. Didn't you hear me say that? You romantic, you." She leaned in toward him. "What do you want her to do? Tell us! This is exactly what Anna needs, you know. You are clever."

Anna shook her head. "Sorry. I'm not following you. You want me to go to Germany? To retrieve something you left—when?"

"Nineteen forty. June. I was in a bit of a rush."

Anna sat back in her seat.

"The best things in life are mad, you know, darling. Instinctive," he said. "You don't understand that yet . . . but, in time, you will. That's where the magic lies. And that, my darling, is what you are lacking in your life."

"What?" Anna didn't know what to say. Max never spoke like this. She had never heard such urgency in his voice.

"That is so true!" Cass rapped her fist on the table. "Bravo, Max! That's exactly right."

Anna shook her head. "Hang on. You're telling me that you grew up in a palace in the former East Germany, and that you want me to go there, on my own, to search for something that you left there seventy years ago? Did I hear you right?"

Max held her gaze.

It was all the confirmation she needed.

"But decades of people will have passed through the Schloss—the Soviets probably used it for military operations, or a hospital. A family

14

must be living there now. Grandfather, surely you know that there is no chance that whatever it is you left there will still be there. I'd hate to see you disappointed. Not now. And I'm just reeling from this." She stared at the map once more.

There was a silence.

"There's a strong chance it will still be there," he said, finally.

"Oh, come on, Anna!" Cass stood up. "You can't just not go!"

"I can't just run off to Berlin!" She turned to her grandfather. "And I don't like leaving you alone. What gave you this mad idea anyway? The abandoned apartment in Paris? Because that is clearly a freakish situation. You can't expect your . . . stuff . . . to be sitting there too, untouched after all these years."

Max leaned his forearms on the table.

Anna sighed. "I have questions. So many questions, Grandfather. First, what is it that you want me to retrieve? Second, couldn't we just write to the owners and ask them to send whatever it is you want back? Surely we could find a simpler way to do this. And third, we need to talk about this. Please."

"You could go away for months and the business would be fine," Cass said. "I can run everything for both of us. It runs like a Swiss train."

"A conspiracy then."

"No, it's not." Cass and Max spoke at once.

Anna's fingers wanted to trace their way over every detail and run over every room on that map in front of her eyes. Her mind wanted to imagine the entire place—set it out. A palace? Who lived there now? What must her grandfather's childhood have been like? It was what she had always wanted to know, but she needed to talk to him properly. She didn't want these vague hints. Asking her to go and get something? What was that? Why now?

"We'll have to talk about this later," she said, but she said it with kindness. She simply had to return to work. Frustration at this blended with an urgent desire to know everything.

When Max answered, he sounded firm. "I know you're interested in going, Anna. And if there's one thing I've learned in this life, it's that you should trust your instincts. Believe me, I've learned that the hard way. And you shouldn't push things—opportunities—away. Not when every bone in your body tells you that you want to do them. Don't let fear stop you from being happy."

Anna stared at him again. What on earth was that about? This was not her Max! All she could do was shake her head.

Raised voices could be heard at the counter. A difficult customer was berating one of the staff. Anna stood up.

"Later," she said to her grandfather. She leaned down and kissed him on the cheek.

Max was in his favorite armchair when Anna let herself into his flat that evening. She had forced herself to concentrate on work all afternoon, but her mind had been swirling the entire time.

Anna wanted the key to Max's past. She had wanted to know about it for years. But how was she supposed to deal with the logistics of his request? Something hidden somewhere in his childhood home? What was he thinking?

She had tried to sneak a look on the Internet between busy periods at the café that afternoon. It had taken her only a few seconds to find some old pictures of the palace online, taken back when Max's family owned it. She only just managed to tear herself away from the images of the beautiful old building when she had to return to work, but the black-and-white photographs had lingered in her mind long after she had shut down her computer.

The old photos were more than evocative. They were stunning, drawing her in and making her feel the mystery of her grandfather's childhood more than ever before. Despite its opulent details—turrets and rows of dormer windows—it looked less like a palace than a home.

The only information that she could find online told her that Schloss Siegel had belonged to the

17

Albrecht family until the Soviet occupation. There was nothing more. Not a scrap. Did anyone live there? Anna had done a search for hotels in the region. Nothing. Museums? It was not a museum either.

She kissed her grandfather on the top of his head and made her way through Max's small living room, opening the paper bag that she had packed for his evening meal. She pulled out a container of lasagna, a salad, and a slice of the special caramel apple cake that she would warm for his dessert. She kept an eye on Max as she busied herself warming up his meal in his modern kitchen. He had the article about the apartment in Paris on the small glass coffee table in front of him, along with his map.

"Another busy day," Anna said, sensing that this was not the moment to barrage him with questions. She placed the lasagna and the salad on one of Max's new white plates and brought it over to him. Anna sat opposite him on the sofa that he had bought just a few years earlier when he had moved into this small, chic apartment. He always kept his surroundings meticulously up to date. He always threw out anything that was the tiniest bit old—relentlessly culling furniture, clothes, books, even selling the odd painting now and then, because, as he always said, Anna would not want any of his old rubbish when he was gone. That was why the sight of him with his childhood photographs had more than unsettled her.

"Best way to be, darling." Max began eating. "Busy."

It wasn't until he had finished his food and wiped his still-elegant hands—aristocratic hands, Anna suddenly thought—with his napkin that he turned to face her.

"Are you happy, Anna?"

What sort of a question was this?

"No plans to change a thing," she said.

"I would hate to see you—give up on love."

"Oh, let's stop going there. Honestly." Anna started to tidy his plate, but he reached out his hand and tugged at her sleeve.

"Sit down again, my dear. I want to talk to you."

He wanted to talk? The Max she knew would never have spoken like that.

"What is all this?" She kept her words gentle.

Max seemed to think for a while. "I have a regret." His mouth was set. "It's to do with that apartment in Paris."

The apartment in Paris.

"You know, seeing these pictures, after all this time . . ." He pointed at the haunting photos. "Seeing these photographs has brought it all back. It seems as if it happened, oh, I don't know, a month ago, perhaps. I can still see it. I don't know. I think regret is the saddest thing we can have in this life. It's what we miss out on, what we don't do . . . that causes the worst sort of pain. Because you never will know what might have been. The chances we didn't take. How different our lives may have turned out . . . if we had made different choices. We will never know if we don't do them, if we don't act."

"Do you really have such strong regrets?"

He tugged at the map of Schloss Siegel, his hands shaking now.

Anna helped him to spread out the faded paper.

"Here"—his hand, blue with a tracery of veins, tracked its way across the top floor of the Schloss—"was my bedroom."

His fingers lingered at the room to the right of the two large rooms directly above the music salon. Though slightly smaller than the two central rooms, it was still substantial compared with those bedrooms that housed the servants. The room next to Max's was marked "nurse" in neat italics, the one after that, "governess."

"I need you to search under the floorboards in my old room," Max said. He sounded matter-of-fact, like he'd asked her to do something as simple as go into the next room to get his newspaper.

"The floorboards?"

"Yes."

If he hadn't looked so earnest, Anna would have said Max was unwell. Two bright spots of color bloomed on his pale cheeks, and he suddenly looked more animated than he had in years.

"You have to tell me. More. Please."

Max leaned across to her and laid his hand over her own. "Anna," he said.

Anna didn't move. "Please." It was whisper-soft now. She wanted to know what this had to do with that apartment in Paris. She wanted to know what he had left in his bedroom. And most of all, she wanted to know what ill-fated thing it was that he would always regret.

But his gaze was gauzy now. Max wasn't with her. He wasn't here. He was somewhere else. While she watched him, one thing became clear to Anna. Max may never have talked about it, but he had not left everything behind.

Paris, 1934

Isabelle de Florian's grandmother Marthe was in her favorite spot by the window when Isabelle returned to the apartment on Rue Blanche.

Marthe had arranged to have her infamous chaise longue moved to her personal sitting room. From this elegant yet naughty piece of furniture she could keep track of every occurrence in the street below. Although the ninth arrondissement was nothing like it had once been, Isabelle knew that gazing at the theater across the road afforded her grandmother some amusement in her seventies. Today Marthe looked as if she was in need of attention.

"I'm not in the mood to talk, unfortunately." Isabelle dropped the two small shopping bags from the department store Printemps down at Marthe's feet.

"What a bore. Something nice, I hope?"

"Only a couple of scarves."

There was a silence. Isabelle was aware that her grandmother was studying her, wanting to know what had transpired that afternoon, but she was still too upset to talk about it.

She moved across to her piano and picked out a few opening notes before becoming absorbed by the music as she always did. She allowed Satie's notes to soothe her, to sweep her into another realm far beyond Paris. She was nineteen. Wasn't that supposed to be exciting?

Isabelle finished the piece and rested her hands just above the keyboard for those crucial few seconds before she turned on the piano stool to face Marthe—and reality.

"It did not go well, then. Or it did not go as you hoped, which amounts to the same thing," Marthe said, fixing her gaze on Isabelle.

Isabelle stood up. Her tea dress with the tiny flowers and gathers below the bust—which she had put on with such anticipation a few hours earlier—seemed dull now.

"Oh, it was fine." It was easier to lie. It was no one's fault. No one but society's, Isabelle supposed. But it hadn't been fine. Not at all.

The fact that Madame Fatouche, Isabelle's latest beau's maman, had chosen the tearoom in Printemps had been a hopeful sign. Decorated in the modernist style with geometric-patterned carpets and trendy tubular furniture, it was not an old-fashioned sort of place.

And it had seemed reasonable to hope that Madame Fatouche would be as modern in her outlook as she was in her choice of cafés—accepting of a girl who happened to be the granddaughter of the once-infamous courtesan Marthe de Florian.

This was the 1930s, for goodness' sake. Everyone had been through the war. And the question of birthright had been blown apart by revolutions. Russia. Surely . . .

Madame had chosen a table opposite the entrance of the tearoom, from which she could observe Isabelle as she rushed in—late—having become distracted by some beautiful ribbons.

By the looks of it, Pierre Fatouche was chatting away with enthusiasm—even if a little fast. Isabelle pushed away the thought that her beau could be afflicted by a case of nerves. Surely he had no reason to be nervous.

Pierre's mother appeared to be ignoring him. Her gaze was directed straight at Isabelle.

"Ah, here she is!" Pierre stood up, leaned forward, and kissed Isabelle on the cheek. She felt the appraising sweep of his pale eyes up and down her thin dress as he lit a cigarette.

Was the fabric see-through? Had she chosen an inappropriate outfit? But no. It was quite modern. Modern and fashionable were exactly right for Printemps. And Madame's dress was similar in style to Isabelle's, after all. The older woman's up-to-the-minute snakeskin handbag perched on the table. Isabelle found herself envying the older woman's sense of propriety and entitlement.

Madame held out a hand. She revealed her white teeth for a glimpse of a second, before she closed her perfectly lipsticked mouth and rested her hand back on the table.

"Maman . . . ," Pierre began.

"My maman saw your grandmother act in a play during the nineties. In the Pigalle. Marthe de Florian was her stage name, as well as the name she used for . . . everything else, wasn't it?" Madame drew the words out slowly and ignored her son.

Isabelle just smiled and smiled.

The afternoon was over before it had begun.

Marthe stayed quiet while Isabelle recounted her story. Isabelle ran her fingers over the piano keys.

"Stop that for a moment, darling," Marthe said quietly. "I have been thinking."

"There's nothing anyone can do. No one's fault."

"Are you sure that it's a man that you want, Isabelle? Because I can tell you, it is not the answer."

Isabelle waited for a moment. "Is there something wrong with wanting love? You know, I have never understood that part of you, Grandmère—" Isabelle stopped herself. What choice had her grandmother ever had?

Marthe pulled herself up out of the chaise longue, and Isabelle went to help her. She admired her grandmother's upright carriage, her slim figure, that elusive quality in her deep brown eyes that had beguiled countless powerful men. Marthe had a collection of jewelry that would rival that of any duchess, and her apartment was filled with exotic gifts, furniture, and artworks that were the envy of everyone who entered her salon. Once, Isabelle's grandmother had been the ultimate Parisian woman. Where she led, others followed.

And yet, like that of the few other courtesans who had made it, Marthe's existence could never be openly acknowledged. Not in proper circles. Not in respectable society.

So where did that leave her granddaughter?

Isabelle sighed. There was no harm in listening

to what her grandmother had to say. "What have you been thinking?"

"It's Paris that's the problem, not you." Marthe moved across to the small walnut writing desk that some man or another—one of her benefactors, as she called them—had given her thirty years earlier. She shuffled some papers around, then handed a brochure to Isabelle.

"Lake Geneva?"

"For the summer."

"Just you and I?"

"Just you and I."

Isabelle studied the photographs in front of her—a fairy-tale hotel overlooking the most enticing blue water imaginable. A wide terrace adorned with bougainvillea and roses. Tables alight with tea candles and elegant people dancing in each other's arms.

Bother Madame Fatouche and her fastidious ways. "Why ever not?" Isabelle said.

Marthe moved forward and hugged her.

CHAPTER TWO

Vineyards carpeted the hillside—water droplets lingered on vivid green leaves, glistening and sparkling in the afternoon sun. Isabelle leaned over the wrought iron balcony outside her sumptuous hotel room. After a few dreamy moments, she turned her attention to the yachts that bobbed about on the lake and to the mountains beyond.

Her gaze drifted from the natural beauty in the distance to the scene just beneath her window. Groups of elegant people sat on the terrace, indulging in a late afternoon tea of patisseries, Swiss chocolates, coffee, and champagne. The men's pale hats shaded their faces as they chatted with beautifully dressed women who lounged gracefully in cream-colored dresses.

"Do go down and enjoy yourself," Marthe said, appearing on the balcony, having finished supervising the unpacking in her own room. "I am going to rest for a while after all that travelling! We have a full summer ahead to enjoy. I do hope all this relaxation is not going to be too exhausting for me."

Isabelle turned to her grandmother. "You've

never taken a proper holiday, Grand-mère. Vacations were never part of your life, were they?"

"I grant you that." Marthe sat down in a wicker chair. "Maybe I shall make a point of changing things. I have the perfect excuse now. You."

"I don't want you to feel you have to leave Paris on my account." Isabelle picked up her hat, tucked it over her dark curls, and smiled. "But, it's only taken me one day here to realize that even Paris is only a small drop in a vast sea. A pearl, no doubt—but not the entire oyster."

"Stop philosophizing. Go and explore!" Marthe waved her away.

"I shan't be long."

"Take as long as you like. I'm not much company for you, I'm afraid."

Isabelle gave her grandmother a kiss. "No one could ever accuse you of being dull, Grand-mère."

"They never used to."

Isabelle made her way down the hotel's grand central staircase to the salon. Wooden ceiling fans flitted above the artfully arranged wicker tables on the black-and-white-tiled floor. Potted palms gave the room the feeling of a conservatory. She moved toward the French doors that led to the terrace.

Here, Isabelle hesitated. Everyone looked so at home. Young men smoked, their eyes narrowed as they gazed upon the women. Suddenly that all-too-familiar feeling of insecurity ran through her—she was an interloper and always would be. She didn't belong in this sophisticated world. But if she was not part of all this, then where was she supposed to be?

Isabelle adored her grandmother, who raised her after she had been cast aside by her mother's family when her father, Marthe's son Henry, died. But the name Marthe de Florian preceded her wherever she went. Would she always linger on the outskirts? It was impossible to imagine anything else.

Isabelle walked onto the terrace and moved to the low, pale stone wall that overlooked the water. A row of wooden seats ran along it. She sat down, if only to obscure herself from the gaze of the other guests. But another young girl was there too—alone—a few feet down from her.

The girl looked a little older than Isabelle's nineteen and had striking white-blond hair. To Isabelle's surprise, her companion in solitude was staring right back at her. There was not a hint of shyness in her manner, but there was no friendliness either. Isabelle ventured a smile.

"It is a beautiful afternoon," she said, in English.

"It certainly is." The girl's accent was not French. But her English seemed confident, assured.

"You are here for the summer?"

"Yes."

Isabelle laid her hands in her lap. "I . . . am looking forward to finding my way around."

"You are here with your family?"

"Just my grandmother. I'm Isabelle. Isabelle de Florian."

The fair girl stood up. She was tall. Her elegant dress was made of pale oyster silk gathered below her breasts. The entire effect—her hair, her blue eyes, and the dress—was almost dazzling in the sunlight.

"I came here for some privacy. You will please excuse me."

Isabelle felt herself flush.

But then, after a moment's hesitation, the girl extended a gloved hand. "Nadja Albrecht."

"Hello, Nadja."

"No doubt we will see you about the hotel." Nadja still sounded superior. "I wish you a peaceful stay." There was an emphasis on the word peaceful.

"Thank you," Isabelle said, just as Nadja turned to sashay her way back into the hotel. The girl was clearly not easily intimidated, but did she have no desire to be liked?

It seemed simpler not to discuss this interlude with Marthe.

Several hours later, Isabelle took extra care with her appearance as she prepared for dinner.

Her toilette was both a distraction and a tonic for her soul. She could reflect when she was alone. She could face up to things and not have to pretend. Not have to act. Isabelle was relieved to be out of Paris—perhaps she was more hopeful than she had been for a long time. But she was still a little nervous. If she calculated the number of beaus' families who had rejected her, she would resign herself to becoming a governess. What alternative did she have? She had to do something with her life, but it seemed that she had little control over any of it.

At eight o'clock, Isabelle followed Marthe and the maître d'hôtel past the tables on the terrace, which gleamed with silverware and crystal. Candles flickered in the warm air, filling the restaurant with dashes of sparkling light. Couples and small groups talked in hushed, intimate voices. The waiter stopped at a table for two, took Marthe's cape, and pulled back their chairs.

Isabelle ran a hand over her silk dress.

"You look beautiful, my darling." Marthe smiled.

"Well, thank you," Isabelle said. But then she felt herself blanch as the German girl and a group of ethereal young blond people sat down at the table next to theirs.

Nadja was dressed in pale pink—silk too. Her

31

fair hair was gathered at the nape of her neck. Isabelle could smell the delicate scent of the other girl's perfume from where she sat.

A jazz band started to play.

Nadja had seen her—Isabelle was sure of it—but she hadn't greeted her. Isabelle didn't want to stare, but it was hard not to glance at the other table every now and then.

"What a charming place," Marthe said.

"Yes."

A young man sat next to Nadja. His blond hair was combed neatly off his face, highlighting his blue eyes. Two boys who looked no more than about sixteen sat next to him. A redheaded girl dressed in deep green completed the party.

When people began dancing on the terrace, Isabelle seized her opportunity. "You must be tired, Grand-mère. Shall we go back upstairs?"

"Certainly not." Marthe began to sway her shoulders in time with the lilting jazz. "We are not a couple of spinsters, you know."

The party at the table next to theirs stood up, and Isabelle breathed a sigh of relief as she watched them move to the dance floor. She had felt awkward while they were sitting close by.

"I want to stay and watch the dancing," Marthe insisted.

Isabelle folded her napkin and put it on her plate. "I'm tired—"

"Spinster, Isabelle?"

"Not in the mood to dance."

"How are you planning on meeting anyone?"

Isabelle stayed silent.

"I didn't come all this way so that you could hide in a corner. You are full of contradictions. What is wrong with you?"

"There is nothing wrong with me. I just might like to spend the summer catching up on my reading. We can visit the local villages together. I could take up a hobby." Why had she been mad enough to think that geography would make any difference in how they were perceived? No matter where she was, she did not fit in. And her grandmother was right. She was fighting contradictions. She knew what she wanted, but she couldn't have it. So wasn't it better to simply avoid the problem and do something else instead?

"A hobby?" Marthe pushed back her chair with such violence that two waiters appeared at her side. "Very well—I am fine," she said, batting the men away.

Isabelle averted her gaze. Marthe seemed determined to cause a spectacle.

"If nobody asks you to dance, then you shall not have to dance," Marthe said, her voice like steel wool on wood. "But if someone asks, for heaven's sake go and enjoy yourself. Don't shut yourself off just because of the way things were in Paris."

"I will watch for a little while," Isabelle said. "But only to please you."

"Honestly, Isabelle. You make absolutely no sense to me at all."

By the time they had made their way across the restaurant, most of the hotel guests were dancing by the lake. A waiter escorted them to a table on the edge of the dance floor and introduced them to two elderly women.

Marthe began a loud and irritating conversation about modern waiters in English with the two older women, and after a few minutes Isabelle found herself inclined to go for a walk.

The low wall where she had sat that afternoon was dotted with lamps tonight, and the moon cut an incandescent streak of light straight along the surface of the dark lake, widening where it met the hotel landing.

Isabelle traced her fingers along the top of the wall, allowing the warmth that the stone had absorbed during the day to linger on her fingers and then seep into her hand.

"I couldn't help but notice you. Are you travelling alone with your grandmother?" asked a voice from behind her—a male one—in French.

Isabelle turned, slowly, deliberately so. She knew who was standing there.

"Nadja told me she met you." The look in his eyes was warm. "Was she rude to you?"

"Of course not."

"I also couldn't help but notice that you were over here alone. Everyone at my table has someone to talk to. Mademoiselle de Florian, is it?"

His voice was gentle, deep.

"Isabelle."

"I'm Max Albrecht," the young man said. "Fortunately—or not—I'm Nadja's brother."

Isabelle extended her hand, and he held it for a moment.

"Every night has been like this, you know. Stunning." He stared out at the lake. "I'd ask you to go for a walk with me, but I presume your grandmother would—"

"Throw me into your arms, most probably," Isabelle finished.

"You don't want to be thrown."

It seemed necessary to explain. "I think she just wants me to enjoy myself. But fun is always so short-lived. I'm bored with it." For some reason, Isabelle wanted to challenge this young man—but on the other hand, he seemed genuine. Friendly. She dug her teeth into her bottom lip.

"Perhaps now and again you could follow her advice?" Max's voice was velvety, and he felt close, even though he stood a respectable distance away.

"I don't see the point."

He tilted his head to one side, watching her.

"Tell you what. Are you by any chance free tomorrow?"

"Tomorrow?"

"We're going out for the day. For a boating party on the lake. Nothing formal. Nadja, her friend Sascha, and my younger twin brothers, Didi and Jo—and me."

"Would they welcome a stranger?"

"But you're not a stranger now, are you?"

Isabelle gazed at her grandmother. Marthe seemed to be engaged in an engrossing conversation with the other two women.

Isabelle turned back to the man standing before her. "Well," she said. "It would probably please my grandmother."

"Excellent. I'll take that as a yes. We're meeting at the landing at half past ten."

Isabelle smiled and her gaze caught Max's, just for a second. She could not decide which was more powerful—the desire to keep staring into his eyes, or the impulse to turn away.

San Francisco, 2010

Anna lugged her suitcase through her living room to the front door, eyeing things as she made her way through the house. The soft cushions on her dove-gray sofas were arranged just as she liked them, and she'd left her favorite books on the coffee table. If only she had the time to read. She had scrubbed the black-and-white tiles in the bathroom the night before, polished the round mirror, and dusted her white bedroom with its many built-in cupboards and double glass doors overlooking a small bougainvillea- and rose-lined courtyard.

Anna opened her front door just as Cass pulled up at the bottom of the short flight of steps that led to the house. Max was in the passenger seat, circling his arm in an adaptation of the royal wave. Cass tooted the horn.

"Oh, honestly." Anna tugged open the back doors of the café van and flung her suitcase between the racks that normally held fresh bread. As if on automatic pilot, Anna's mind leapt to what should be happening at the café—it was too early for afternoon bread deliveries, but the morning rounds would be complete. What was she doing leaving everything behind? What had she agreed to? And yet, she could not do anything other than give her beloved grandfather his wish.

She slammed the back door of the van, but her mind was still picking away like a hen at a patch of plain dirt.

Anna had done more research, but there was no listing in the local German phone book for the owners of Schloss Siegel. Her searches on Google maps revealed only that the Schloss was located on the edge of a small village, also called Siegel.

"Are you sure you're ready, darling?" Max said now, moving his thinning frame into the middle seat so that Anna could get in.

Ready? Anna wanted to chuckle at the very thought. Instead, she reached a hand out to cover Max's own.

"You know me," she quipped instead. "Always prepared." She hoped her voice did not give a thing away.

At least she knew where she was going. In Germany. There was a direct train northeast to Siegel from Berlin. It took an hour and twenty minutes. Not too long.

"Excellent." Max folded his arms, but he seemed a little shaky.

Anna looked out the window as they headed toward the airport. The brilliant sunlight sparkled on the bay. Would anyone remember her grandfather when she arrived in Siegel?

Once she had transferred in LA to the plane to Berlin, Anna couldn't settle on any one train of thought. She tried and failed to concentrate on the smorgasbord of entertainment that the plane offered. Every time she attempted to focus on a film, her mind began to drift, returning again and again to the fairy-tale images of the Schloss.

By the time the train pulled to a heaving stop

in Siegel, Anna was exhausted. As she descended from the train, she looked around the deserted platform. An old station building that looked to have been charming once was now decorated with aluminum-framed windows covered in dust. And yet, even though there was a sense of something old and beautiful clashing with the functional Soviet period, Anna felt a strong sense of history already, just being there. She couldn't help but wonder about all the other trains that had stopped at this station—and how many of them had held her grandfather—and his family.

Anna had worked out her route before she left home and knew that it should take only a few minutes to wend her way through the small village to the main square. As she set off, she kept her eyes focused straight ahead and did her best to ignore the churning feelings in her stomach.

She was the only person who had alighted from the train. Her suitcase rattled in the silence as she dragged it up the street that led to the square. She passed a row of derelict-looking houses; long grass grew along the fronts of the old stone buildings. Next, she passed a small shop. An ancient sign over its closed front door flapped in the breeze. There was not a soul in sight. There were no cars, no traffic, no bakeries. No gas stations or houses that looked as if they held any form of life. Where was everyone?

Anna decided it was best to keep going, although the temptation to stop and stare was almost overwhelming. The wind picked up and the eerie silence that had permeated the late afternoon was replaced with odd, inexplicable creaks and groans. It was early spring, but the village held no promise of new life. It was as if the past was hanging on by its hinges and yet not even sure it belonged anymore. So what was going on? Anna did up the buttons on her black jacket with her free hand as she rounded a bend in the road that led to the square—the heart, presumably, of what had once been her grand-father's village.

She stopped in front of the church. Oddly, the building appeared to have a new terracotta roof, and its walls looked freshly painted. It was a pretty church, with a round tower culminating in a point with a gold weathercock. Next to it was a general store with a light on inside. Anna took a few more steps. She stopped right in front of an old building just past the store.

Suddenly exhaustion hit her, causing her to sway and almost drop her luggage right there on the pavement. She had made it. She was here. She had been travelling for almost twenty-four hours to get to this place, this place that she had never been to before, had only learned of a few days ago. But while the village felt foreign, it also seemed familiar. Several wooden tables with long benches were lined up in the front courtyard of the ivy-covered stone building right in front of her. The freshly painted sign announced that she'd reached her destination— The Hotel Goldener Hahn. Anna took a few last heady steps and pushed open the wooden front door.

She found herself entering the restaurant, which was lined with more long tables and wooden chairs that looked as if they had danced straight out of a nursery rhyme. It was as if she had wandered into another Germany now—a traditional Germany full of stories and magic and all sorts of wonderful characters from childhood books. How many times had her grandfather strolled into this very place? Had he tasted his first beer here?

"Can I help you?" a girl asked in German. It seemed logical that she was dressed in a traditional folk costume; her light brown hair was swept back into a bun.

As the girl showed Anna up to her room, they passed a middle-aged couple coming down the stairs. Dressed in modern clothing and carrying a map, they looked perfectly normal, and from the right century too. Anna felt some of the tension that had built up in her shoulders dissipate.

Her room was laid out in a charming fashion. A wooden staircase separated her bedroom upstairs from a small private living room downstairs. A tiny bathroom with a pedestal basin completed the picture. She had a view of the village square.

She unpacked, hung her clothes in the wardrobe, took a shower, and lay down on her bed. She needed to take an afternoon nap, wanted this interminable day of travelling to end. And yet at the same time, she wanted to get up right now. Explore. Find out. But dinner would not be for at least four hours. She had to rest or she would collapse.

After fifteen minutes Anna knew that idea was hopeless. She couldn't turn her mind off. How long had things been like this here? The place was starting to feel like her village too.

Anna lay where she was a few more moments. Walking through a couple of streets in Siegel had done it. Seeing the half-empty square. Anna's past and present suddenly seemed to have melded like two parts of a broken cup.

For all these years she had lived thinking that she didn't have a past. But she did. Suddenly, Max had given it to her. And here she was. The desire to see the Schloss was overwhelming. She wanted to be there now. She wanted to see the ghosts of her family, her lost family, the family she should have had, and this feeling was so intensely linked with her love for Max and her tiredness and the desolation of the whole place that she had to get up. She had to go to the palace now. She could not, would not, wait.

A middle-aged woman was on duty at the reception desk. A string of pearls sat flush against her black cashmere sweater. Her hair was neat and blond.

Anna introduced herself in English, hoping that the woman would understand. "I want to ask about the possibility of visiting Schloss Siegel. I tried to contact the owner before I left home, but—"

"You had no reply." The woman began turning pages in her reservation book. She spoke English perfectly, but her words were clipped.

"That's right."

"That is not a surprise."

Anna waited a beat. "Would it be possible to contact the owners? I have good reason to see them. A personal connection from the past."

The woman looked up, her eyebrows arching in two perfect, black crescent moons.

There was nothing for it, but to plow on. "I have a connection to the family who lived there before the—"

"Russians came." The woman rolled the *R*.

"Yes."

"The Albrechts."

"That's right."

The woman folded her arms. "There are some

walks in the vicinity of the hotel. I'm sure you'll enjoy those. I have a map showing other local attractions."

Anna chose her words with great care. "I'm so sorry, but I need to visit the Schloss. That is why I am here. I came all the way from San Francisco."

The woman turned from Anna. She selected several glossy brochures and a map from the stand behind her desk, clicked her pen open, and with deliberate strokes, began drawing large red circles around the tourist attractions marked on the map. She handed them to Anna without a word, then turned to her computer and began typing.

"Thank you," Anna said. Her words came out careful, deliberate.

The woman did not look up.

Two minutes later, Anna found herself back in the village square. She knew the way to the Schloss, had studied the map of the village online enough times to be able to make her way there without assistance. It seemed the only thing to do was to put one foot in front of the other and go find out for herself, even though she had no idea what to expect. She had done that before at various times in her life—of course she had.

Anna turned right and headed past the church, not giving in to the temptation to check whether the door was unlocked. Her ancestors had worshipped there. Had her great-grandparents married in this little church? But she needed to stay on track.

The street beyond the church would take her directly to Schloss Siegel. How many times had Max walked here when he was growing up?

Anna shook her head and focused on her surroundings. She passed several utilitarian-looking houses with steeply pitched roofs and small windows, which she assumed had been built after the Berlin Wall came down. A curl of smoke rose out of one of the chimneys, and the sound of someone chopping wood in a back garden reverberated in the air.

Anna kept going. After a few minutes, open country girdled the narrow road. The trees on either side of her were dotted with the odd leaf, but they were not replete, not yet. It was, after all, only March. Soon everything was quiet except for Anna's footsteps on the road.

The road turned, and as Anna followed it, a series of what looked like old outbuildings—stables, perhaps—appeared on her right. Her heart plunged into a dive. She was getting closer to the Schloss.

A rickety barbed wire fence protected the outbuildings from the road, while grass and weeds spread to the edges of the old buildings. The windows on the top floors were boarded up with graying wooden planks and crossed with diagonal boards. A bright yellow sign was attached to one of the windows. Anna could not read German, but its message was clear.

She drew her arms around herself and continued on until she reached the entrance gates to Schloss Siegel.

CHAPTER THREE

Lake Geneva, 1934

Marthe had all the waiters dancing to her tune. A gaggle of young men was leading the ex-demimondaine to the best table by the water. If anyone had asked Isabelle why this sort of thing happened every time she went anywhere with her grandmother, she would have said that it was not only due to Marthe's natural charisma, but also because her grandmother still had what it took.

The morning was perfect for a boat trip—the air was clear and the steady buzz of crickets was punctuated with the odd call of a bird. The tables on the terrace were laid with fresh white linen for breakfast. Coffee scented the air.

Isabelle had woken after a delicious sleep. As she had drifted off the night before, her thoughts had swirled pleasantly around Max. Even though she had talked with him for only a few minutes, she had felt both safe and excited at the same time.

This morning, she had dressed with extra care. Her white day dress was just the thing for a summer's day on the lake. She had pinned her straw hat so that it sat at exactly the right angle, showing off her glossy, dark curls to perfection.

Marthe took advantage of the many eager waiters who hovered around her at breakfast, bossing them about and insisting on having a range of patisseries that would make the Ritz in Paris proud. As Isabelle settled herself back in one of the cushioned wicker chairs and tucked her legs under the tablecloth, she felt the promise of the gorgeous day ahead even more keenly.

Max's party wasn't at breakfast yet. This wasn't a surprise. Marthe had always been an early riser, and even though Isabelle often felt like sleeping late, her grandmother insisted that she not become a slouch.

"I met another guest last night," Isabelle said.

"You were talking to a young man." Marthe broke open a croissant, buttered it, and took a sip of her coffee.

"I thought you were too busy talking to those ladies to notice," Isabelle laughed.

"I see everything," Marthe said. "And what I do not notice, I work out on my own."

Isabelle laid her knife down on the porcelain plate. "This . . . family invited me to go out on the lake with them today. In a boat."

"I would imagine it would involve a boat if you were going out on the lake," Marthe said. "I do hope you're not swimming. But I only saw you talking to a young man, not the entire family."

"He is travelling with his family."

"But we do not know them."

Isabelle exhaled. "I thought you said that you didn't want me to stagnate," she said, keeping her voice low. Marthe was always full of contradictions. She would change her mind when it suited her, depending on the circumstances. One minute she would want to go out; the next, she would decide to stay in the apartment to read a book. Her vagaries—her whims—had become famous.

"I didn't mean that I wanted you to skip off for the entire day with the first group of strangers you came upon. Can you not have lunch with them tomorrow instead? That way I can observe them through my lorgnette."

"What, while you pick them over with those women you met last night? And analyze them endlessly?"

"Old women have to have some entertainment," Marthe said. "And what is better than the antics of the young?"

"Then you'd be wise to invest in a telescope this morning," Isabelle muttered. "You will look ridiculous enough from the shore."

"I'm not sure that it is the right thing to simply accept this young man's invitation so easily. I do have my standards, you know."

Isabelle raised a brow, then instantly regretted it. Her grandmother was the love of her life. She had taken Isabelle in after her father's death, when Isabelle's mother's family had rejected her, denouncing their little granddaughter as the spawn of a courtesan's son. Isabelle would stain their perfect middle-class reputation if they were to have anything to do with her. Marthe had scoffed at their petty politics. And she had done what she always did. Worked it out and survived.

"I don't see what the problem is," Isabelle said.

"I am confident in Paris. Everyone knows everyone there. All I am asking is that you get to know these people a little better before going off for the day. What if you and the young man were left unchaperoned? What then?"

Marthe's overprotectiveness was hardly surprising. She had been desperate at Isabelle's age, living in poverty and working as a seamstress in the airless confines of Paris's ramshackle garment district. Marthe had already borne two children to two different men by the time she was twenty. She lived in a shabby tenement building and sewed buttons for a living while leaving her two babies in the care of her landlady, a harsh woman who she suspected did not look after them at all. Remarkably, her life had been turned around by one chance encounter.

"I can't think what would happen! Nothing, I

imagine," Isabelle said. Something distracted her and she turned, relieved at the diversion from the conversation with her grandmother.

A young woman had appeared on the terrace. She seemed to be floating toward the table next to them. Three waiters hovered around her.

Marthe had competition.

"An apparition," Marthe said, picking up her lorgnette.

"She appears to be alone, and surviving," Isabelle almost growled in return.

"I noticed."

The girl spoke to the waiters, ordered juice.

"American," Marthe said.

"Grand-mère, if you are going to spend the entire summer worrying about foreigners, then we may as well return to Paris."

"Paris is full of Parisians," Marthe said. "I'm bored with them all."

Isabelle turned her gaze to the blond girl at the next table. She was tall, effortlessly elegant, and the pale pink dress that she wore showed off her complexion to perfection. She was stunning; there was no doubt of that. American or not.

"Hello there! I saw you last night!" the girl called out in English, looking at Isabelle. "Talking to that divine German, Max Albrecht. You know him? What a family. German aristocracy. They own half of Prussia or something. Did you realize?"

Marthe set her coffee cup down with great care and stared at the girl.

"Virginia Brooke," the girl continued, turning to Marthe. "I'm sorry, I didn't introduce myself before I spoke to you. But that hardly matters these days." She did not look sorry at all.

"Well," Marthe said, rolling out the English that she had studied during her days as a top courtesan. "You are most welcome to talk to us. It's quite diverting for this time of the morning."

Isabelle felt something close to relief. Marthe was not going to create a scene. "I am Isabelle de Florian," she said. "And this is my grandmother, Madame de Florian." How comforting to be able to say those words without fear of a cringed response, a tightening of someone's shoulders, a polite nod, and then a goodbye.

Virginia Brooke clearly had no idea who they were. "Well, I'm pleased to meet you." There was a pause. "I think we could even be friends."

Marthe bustled about with her napkin. She was ruffled. Isabelle had to bite her lip to stop herself from giggling.

Virginia Brooke didn't seem to notice any of this—and if she did, she ignored it. "I couldn't help overhearing you just now—I was listening to your darling French conversation while I came to sit down. I heard that you wanted to go out on the lake with Max and his family. You really will be safe, you know."

"Oh?" Marthe asked.

Isabelle pressed her lips together.

"Yes. You know, if you'd prefer, Madame de Florian, I could always go with Isabelle. As a chaperone."

"I see!" Marthe looked appalled.

But Virginia just gazed calmly at the older woman.

"Are you travelling alone, Miss Brooke?" Marthe asked.

"Oh, quite alone. But I've met the most interesting people," Virginia said. "I'm from Boston. On the escape."

Marthe seemed to consider this.

Isabelle stayed quiet. She was itching, just itching to go out for the day with the Albrecht party, but she was intrigued by Virginia. On the escape? From what?

"Have you been invited to go out with the Germans, Miss Brooke?" Marthe asked, giving Virginia one of her best stares.

"Oh, heavens. That doesn't matter. I'll just tell them I want to come. And do call me Virginia, please."

Marthe put her napkin down. "Well then. Perhaps once you have 'talked to them,' you could send us a message and we'll see."

"Well, look! Here they are right now!" Virginia indicated the group with her coffee cup.

Max wore a pale suit, almost the same color

53

as Isabelle's dress. He caught Isabelle's eye at exactly the same moment she looked at him. She stared back down at her plate, but she couldn't stop a smile from forming on her lips.

"Leave it to me." Virginia stood up, went straight over to the German party, kissed Nadja on the cheek, and began chatting with the group.

Max looked at Isabelle again, raised an eyebrow. Isabelle smiled back. Two minutes later, Virginia made her way toward them.

"It's all sorted," she said. "We'll meet at half past ten here on the landing. The motorboat will pick us up at ten forty-five and take us to a picnic spot farther up the lake. They're going to explore some village or other. The hotel is supplying luncheon and we will all be there. It's done." Virginia sat down and toasted Marthe with her coffee cup.

"I see," Marthe said. "Well then." She studied the Albrechts, who were laughing now. It seemed that one of the twins was pulling some sort of antic.

Marthe tilted her head to one side. "I can see that I would look churlish if I were to stop you from going."

"She'll have a ball." Virginia smiled.

Marthe stood up and Isabelle followed her, but Virginia caught her eye as she left, and something kindled between them. Isabelle stopped herself from turning around again. It was a surprise to feel a connection to someone she hardly knew. Not to mention someone so foreign. But she found herself drawn to this confident young woman. Perhaps she did not need to know why.

"She's the perfect motor sailor." Max stood behind Isabelle as she gazed at the boat two hours later from the dock. The boat's hull was painted white, with a row of portholes and a wooden cabin above it. Her varnish was polished to a sheen. Uniformed crew had placed a small walkway up against the shore, and Virginia was already halfway across it.

"She is beautiful." Isabelle smiled. She was so very aware of Max right behind her. "Do you think they'll put up the sails?" She turned to him.

"I hope so," he said, his voice quiet, deep. "Shall we?" He extended his hand to help her step off the landing onto the wooden plank.

"I think we shall." Isabelle smiled, and she placed her fingers in his palm.

Siegel, 2010

Traces of stubborn black paint peeked through the rust that covered the wrought iron entrance gates to Schloss Siegel. But the vivid coppery-brown tarnish could not hide the elaborate scrolls and swirls that must have once gleamed. Anna ran her fingers over one of the patterns. The immediate problem was not the rust, but the enormous padlock that bound the gates tight.

Beyond this, a driveway was bordered on the right by forest and on the left with the patchy remains of a lawn, scattered with tall tufts of grass that swayed in the silence. Nothing else was visible.

Anna folded her arms across her chest.

The gates were too high to climb. Perhaps there was another entrance somewhere else.

Anna decided to explore a bit more and turned left to follow the thick stone wall that extended beyond the gates. The wall was higher than Anna's head, and a layer of rusted barbed wire ran along the top of it.

There was a grassy path, easily wide enough for Anna to walk along, between the wall and the road. If she had to make a circuit of the entire property in order to find a way in, then she would do so. She continued for several minutes, admiring the tops of tall trees that were just visible above the old stone. Anna listened but could detect no sounds coming from the other side of the wall.

She breathed away a shudder that ran through her insides. The afternoon was darkening a little, and the place felt even more alone. But at the same time, Anna was drawn to it. Something else had kicked in, a sense of . . . what was it? Home?

She turned right after several hundred feet, following the impenetrable wall until the road stopped at another pair of gates. These were not as elaborate as the previous ones—in fact, they looked as though they belonged on a humble farm.

Anna saw another set of outbuildings to her left. A small, derelict house—its windows boarded up and weeds grasping its walls—stood just beyond them. Although these buildings had not been on Max's map, they appeared to be part of the estate. Washhouses, perhaps? Had a caretaker once lived in that house?

Anna walked up to the simple set of farm gates and craned her neck to see over them. She could just glimpse a bank of trees, a sloped lawn, and . . . she caught her breath.

There it was.

She was looking at one side of the palace, which was still breathtaking despite its age and the abuse of multiple wars and governments and upheaval and changes of ownership. The sight of the old Schloss, sitting there like some steadfast shipwreck, caused Anna's heart to falter. The wall was peppered with bullet holes as though pocked by some foul disease.

The windows were boarded up. Weeds and bracken climbed up the walls. Several pieces of iron in unidentifiable shapes lay about near the Schloss, relics of the Soviet era or, perhaps, old farm implements from . . . before that time.

This gate was not only padlocked but crisscrossed with barbed wire to ensure that no one could get in.

Anna hated to imagine what Max would feel, standing here, looking at this. It was as if his entire childhood, his former life, had been left to rot.

What was she supposed to do now?

She continued to stare at the part of the house that she could see. The image of a young Max running through the gardens, down to the lake that she knew lay beyond the palace, flashed through her mind. And then, Max as a young man, strolling down to the lake, looking thoughtful. A book in his hand, perhaps, going for a solitary row in a boat. Anna almost felt as though she'd been there, as though she'd known Max back then. She felt more crushed at the sight of the rundown property than she'd ever imagined possible. After all, she'd never given much thought to the past—but there was something about this house and all that it had suffered that threatened to overwhelm her.

Her family, Max's family, had lost everything. She tried to imagine what it must have been like for them to leave their home, a place layered with centuries of family memories and stories.

And yet, had it been fair for them to have had all of this?

Anna shook her head and turned away. All she knew right then was that she wasn't going to get any answers by standing there. The Schloss and the park were impenetrable. She'd have to find another way to get inside.

If whatever Max had hidden under the floor-boards in his room in 1940 had survived the years of political turmoil, gunshots, and looters—not to mention the current owners, who may have ripped everything valuable out of it and left the rest to rot—it would be a miracle.

But she had to find out. Anna forced herself to return to the village.

As she followed the road back into the tiny town, a plan began to form in her head. There had to be some sort of civil office that she could visit there. If not there, there would be someone she could talk to in another town nearby. Someone had to know who owned Schloss Siegel, and Anna had to get in touch with them.

She walked around the village's central square, but there was nothing there except the shop, the hotel, the church, and several private, rundown houses on the other side. She turned up the first street she came to and found only a few more cottages.

She couldn't help imagining what it must have been like once. The village, alive with children and voices and laughter and families and shop-keepers and noise. The fact that the hoteliers wore traditional costume seemed to make every-thing more poignant somehow. It was as if this place, hidden away in the forest, locked up by the recent past, had been forgotten now, as so much was forgotten once it was gone. Once it was done.

But why did it have to be finished?

Anna made her way back to the square, taking the next road. After several minutes she turned back around. She had passed a ghost of a post office but nothing else. The clouds had turned to dark gray now—she had been walking for at least an hour. It was nearly six. There was still no sign of life in the village beyond the hotel—and the shop.

Of course. It was still open. But for whom?

Anna pushed the door open. She was hungry now, and her eyes burned with exhaustion. She experienced another bout of dizziness, as if the floor under her feet were spinning.

An elderly woman sat behind the counter, but she stood up when Anna appeared and turned to busy herself with the racks of cigarettes behind the till. Anna watched out of the corner of her eye while the old woman pulled a couple of packets out, sorting them in a halfhearted way.

Anna glanced around the store. It looked as if nothing much had changed here for a long time. The merchandise—mostly packaged goods—was arranged in three aisles, and there was a small selection of fruits and vegetables in a fridge at the back.

Anna decided it would be tactful to buy something before approaching the storeowner. She wandered, fascinated by the German biscuits, the jars of sauerkraut, and the packages of sausages in the freezer section, drawn by the colors of the packaging and the potential of new ingredients. She had to shake herself back to the present.

Finally, Anna selected a packet of chocolate cookies. She needed them. After stalling for a few seconds so that she could plan what she was going to say to the woman at the counter, she made her way over to the till.

"*Guten tag*," she said, wincing at what was probably the worst German accent the woman had ever heard.

"Hello," the woman replied in English, holding out a hand for the cookies, not smiling.

But Anna was not going to budge. "I was wondering—could you tell me where I could find the mayor of the village?"

The woman scanned Anna's cookies and punched numbers into her cash register, deadly slow. Anna bit her lip and paid for her small purchase.

The woman studied Anna as if assessing her—up and down the entire length of her being. "I am the mayor of Siegel. If you have questions, you must talk to me."

CHAPTER FOUR

Lake Geneva, 1934

There was something about being out on the water that spelled freedom, glamour, and exhilaration, all blended into one heady mix. Looking out over the deep-blue water and sparkling sunshine, while Max leaned against the side of the boat next to her, Isabelle felt a sense of hope, of happiness and possibility that she had not felt since she was a child.

Even if today was just an aberration, she could live on the feelings she was experiencing now for months. She had a good imagination, but she hoped that she wouldn't have to use it. Deep down she hoped that she could live like this, feel like this, forever.

Max pointed out several picturesque towns as they motored along, telling her which of them sold the best Swiss chocolates, which held the most colorful weekend markets, which had the liveliest restaurants and cafés, even which were best for clothes shopping.

Isabelle caught her breath when they passed private waterfront estates, their immaculate gardens surrounding gabled and turreted houses with motorboats and yachts moored to private jetties. But, as Max pointed out, the lake had its wild side. Impenetrable mountains—their tips capped with smatterings of snow—loomed behind the forests above shingled, deserted beaches.

"Here we are. St. Prex," Max said, as the boat slowed and turned toward the shore.

Didi and Jo were talking in the wild, excited voices typical of young men. Virginia had taken off her hat and turned her face toward the breeze. Nadja sat on one of the wooden slatted seats up at the front of the boat chatting with her friend Sascha.

When the boat pulled up at a small jetty on the edge of the town, Max turned to Isabelle and asked, "Would you like to walk with me? I'd love to show you the town, if you'll allow me."

"That sounds perfect," Isabelle said with a smile.

"I'd like to take Isabelle for a walk," Max announced to the group while the crew tied the boat to the moorings. There was a pretty park behind the rocky foreshore, and narrow streets led off into what looked like a medieval Swiss town.

"Go ahead," Virginia laughed. "Unless you think you need that chaperone, honey." The American girl looked arch.

Isabelle felt herself blush, but she just shook her head.

The crew helped Isabelle, Nadja, Sascha, and Virginia off the boat. Didi and Jo were off next, scampering down to the water's edge.

"We'll be back in time for lunch," Max said, following everyone else off the boat.

A sense of disappointment fluttered through Isabelle. She didn't want to come back for lunch. She would much rather spend the whole day with Max. But that was ridiculous. She said goodbye to Virginia.

Virginia waved back. "I'll be here in the park with Nadja and Sascha. We're going to have a delicious talk."

Virginia did not seem at all put off by Nadja's cold manners. Isabelle wondered whether her new American friend was fazed by anything at all.

Max held out his arm for Isabelle. "Shall we?"

Isabelle slipped her arm into his. When she did so, she realized that she was feeling as she never had before.

It would have been easy to become lost in the cobbled streets of St. Prex. Many of the gabled houses were covered in climbing greenery, their window boxes a riot of summer colors. After half an hour of wandering and easy conversation, Max offered to take her to a café for a glass of something cool.

But he seemed hesitant, watching her as he waited for her to respond.

What was he looking for? Did he expect her to be embarrassed at the idea of sitting alone in an unfamiliar café with an unfamiliar man in a foreign country? The truth was, she didn't feel any sort of embarrassment at all. Oddly, she felt more at home here than she often did in Paris.

"So," Max said, his blue eyes crinkling at their corners as he offered her a seat under the verandah of a charming café. "Now you know my family."

Isabelle waited a moment. She wanted to ask about his parents. But this was always a sensitive subject. The war . . . his father.

But Max seemed to sense her thoughts. "My parents are hosting . . . guests this summer. Well, of a sort. My father did not want to leave the men who are staying with us for the month of August. They are from the training camps south of Berlin."

"Oh," Isabelle said. Training camps. The idea made her feel like shuddering. "That must be interesting for you—to have them there, in the house."

Max chuckled. "What a diplomat you are. My parents have their . . . political views. There are movements in Paris too. But I'm sure you're aware of that."

Isabelle tensed. The Communist and Fascist

uprisings in Paris earlier in the year were still fresh in everyone's minds. But she couldn't imagine what it must be like to live in a country where alternative political parties were banned, let alone protests. Hitler had just given himself absolute power. She had read about the SS's efforts to destroy all opposition within the Nazi party in June. It was impossible to know what to say.

There was a silence.

"My parents want me to join the Nazi party," Max said. "But if Hitler is capable of ordering the SS to kill men who had stood shoulder to shoulder with him, how can I think of joining them, let alone allowing people like my younger brothers to join his cause? People are saying it was necessary—that in order to move forward, sacrifices had to be made. We all know that Germany needs a new future, and the only way forward that we have is with Hitler. I don't know what the answer is, Isabelle, but I do know my parents are urging me to join the Nazi party."

A group of young children ran around and around in circles in the square next to the café. The colors, the window boxes, the waitresses wearing checked pinafores and wielding jugs of lemonade—none of this seemed to fit into the world that Hitler was creating.

"I'm the eldest in my family," Max went on.

"You see, whatever I do will be taken as a model, by my brothers, by the villagers—and I just don't know." He leaned forward then, and he rested his brown hand on the table.

Isabelle wanted to reach out her own hand. Instinctively, she almost did so. But then something stopped her. She had only just met Max. She did not know him. And yet, not only did she feel that here was perhaps one of the most interesting men she had ever met, she knew that in front of her sat a good man, a man who carefully considered the world around him. Before she shared her thoughts, she wanted to know more.

Siegel, 2010

Anna felt oddly uncomfortable under the mayor's gaze. It was unusual for her to feel intimidated. She dealt with the public every day at her café.

Should she tell the mayor her story, or simply say that she needed access to the Schloss and had good reason? If she were to reveal nothing, then the woman would surely become even more suspicious than she already appeared. If she said too much, then the mayor might find Anna's objective ridiculous. Retrieving something sentimental from the Schloss that was left there in 1940? The woman would think she was mad! And every time Anna had prodded her grandfather for the truth about what she was seeking, he had turned away. Told her that these things were difficult to talk about. But once she was there, he said, once she was in Germany, it would be easier to talk. On the phone. Not face-to-face.

Now, Anna faced the mayor. "My name is Anna Young," she began. "My grandfather is Max Albrecht."

The woman stayed dead still. "Why have you come?"

"My grandfather's family—"

"We know the Albrechts," the woman said.

"Of course. Well. My grandfather, Max, asked me to come back here. He asked me to go to the Schloss on his behalf. He is ninety-four, you see."

"My name is Agatha Engel."

Anna held out a hand. Frau Engel shook it, but she did not smile at Anna.

"What does he want?"

"It's a long story. But he . . . wants me to . . ." She didn't think it would be wise to reveal that there might still be something hidden under the floorboards in the Schloss. If anyone in the village did have a key, they might be tempted to go in search of Max's personal belongings for themselves.

Anna started again. "He's an old man. He wants

me to take some photographs of his childhood home for future generations of the family. I think you will understand."

After what seemed like an age, Frau Engel leaned her large hands on the shop counter. "I do not have a key, Miss Young. Return to America and forget about the Schloss. Your grandfather should forget the past. I cannot help you. No one here will be interested in your desire for photographs."

Anna gathered up her cookies. The woman had folded her arms now. Anna nodded. She was not going to make any further progress here. Not now. She thanked Frau Engel and left the shop.

The air outside had chilled, and a late afternoon stillness settled on the village. The atmosphere felt timeless. It was as if the village had slipped back to a lost time. Smoke curled from the chimney of the hotel.

It was tempting indeed to go home to San Francisco—it was certainly a much happier place than Siegel. But Anna couldn't do that. Not yet, anyway. Not for two reasons.

First, she knew she wouldn't be able to live with herself were she to return home without having even properly tried to get inside the Schloss, and second, Anna was now invested in this place. Having walked around the perimeter of the Schloss—having glimpsed even the tiniest part of Max's past, that place that he had never talked about—she could not leave without searching harder. And she could never face Max if she had not done everything she could.

She made her way back to the hotel. This time a different scene greeted her inside the restaurant. A fire crackled in the huge old hearth at the back of the cozy room. Three people sat at the bar to Anna's left, a middle-aged couple who chatted in English and a solitary man—a local, perhaps. His tweed cap rested on the counter next to him.

Music played in the background. Schubert. Lieder—a lilting song that Max still enjoyed listening to. The reminder of Max didn't help. Anna made her way up to the bar and perched on one of the three spare bar stools. For reasons she couldn't quite understand, she felt nervous. This was unlike her—she was normally so confident and capable. She had taken care of herself for years, started her own business, cared for Max, built a full life for herself, so why did she feel so edgy? She focused straight ahead. What on earth was her next move going to be?

The man next to her turned to her and nodded, and the woman next to him smiled at Anna.

"Hello," the woman said. She had a British accent, sounded friendly.

"I'm Anna," Anna smiled back. "Nice to meet you."

"Flora Miles," the woman said, "And this is my

husband, Doug. We're touring for two weeks. Fascinating area, isn't it?"

"Yes, fascinating."

The bartender asked what she was drinking. Anna ordered a German Riesling. She could not stomach beer.

"We came up from Berlin today. Tomorrow we head to Poland." Flora seemed inclined to chat.

"Oh?"

"Yes. We're taking it day by day. No rush."

"A good way to travel," Anna said.

"This is a nice little hotel, isn't it? Are you backpacking your way around Europe?"

"No." Anna laughed. "I'm here for . . . more personal reasons."

The man on Anna's other side stirred. She sensed him looking at her, but she didn't meet his gaze.

"My family came from here," Anna said, speaking loud enough for the man to hear her, hoping he spoke English as well. "They owned the Schloss at the edge of the village. I don't know if you've seen it."

"The Albrechts," the man said, out of the blue, in English. "They never came back."

"They never came back?" Anna asked. Didn't he mean they were forced to leave?

The couple next to her stayed quiet. Anna sent them silent thanks.

"The government offered to let families buy

back their homes in the 1990s, but the Albrechts weren't interested—they never came back to Siegel—so the Schloss was put up for sale."

Weren't interested?

"And do you know who owns it now?" Anna asked, spinning her wine glass by the stem.

"Some big company." The man shrugged. "Their lawyer came here once to look it over."

"Do you know who the lawyer is?" She tried to sound casual.

The man placed his beer mug down on the bar with precision. "The lawyer met with the mayor when he was here. That's all I know."

"Thank you," Anna said. "You've been very helpful."

Frau Engel was turning the red door sign on her shop from "Open" to "Closed" when Anna rushed back to the store. While she understood how important these signs were, knew how hard it was when someone begged to come inside when you were closing for the day—this was for Max. So Anna put on her sweetest smile and approached the older woman with care.

"Yes." Frau Engel did not turn to face Anna when she spoke.

"I spoke to one of the locals," Anna said. "He told me that you have met with the lawyer who represents the owners of the Schloss. I'm guessing this lawyer has access to a key. I understand what you are saying about the past; believe me, I do, but—"

The woman turned then, abruptly. "Do you have any idea, Miss Young?"

"Believe me, I do understand. It's not me I'm doing this for. It's my grandfather. He is so old, you see, and his memories of this place must be so strong that he . . ." Anna tried a different tack. "Look. All I want to do is help my grandfather. He just wants me to have a look at his old home. That's all."

Frau Engel sniffed.

"He practically ordered me to come here. He's too old to come himself. Please, Frau Engel."

"You cannot expect a lawyer in Berlin to indulge your grandfather's wish to take some photographs of his old home. Can't you see that your plan is ridiculous? Do you want to waste people's valuable time?"

Anna waited on the doorstep. Once Frau Engel stopped talking, the village square returned to silence.

"I am closing the shop, Miss Young."

"I came all the way from San Francisco. Please would you reconsider?"

"It was a crazy thing to do."

"And some of the most important things in life are just that," Anna said. "Crazy." Now she was quoting Max! She shook her head at her own words.

"Goodbye." Frau Engel nodded at Anna and closed her shop door.

Once she was back in her hotel room, Anna knew she had to come up with a plan. The last thing she wanted to do was worry Max, but she had to let him know that she was not going to give up. Siegel had been wasting away for decades. There appeared to be a set amount of information that everyone was willing to share and that was that.

Someone would have to let up.

Only one person appeared to have the key to the old palace, and that was the lawyer in Berlin. Anna would have to contact the lawyer somehow, but she wanted to talk to Max first. If she was going to convince a hard-nosed lawyer that she needed to get into that Schloss, then it would certainly help if she knew what, exactly, she was going to retrieve. She picked up her phone from the bedside table and went out to the checked sofa, settling into a corner with her legs tucked under her.

"Grandfather," she said.

"Anna!" Max sounded both far away and delighted to hear her voice.

Anna chatted with her grandfather about his health, her flight, and her arrival for a few minutes before she asked the questions that were burning in her mind and shared the information that she had gathered so far.

"Grandfather. Are you aware—did you have any idea about the state of the village?"

There was a silence that could not have been louder had Max played a fanfare down the phone line.

"I haven't heard anything for nearly twenty years," he said. "I did have some . . . contact with an old friend, a neighbor back in the 1990s. He warned me that things weren't good."

"There hasn't been any investment in either the estate or the village since then, I'm afraid. The hotel is up and running, and the church appears to have been well kept, but that is all. I didn't know how to tell you the Schloss is not—"

"I see." He cut her off.

Anna wished she were with him, able to give him a hug. "The only person who has a key to the Schloss is the Berlin lawyer who represents the current owner. I have no idea who that owner is, but apparently it's some business or other. This lawyer is going to want a good reason to let me inside the estate, I'm afraid. Can you give me any more compelling reasons why they should allow me to enter?"

She paused for a moment before she went on. "I don't even know what I'm looking for when I get there."

"Everything's harder . . . and easier in equal measures as you get older," Max sighed. "In fact, you realize how easy things could have been.

How simple and straightforward they should have been, had you made the right damned decisions in the first place. It always seems harder at the time than it really is, Anna. I wish I'd known that when I was young."

Anna leaned against the back of the sofa.

"Still, the past is best left in dreams, Anna. I would like only my little remnant. That is all."

Anna kept her voice quiet. "Are you able to tell me what it is that you're looking for?"

"Anna. Please."

"The problem we have is that your reasons sound sentimental, Grandfather. We are talking about a lawyer here. They don't tend to deal in sentimentality."

"Anna."

This was the closest she had come to having an argument with Max. The feeling was odd and uncomfortable, and yet, something was rising in her chest that was becoming hard to push down.

In a way, Max's past was her past too. She had a right to know about her ancestors. Who were Max's sisters and brothers? Surely he was not an only child. What could he possibly not want her to know? The question of trust, of his faith in their relationship, kept bubbling away in her head, but then they were talking about a war. She had to try to put herself in his position, no matter how hard that was at times. He hadn't lied to her—but he hadn't told her anything for decades.

"You are thinking too hard," Max's voice interrupted her thoughts. "I know you too well, my dear."

"This place is haunting me, even though I haven't even walked into that Schloss yet. I'm not leaving until I've got you what you want. But you have to help me. I have to convince a lawyer, for goodness' sake, that I have a legitimate reason for wanting to enter that estate. I can't even convince the owner of the local shop to let me past the barbed wire fence at the moment."

"Anna," he said. "Darling. Okay."

"Okay?"

"Yes," he said. "Okay."

Anna rested her head against the cushion. She was exhausted from jet lag and fresh air and lack of food. She would have to go down and eat something in the restaurant soon, or she would faint.

There was a long silence down the line. But when Max finally spoke, he sounded as if he were in the next room. "It's to do with that apartment in Paris," he said. "I knew the girl who lived there when I was young."

"Didn't it belong to a courtesan?"

"Yes, Anna, and I knew her. But it was her granddaughter whom I . . . loved."

"Ah."

Max stayed quiet.

"But, hang on, wasn't the granddaughter the one who locked up the apartment for seventy years and never went back?"

There was a silence.

"And you had a love affair with her?" Anna stood up and paced around the room.

"It wasn't just an affair, darling. It was real. You know when it's real."

Anna's insides fluttered. She walked over to the window. It had become dark outside and a couple of streetlights had been switched on in the square.

"A Parisian love affair?"

"It began in Lake Geneva. I knew from the moment I first spoke to her. Her name was Isabelle de Florian."

"Lake Geneva?"

"We were holidaying there," he said.

"Oh!"

"Don't sound so surprised."

"But what happened? Why did it . . . end?"

Max went quiet again. "Too much happened. Far too much."

Anna's head was spinning. Perhaps she could tell the lawyer about the apartment in Paris, the love affair, Max's need to retrieve something. What if she could get her hands on a copy of the article about the abandoned apartment and show him?

But she had more questions. "What happened, though? What did you do? Why do you have regrets?" Her words came out almost as a squeak.

"It was an engagement ring that I hid under the floorboards of my bedroom." Max fell silent again. He coughed.

He sounded exhausted now. How valiantly he had tried to push aside thoughts that would take him back to a time that he needed to forget.

But still Anna's mind filled with questions. What about his relationship with her grandmother, Jean? They had never seemed very happy together. They always seemed to just get by. Max was often withdrawn around his American wife. And Anna's grandmother had always been so practical. Max had seemed to prefer Anna's company to that of her grandmother. She had always felt sorry for him, and now he was telling her that he had shared a grand passion with a woman who also seemed to have fled from her past for a reason that no one knew anything about?

Anna couldn't help but hit her forehead with the heel of her hand. But Max seemed to want to talk again—albeit in riddles.

"All we have left of the past are remnants in our minds, Anna, and all we can do is look at them sometimes, every now and then. Take them out, dust them, turn them over in our hands until we must return, full circle, to the present. And when we are back here, we try to live our lives as best we can—again."

"What a philosopher you are," Anna said, but she almost choked on her words.

"One has to be. Goodbye, darling."

Goodbye? Anna wanted to shout that she had so much more to ask.

But she didn't want to push him any further. Not now. He was so . . . vulnerable in many ways, even though he seemed formidable in his convictions at the same time.

Anna decided to play things safe. "I'll find out the name of that lawyer, and, Grandfather, no matter how hard I have to fight for it, I will do my utmost to get you your ring."

Once she said goodbye and hung up the phone, Anna collapsed on the hotel bed.

Frau Engel was dining in the hotel restaurant when Anna walked downstairs a few minutes later. She was seated with the woman who had been working at the hotel earlier that day, along with a middle-aged man whom Anna had not seen before. He was dressed in a pale pink shirt, cream trousers, and tan leather shoes. Frau Engel had changed into a fitted navy-blue suit. A brooch was pinned to the breast of her jacket. Both women glanced at Anna and then turned away, fast.

Anna felt even more unwelcome than she had in the shop. And yet she would have to approach the group in front of her, and soon. She might as well take advantage of their presence to get some more answers.

A waitress appeared at her side and showed her to a table. The English couple she had met that afternoon were seated in a far corner but didn't look up when Anna entered. Several of the long tables were occupied, and there was a small group at the bar.

If she could not get the mayor to tell her the name of the lawyer who handled the estate, she would have to talk to the people at the bar and hope they were locals. It wasn't really Anna's style to pursue strangers like that, but what did it matter? She was miles away from home and she was going to have to be resourceful. Failing all that, she would have to find the local council offices. The mayor had to have a proper office somewhere. She couldn't run the district from the shop, could she?

Anna took the menu from the waitress, only half listening while the young girl listed off the specials. Anna ordered *buletten*—specialty meatballs—and a glass of wine for courage.

Once the waitress had left, Anna pushed her chair back and stood up. She would have to act now, while the mayor and her friends were still there.

"*Guten abend*," Anna said, as she stopped at the mayor's table.

The two women looked at her as though she had insulted them. The man nodded, but Frau Engel remained stock-still and regarded Anna through narrowed eyes.

"I am sorry to interrupt you," Anna said. "I won't take up too much of your time."

"Please, if you would allow us to enjoy our evening." Frau Engel sounded cold.

Anna stood her ground. "I didn't tell you the whole story. You see, my grandfather has great regrets about the past."

She sensed a shift in the women's mood. The man in the pink shirt put his beer glass down and studied Anna.

Even so, Anna decided she would not give too much away. An idea had formed in her head. "The Albrechts, my family, were an instrumental part of this village for centuries, I believe. I am just asking for the lawyer's name. That is all."

Frau Engel turned back to her food, but the man at the table spoke up. "It is because of your grandfather, Max Albrecht, that the village is in this state. If it wasn't for me, and for my wife, here—if we had not restored this hotel and rescued it—there would be nothing left of Siegel. It would be a ghost town. So forgive us if we are not so sympathetic to your plight."

"What are you talking about?" Anna said.

"How could you blame the state of an entire village on one person—my grandfather? You don't even know him!" She felt heat rising in her throat and took a deep breath. She must stay in control of herself.

There was a pause. The woman seemed to be deliberating.

"The lawyer's name is Wil Jager," she said. "He works at a firm called Lang Meisner in Berlin. I do not know if he will help you."

Right then, Anna's food arrived at her table. She was starving. As she turned to leave, she fought an urge to lean down and kiss the woman who had spoken on the cheek.

"Thank you," she said. "I appreciate your help." She wanted to ask more, but it seemed that the conversation was over.

The moment she sat down, Anna took out her phone and added the name of the firm and the lawyer to the list she had created for her trip. But her thoughts took on a life of their own.

It seemed brutally unfair to blame Max's family—specifically him—for the ruination of Siegel. The Albrechts had been forced from their home. They had no choice but to leave. Anna hated to think of this bitterness—this unfair-ness—being directed at the man she loved most in the world. The only man she loved in the world.

She ate her dinner methodically. The meatballs

were delicious, and in a fit of determination—not wanting the people at that other table to think they had bullied her away—she ordered a lemon mousse for dessert.

The next step was to talk to this lawyer. Maybe she could find a way to convince him to allow her to retrieve Max's ring from the Schloss. And now she had another mission—to restore Max's good name in the village. Although she hadn't realized that was part of her plan, it now struck her as an essential reason for her being there.

Anna finished the last crumb of her dessert. She charged the bill to her room and stood up. She would call the lawyer's office first thing in the morning and make an appointment to see him in Berlin.

CHAPTER FIVE

Anna phoned Berlin while holding her mobile phone to her ear and packing her suitcase with her free hand. She could have an appointment that afternoon. Wil Jager had a cancellation and this was most unusual. There might not be another opportunity to meet with him for weeks.

Anna had tossed and turned most of the night. Jet lag combined with irritation kept her awake, and she kept asking herself the same questions. What had happened to Max seventy years earlier? What had caused him to turn his back on his entire past, and why did the villagers blame him for the decay of their home? And then there was the love affair with Isabelle de Florian. What about it was the biggest regret of his life?

When Anna checked out of the hotel, the receptionist on duty was one of the waitresses who had been working in the restaurant the evening before.

The sound of her suitcase wheels scratching along the road was the only thing to break the silence in the village square. It was as if the place were speaking to her now—the connection she felt with it was indefinable, and yet strong. The church sat there, benevolent, overlooking the scene as it must have done for centuries. It was easy to imagine the villagers in the past, meeting there, chatting outside in the square. And her family, Anna's family, would have been part of it all. They would have known everyone here, presumably, been part of a close-knit community. But Anna had never known about them, and when she added that to the fact that she had not had a proper family—not after her mother died when she was twelve, not after her father left, not unless she counted Max—it made his walking away from his past even harder to understand. But now he had made it clear that he had lost many things that mattered too.

She stopped at the edge of the square, just before she turned in the direction of the railway station. The rattle of her suitcase came to an abrupt stop, like the rattle of a train on a line that was at its end point. The sun shone over the old buildings, highlighting their signs of decay, their age, their beauty.

Someone had to revive them.

Several hours later, Anna walked out of her hotel in Berlin, which was located a few streets into the old East Berlin, directly behind the Brandenburg Gate. Elegant shops and restaurants lined the street outside the hotel. Their glass fronts and attractive window displays spoke of prosperity and success, and the freshly paved sidewalks were busy with shoppers, office workers, and tourists wielding cameras.

The old East Berlin had been obliterated, that was certain, but Anna could still sense its presence beneath the gleaming surface. Somehow, the past crept into her bones here just as it had done in Siegel. She walked farther into the old East and turned up a narrow street, passing two empty spaces that must have held buildings, once.

The lawyer's firm was on a wider street nearby that was filled with handsomely renovated and gleaming new buildings. Anna stopped outside an ultramodern glass and stainless steel office.

The glass doors slid open for her and she stepped into a tall atrium. Immediately, she felt a sense of calm. The place radiated luxury and success.

She had rehearsed several possible opening lines in her head until she finally settled on one. It was anybody's guess how the lawyer was going to react.

As Anna stepped out of the elevator onto the fourteenth floor, she was awed by the sparkling office foyer, a vast space with gleaming marble floors and floor-to-ceiling windows overlooking the city.

She took a deep breath and headed toward the well-groomed woman who sat at the sprawling reception desk. Once the receptionist had tapped Anna's name into her computer, she nodded and asked Anna to sit in the waiting area.

"Would you like a coffee?" Another woman appeared at Anna's shoulder.

"Oh, thank you," Anna said. She hated to think how much this little visit was going to cost.

Ten minutes later, Anna was attempting to make sense of a German financial magazine when a male voice called her name. She looked up and put her magazine aside.

"Anna Young." The man standing in front of her said her name pleasantly enough. "I'm Wil Jager." He walked toward her and held out a hand, which Anna shook. The first thing that struck her was that his eyes were sea green. With his skin tone, she would have thought he would have brown eyes, so the green was both unexpected and very charming. Anna checked her thoughts. What on earth was she doing? She was not here to analyze German men, let alone one whom she needed to ask a singular question— one that he would no doubt find nonsensical.

Anna looked away. Had he known what she was thinking? He indicated for her to follow him. She was glad he knew how to speak English.

"You've come over from the US?" he asked.

"I just arrived in Germany yesterday and came from Siegel this morning."

Wil Jager stopped at the entrance to one of the

corridors behind the reception desk. He had his back to her, and he ran a hand over his jaw before turning. "Siegel?"

"Yes."

"Oh."

"Yes," Anna said. "That's what I came to talk to you about." She had thought about how to approach this all morning. Seemed best to come straight out with it.

Wil started walking again. He went to the end of the airy hallway and held the last door on the right open for Anna. Anna was tempted to stop and admire the view from the large windows at the end of the corridor, but she did not want to appear too dazzled by Wil's office. And she was very aware that she must not waste even a few seconds of his expensive legal time.

"Come in," Wil said, but he sounded wary now.

Wil's office was also framed with floor-to-ceiling glass. Several cranes hung suspended over the city, and there was a stunning view of the rebuild of the Royal Palace and the old Imperial part of the city. Anna forced herself to turn away and face Wil.

He was right behind her, and she almost bumped into him. "Sorry," she said. "The view . . ."

"I know," he said. He was watching her now, and a slight frown had appeared on his face. But then he shook it off and asked her to sit down.

"How can I help you?" he asked.

"This is going to sound a little odd."

"Please go ahead."

"Okay." Anna shifted in her leather seat.

One side of Wil's mouth curved up a little now. He seemed to have moved on from his previous surprise at the name Siegel.

Anna took this as encouragement. "My grandfather's family used to own Schloss Siegel. His name is Max Albrecht."

Wil leaned back in his seat. Those green eyes narrowed and the smile disappeared. "Really," he said, his voice quiet.

Anna went on. "I understand that the new owners are clients of yours."

There was a silence.

"Okay." Anna cleared her throat. Why was this so hard? Why did everyone respond to this information with reticence? Best to just plow on. "The thing is, my grandfather asked me to come all the way here because he left something in the Schloss. In 1940, as it turns out. It's been a long time, obviously." This sounded utterly mad. "And he wants—needs—it back. Kind of soon."

"Nineteen forty?"

"Yes."

Wil raised a tawny brow.

"I was wondering if the owners might let me inside so that I can retrieve his property. It shouldn't take long."

Wil shook his head and almost chuckled. But

then he looked serious again. "The owners would never let you inside. And I wouldn't advise them to."

Anna was prepared for this. "My grandfather is ninety-four. This means a lot to him. I was hoping you could help. He's not asking to be given anything—the past is the past—but he has this one wish."

Wil shook his head. "Are you telling me you've come all this way for this?"

Anna held his gaze. "Max wants his—item—back."

"We've established that," Wil said. "But I am one hundred percent certain that my client will not let you in. Sorry. I can't help you."

"Could someone accompany me into the Schloss while I get it?"

Wil chuckled.

This irritated Anna even more, but she waited for him to answer.

"It's unsafe. The Schloss is abandoned. Empty." He leaned forward now, clasped his hands on the desk. Looked straight at Anna as if he were ready for a debate.

"So how do I get this—thing—back for my grandfather then?" Anna kept her voice even.

"I can't see how you possibly can."

Anna held back the derisive laugh that was forming in her own throat. "Could you give me the owner's name, please? I think I should contact them directly." Maybe they would be more reasonable than their lawyer. She could only hope. They would surely understand that she didn't want to interfere—she just wanted to give an old man his wish.

"I can't give out clients' names, Ms. Young."

"It's Anna. Are you the only lawyer handling this client's interests?" Maybe there was someone more senior who could help. But Wil was a partner in the firm.

"I handle this client myself, Anna." Wil looked at his watch.

"But the property inside the Schloss belonged to my grandfather. Surely you can't just dismiss that out of hand."

Wil still didn't move. "It belonged to him once. Not now."

"Oh, but if he left it there, doesn't it still belong to . . . ," Anna stopped. She did not want to show that she was rattled. That seemed important if there was any hope of his taking her request seriously.

There was almost a twinkle in Wil's eye. "What was your grandfather thinking?"

"He's never asked me to do anything before and . . . ," She stopped. She did not want to reveal too much about Max. The man in front of her was an expert at drawing people out. He would want to know all the particulars, then write them down and keep them on file, in case her grandfather decided to write to him and push the matter further. She would have to be careful about what she said. She raised a hand to her head.

Anna did not want to deal with these complications—and she had not asked for them, that was true—but this was her beloved grandfather, and she was not going home without finishing her task.

Wil stood up. He held out a hand. "It's impossible. Surely you knew that."

Anna stood up too, but then her phone rang. Cass's number flashed on the screen. She let the call go through to voice mail, but it was very early in San Francisco. Anna sometimes went into the café early to help with the baking, but Cass . . .

She pulled her thoughts together. "Couldn't you at least call the owners and ask their permission? It is their property, after all—their decision. If they know it's a family member wanting to go inside, surely they would see reason."

The phone rang again. Anna looked at it for a second, her finger poised over the keypad.

"Someone wants you," Wil said.

Anna shook her head.

"Feel free to answer it."

"I'll just be a moment."

Anna took the call and went to stand by the window.

"Anna . . . ," Cass said.

• • •

A couple of minutes later, Anna had collapsed in the chair opposite Wil Jager's desk. She knew that the numbness that had formed around her body was a blanket of shock. Her mind swirled with questions. Max had always been so healthy—why did this have to happen while she was away? Then she felt annoyed—at both herself and Max. Why had he sent her away? Why had she fallen for her grandfather's mad scheme without thinking about the implications of leaving him alone when he was so old?

Suddenly, Anna was fighting back tears. This was unbelievable. She hadn't cried for years. In fact, she prided herself on being able to hold her emotions in check. What would this hard-nosed lawyer think? She brought a hand to her eyes, took a deep breath.

As soon as Cass had told her Max was in the hospital, Anna's thoughts had run to a heart attack or a stroke. It had taken her several moments to take in that Max had fallen in his kitchen while preparing dinner. Anna always popped in to see him at that time of day. Why hadn't she arranged for someone to take her place while she was away? Why had she thought that a ninety-four-year-old would be fine while she was out of the country? She had, of course, stocked his freezer and his pantry with enough food to last for a month and had organized fresh fruit and vegetable deliveries, but still. Wil Jager was right. She had been drawn into a crazy, hopeless scheme. And on top of that, Max was in real trouble and on his own.

"Are you okay?" Anna was aware of Wil leaning against his desk in front of her. She was aware of his voice, but the room had turned hazy and fluid, swimming with movement.

"Sorry about that," she said.

"Stay there a moment. Don't move." He left the room.

Anna sat back in her seat. She did feel dizzy. What were the implications of a broken shoulder at the age of ninety-four? Apparently, it wasn't yet known whether Max would need an operation. The doctor was assessing the situation, and as soon as the painkillers had taken effect, the hospital would carry out a scan. What were the risks if Max had to have surgery?

"Try to relax. Breathe," Wil said as he reappeared with a glass of water.

"Thanks. I'm fine." She took a sip, but the room still spun.

"This might help. Our kitchen staff thought . . ." Wil seemed a little embarrassed now. He handed her a small warm towel.

"Oh, thank you," Anna held it up to her face. It was scented with something familiar—eau de cologne. Max used to buy it for her grandmother.

Anna forced that thought away and looked up at the man standing near her. She would have to calm down. She had always made a point of leading an orderly life, but everything seemed to be spiraling out of control. She was letting Germany get to her. She had to get her act together.

"My grandfather's had an accident. He's in the hospital. I should be there. That's all." Anna placed the towel on her lap.

"Sorry to hear that."

She sensed him watching her. "Is it bad?" he asked.

"Fractured shoulder. He might need an operation—but at ninety-four . . ."

Wil was quiet again. When he spoke, his voice was softer. "I brought you these too. They might make you feel better."

Anna looked up. Wil had a small white box in his hands. He had taken off the lid, and nestled inside was a cluster of perfect-looking chocolates.

"A client makes them. She moved to Berlin recently and we have a standing order now. They're quite good. If you'd like one . . ."

Anna reached out, and in spite of everything, managed a smile. "Thank you," she said. For some reason, she felt curious about German chocolate and surprised at a loyalty to Germany that she had never felt before. Was she beginning to feel a little at home in her ancestral country—as well as confused and hopelessly shut out? She put the truffle in her mouth, allowing its smoothness to slip over her tongue.

"This little episode must be costing me a fortune," she said, a chuckle rising in her throat.

"No charge for fainting—or chocolates." Something twinkled in his eyes.

Anna felt a renewed determination kick in. She would keep trying. "I know Max's request is crazy, but don't you think there's any chance we could help him a little? His age . . ."

Wil picked up a gold ballpoint pen and rolled it around in his fingers, whirling it so quickly that it became a blur.

"That makes me dizzy," Anna almost laughed.

"Sorry. Helps me to think."

So he was thinking about it. Anna didn't say a thing.

"You could always break in with a flashlight," he said, finally.

"I could. Always wanted to get arrested in a foreign country." Anna was beginning to feel a little more like herself. "I'd probably impale myself on the barbed wire though."

Wil's brow went up. "Do you know what it is that your grandfather wants? Not that I think there's any hope my clients will let you in. Just wondering."

Anna held out the chocolate box, offered one

99

to Wil. He took one. She thought about it. If she wanted Wil to help her, perhaps she should explain. He would have to be bound by some kind of client confidentiality clause—weren't they all supposed to keep quiet? As long as he didn't tell the owners.

"Anna." Wil's voice interrupted her thoughts.

"Just thinking."

"You can tell me," he said. "I won't pass it on. Not even to the owner. Whatever is said in here is confidential. Always. I would never say anything that you didn't want me to repeat."

"Okay, then," she said, finally. "Max asked me to retrieve an engagement ring . . . he never gave it to someone. In 1940, apparently. Tells me it was the biggest regret of his life. And now, he wants it back. So."

"You're joking."

Anna shook her head.

Wil moved back to sit at his desk. "Okay. Do you know where he left it?"

"His bedroom. I have a photocopied map of the Schloss. And I know which room was his. I could find the room in no time if you let me in."

He looked at her then, and Anna looked away. She didn't know why, but she felt compelled to look away whenever she met his eye. She must just be feeling vulnerable after the shock of Max's news. That would be it.

"I take it the hiding spot is utterly cryptic?"

"Max hopes so."

"Hmm."

Anna bit her lip. The taste of chocolate lingered, delicious. "Is there any chance you might change your mind and let me in then?"

Wil inclined his head. "I have been inside the Schloss. Only once."

"The mayor said that."

Wil stayed quiet.

"What was it like?"

"Stunning," he said, putting his gold pen back to rest in its holder. "Beautiful. Unspoiled—which is more to the point. Even though it's . . . like it is."

"Imagine having to leave it."

"Yes. Imagine that." Wil typed something into his computer.

"I'd love to see inside, engagement ring or not," Anna started. "I didn't know anything about it until last week, you see."

Wil looked up. "Your grandfather never spoke to you about Siegel, Anna?"

Anna shook her head.

He sat back in his chair and studied her again. "Your family was the largest landowner in old Prussia. They had priceless art collections, funded wars—European campaigns such as the Napoleonic Wars. They were bankers. Some of your family's paintings ended up in major galleries around the world after the Soviet occupation. Your grandfather would have had an incredible lifestyle until . . ."

Anna took in a sharp breath. "Perhaps it's understandable that he never spoke of it then! The loss . . ."

Wil stayed quiet.

"Do you still have the key?" she asked.

Wil glanced at his computer again. "Just looking at the meetings I have coming up."

Anna stayed silent. This seemed like the wrong moment to press him further.

"Look, Anna, I can't believe I'm saying this, and to be honest, I don't know why I am, but I could try to swap my commitments for tomorrow and take you up to Siegel in the morning. I can get you inside. And, if we can retrieve the ring, perhaps the owners needn't even know we were there. But you have to understand, you mustn't say a word to anyone. And I never do this sort of thing. It's just that . . ."

"Okay," she said. "That would be . . . very good." Very good? Lucky English was Wil's second language!

But he was on to it. "Very good?" He smiled, his eyes playful.

"Just tell me when to be ready. And it would be fantastic," she added in a rush. "Thank you."

He kept right up with her. "Nine o'clock tomorrow? Is here good for you?"

"It is." Anna stood up. Suddenly she felt much better. Surely her news would help cheer up poor Max. All she could do was hope that finding his long-lost ring would give him the strength to get through his recovery.

Lake Geneva, 1934

If anyone had told Isabelle before she came to Lake Geneva that she would feel what she felt now, she would have said that they were mad. But now, sitting on a lawn that ran down to a secluded lakeside beach—the water glowing with the sort of magic light that only appeared in the late afternoon and apparently only in Switzerland—Isabelle knew that all she could do was run with it. Why ever would anyone fight perfection? Why on earth had she given up hoping for its existence?

The friendship that she had formed with Virginia Brooke had swelled into the sort of indulgent affection that she had never experienced with her girlfriends in Paris. Isabelle knew that Virginia understood her. Virginia was fun and open, and utterly herself. There was no pretense about her. She had been quite open about the fact that she wished to avoid leading the sort of life that her family had planned for her. That was why she had chosen to travel, using an inheritance that she had received from her grandfather when she came of age.

Virginia encouraged Isabelle to be herself as well. They had taken to spending most days together, albeit in a big group that consisted of Max and his family, along with several other young people from the hotel who joined their daily outings.

But Virginia always made Isabelle laugh. She seemed, like Max, to sense when Isabelle was quiet or withdrawn, when she lapsed into the thoughts that used to plague her constantly in Paris. Where was her life going? Would she ever be accepted, the granddaughter of one of the most famous demimondaines in Paris . . . a prostitute?

Those things didn't seem to matter to Virginia at all. When Isabelle had, one evening, finally told her friend the truth about Marthe, Virginia had looked at her, held out a hand, and then laughed. Then she had apologized—she had thought it was going to be something far more dreadful than that.

After that, Isabelle had felt more comfortable with Virginia than ever. She talked freely with the American girl about politics, fashion, men, Paris, art, the future—and her developing feelings for Max.

But still one question hung over her head like a rock on the edge of a precipice. What would happen if she told Max the truth about her grand-mother?

He came from an aristocratic family.

They were hardly going to welcome the grand-daughter of a courtesan into their midst.

And now it was nearly time for Max to leave. It was nearly time for Isabelle to return to Paris. It was nearly time for all this magic to end.

The only consolation was that Virginia was returning to Paris to stay. She was inordinately excited at the prospect of spending the fall in the world's most romantic city.

The thought of leaving Max caused Isabelle's stomach to churn and threatened to spoil her last days with him. Now, he was stretched out next to her on the picnic rug that the hotel had packed for their latest outing. He had propped himself up on one elbow, his eyes focused lazily on Didi and Jo as they fished at the edge of the lake. Max's boater was tipped at a rakish angle, and one hand rested in Isabelle's own.

The first time Max had kissed her, Isabelle had nearly died on her feet. They had been dancing on the terrace when they'd been drawn to each other. After dancing, they had walked to a quiet spot at the edge of the lake, Max's fingers entwined loosely with hers, as natural as could be.

It was one of those dreamy evenings when the pink sunset had lapsed ever so slowly into velvet moonlight, holding only the deepest of promises and secrets. Max had stopped, turned her to face him, and cupped her chin in his hands. As his lips had touched hers, the feelings that had been flickering within her since she first talked to him billowed in intensity, blooming into something so magnificent she felt utterly swept away. One thing had been certain—right at that moment, nothing else had counted.

Isabelle had been fighting with herself ever since, trying to trick herself into thinking that everything would be fine, that she would be capable of returning to her old life when she returned to Paris. Eventually, she had given up. There was nothing she could do about her feelings for Max.

Marthe knew that Isabelle and Max had become good friends, but Isabelle had not confided to her grandmother that she had fallen in love. Men had always been a commodity for her. While Marthe had always preferred the company of men to that of women, Isabelle was pretty sure that she had never let any of them in as a real confidante— and certainly never allowed herself to be caught up in the thrall of love.

Even though Isabelle had tried to make clear to her grandmother that she was less brazen than Marthe, Marthe had always advised independence above all things. Isabelle needn't worry about money, as she would inherit the apartment in Paris, with all its exotic furnishings and Marthe's exquisite jewelry collection. These gifts from Marthe's habitués—some of the most important and powerful men in late-nineteenth-century Europe—were already worth a small fortune, and their value would only increase. Even though Marthe had supported Isabelle's forays into the world of young men, she always told her granddaughter to keep her head—never let herself fall headlong in love.

And now look what had happened.

Isabelle loved her grandmother's strength of character and her independent spirit, of course she did. But how would she explain Max to Marthe? What's more, how would she explain Marthe to Max?

Isabelle sat up and sighed. Her hand slipped out of Max's. He sat up too, frowned.

"What is it?" he asked.

Isabelle closed her eyes. She often wondered if he knew what she was thinking before she did.

"Nothing," she said.

But Max wasn't fooled. "Tell me."

Isabelle stood up and walked over to the shore. Virginia was leaning against a rock, reading a novel by some American writer—one of the new members of the avant-garde who seemed to have taken over the Left Bank. Marthe always scoffed at them, mocking their desire to live in squalor while posing as intellectuals. Marthe mourned her own era, the turn of the century and the years before that, when life had gleamed with impossible glamour and a dash of devastating theatricality, when Montmartre had been the center of everything, when dance halls and theaters and circuses had reigned. She mourned a time when the city had been filled with images of *les demimondaines*—the Parisian courtesans who were posted on billboards on every street corner—when everything had seemed modern and exciting and possibilities had been endless, until the war happened, until the *Titanic* sank, until everything Marthe's generation had believed in had been turned on its head.

But then, Max had told Isabelle about his life. His life in Germany that was so vastly different from the world Marthe talked about. The idea of Max's home in Germany enticed Isabelle so much that she hardly dared to hope or admit to herself how much, one day, she would love to be a part of it all. He talked of winter afternoon teas of home-baked rye bread and jam along with cake topped with sliced apples in the library at Schloss Siegel with his father, whom he called Vati, and his quiet chats with his mother in her writing room, with its view of the lake and the deer park beyond. He described convivial games of billiards with Didi, Jo, and his cousins, snowball fights, nights spent around bonfires in the park, sleigh rides in the whisper-quiet forest, dances in the grand salon with musicians from the Berlin Philharmonic playing Strauss and Schubert for all their guests, family picnics by the lake in the summer, riding expeditions from the old stables where the family coaches were kept, the annual village fair, and ice skating. Isabelle could hardly believe it wasn't a fairy tale. And then there was Max's work—learning how to run the estate, working with the villagers, looking after the family and its business, preserving the Schloss— and his dreams of having a family of his own, one day, in a country that was at peace not only with itself, but with its neighbors. Isabelle just listened in a state of wonder. It sounded, to her, like heaven.

But until now, Max had always assumed things would be the same. Traditions would remain in place, and life would go on as it had for hundreds of years—in spite of the losses of the last war. But now everything he held most dear was suddenly under threat.

"Shall we go for a walk?" Max asked.

He stood up, brushing off his cream trousers. He had allowed his shirt to become untucked.

Isabelle called to Virginia, telling her that she and Max wouldn't stray too far. Didi and Jo's whoops resounded along the beach. Nadja had gone shopping for the day with Sascha.

Max was silent as they strolled along the rocky

cove. They headed toward the end of the beach, where there was no chance their conversation would be overheard. Max stopped when they reached the large, flat rocks that sat before a bank of high cliffs. The beach had curved, and they were safely out of sight of the others.

Isabelle was slightly ahead of Max now. She leaned down to pick up an unusual-shaped stone that had lodged in a rock pool.

Max stopped beside her, turning her to face him as he looked down into her eyes. "What is it?"

Isabelle hesitated. Now was not the time to tell Max the truth about Marthe.

"Are you worried about the future, about what's going to happen after the summer's over?" he asked.

Isabelle hugged her arms around herself.

"We need to sort out how we're going to meet, and when," Max said, taking a strand of her hair and tucking it behind her ear.

Isabelle sighed. Every part of her lived for the moments she spent with Max now. She felt more alive when she was with him, talking to him, than when she was doing anything else.

"We need to talk to your grandmother, but we should come up with a plan first," Max went on. He took a step closer again. "I've been thinking, would you and Virginia like . . . do you think your grandmother could spare you both for Christmas this year? I won't have to work then, the Schloss is beautiful in the wintertime, and all my family will be there."

"I would love to ask my grandmother, and I think Virginia would love to come too, if I can pull her away from Paris and what she sees as glamour and excitement and thrills. None of that matters to me, you know."

"I know," Max said, cupping her chin in his hand.

Isabelle leaned in toward him.

"I don't like you worrying," he said. Max's voice was just a murmur now, but it was as clear to Isabelle as if he were talking at full pitch. "Let's sort things out for Christmas."

After a few moments, he moved down to the water. He picked up a flat stone and threw it into the lake, sending it bouncing across the surface several times.

Isabelle stayed where she was.

Max continued staring at the smooth lake. "I hope these will not be the last few Christmases that we get to spend in the way we are used to— at Siegel."

Isabelle felt indignation rising like a snake. "I hope not. Surely it isn't as bad as that?"

"My parents want me to . . . commit." Max frowned. The way he held himself was proud, so dignified. Isabelle hated to think of his having to fight alongside the Nazi army. She hated the thought of another war. Anybody could see that he was an upstanding young man who wanted to do what was right, that he had strong convictions. It was one of the things she adored about him.

"I know." Isabelle went to stand beside him. The water's serenity seemed to mock the fact that Isabelle was about to be separated from the man she loved. There. She had admitted her feelings to herself.

"Just think about those millions of Germans who were unemployed last year. It's more confusing than you might think—after all, the Nazis are doing a great deal to reduce unemployment and give people work and a reason to feel hopeful for the future. They are doing far more than the Weimar Republic did. And they are achieving results."

Isabelle's throat went dry. "But their actions . . ."

Max sounded matter-of-fact. "We have three problems in Germany—first, guilt about the war; second, the enormous reparations that we are forced to pay; and third, the severe limitations to our military that were forced upon us at the Treaty of Versailles. And we need a government that is willing to address these things."

"How bad is it, being there?" Isabelle sensed a shift in her own feelings, sensed, somehow, that this relationship was becoming more mature. Right now, here by the lake.

Max shook his head. "People were starving after the Kaiser fled. There was a lot of hatred directed towards the new government for signing the armistice. Violent uprisings were the result—then terrorist assassinations of government politicians, including our foreign minister, a general strike, hyperinflation, threats from Communists."

Isabelle nodded. But now, all protests had been banned.

"As for what it's been like, living there," Max went on, "I have a friend from our village, someone with whom I grew up, who cannot find work in Germany. I hate to think what will become of him, and I wonder if he'll ever be able to come home. Another family friend, a man in his forties, has not been able to support his four children since losing his job in a nearby town. It wasn't until he had spent all his savings and was facing starvation that he came to us for help. But where does that cycle end? Millions of people living like that? I am in a position to make a difference, Isabelle. I can't stand by and do nothing. Do you see?"

"Yes." Isabelle felt something heavy settle in her chest.

Max was silent again for a moment before he spoke. "I have to believe in something. My parents are right. I have a responsibility to my family, my village, and Germany. No more sitting on the fence. If the Nazis are the only way to bring hope to my country and assure a stable future for my family and my village, then how can I say no?"

Isabelle folded her arms around herself. He was right. He did have to do something. He had to take a stand. But . . .

Max spoke in a low voice now. If the afternoon hadn't been so still, his words might have gotten lost in the smallest breeze. "Hitler promises that the nervous years have ended, that with him, the German way of life will be determined for the next thousand years. He promises national health care, government schooling, partnerships between the government and businesses. He says he will inject government funds into social welfare and the industrial sector, as well as the military. And he says that he will not bring war to Europe, that the only way it would happen would be if the Communists began a conflict. He says he will protect us and our need for peace—he will bring us out of our deep national crisis. We need strength."

Isabelle had to say something. "I agree that a strong leader in a time of crisis is crucial," she said. She took a few steps toward the water, then turned back to Max. She had to have this out with him. "But there are rumors circulating throughout Europe about his treatment of the Jews—how do you deal with that, Max?"

"I've told you that my decision was not easy. But when it comes to my family—I have to think of their future first. I have to work with my parents to make things better for everyone around us. If I turn against them, then it will cause chaos for my family and all the people whom we support. Should I turn my back on my parents and our government just because of some unsubstantiated rumors?"

Isabelle wanted to reach out and take him in her arms.

"My parents want me to go to the Nuremberg rallies. I think that at least I should go and hear Hitler speak. Does that make sense, Isabelle?"

She moved to stand next to him. And he reached out, taking her hand in his own and holding it, close to his heart. She leaned in toward him, and she felt more at home there than anywhere else in the world.

Three days later, Isabelle stood with Virginia at the water's edge, their packed suitcases surrounding them on the landing. The paddle steamer that would take them to the train station in Geneva made its stately way toward them.

"You are good at keeping secrets," she said to Virginia, out of the blue.

"I've learned to keep my own counsel." Virginia looked especially radiant today. Her blond hair was swept back into a neat chignon underneath her small hat, and she wore a powder-blue, high-waisted suit that showed off her slim figure.

"I admire your independence." Isabelle tugged at her white gloves.

"But it's not what you want for yourself." Virginia stared straight ahead.

"Surely a family and independent thought shouldn't be mutually exclusive. Not if you are with the man who loves you and whom you love back." Isabelle watched the steamer approaching.

Virginia held out a hand. "I love your idealism. And the funny thing is that on top of that, you don't want to shock your grandmother with your hopes for a perfect family life. It is all so out of the ordinary."

"I suppose it is," Isabelle said. She had not confided in Virginia about her conversation with Max—out of the ordinary was one way to describe the world in which they lived now.

"You want to pretend that the Albrechts are just German friends where Marthe is concerned," Virginia went on. "But do you honestly think you have kept your secret from her?"

"I don't want to hurt Grand-mère. If you come with me to Siegel this winter, it will look quite sensible, Virginia. After all, we have been out with the Albrechts nearly every day this summer. Most of what has happened between Max and me has taken place away from this hotel. We have behaved ourselves perfectly while Grand-mère has been watching."

Virginia smiled and shook her head. "You, Isabelle de Florian, run deeper than most people realize. Of course I'll keep your secret."

"It is necessary for now. She would never understand."

Marthe was approaching.

"I cannot wait to see Paris," Virginia said, leaning in to kiss the older woman's cheek.

Marthe patted Virginia on the arm. "And we cannot wait to show it to you," she said.

A man in uniform announced that the steamer was ready for boarding. Isabelle moved toward it without looking back at the hotel. She suspected that this summer had been a beautiful diversion, but it was not something that she would ever get back.

CHAPTER SIX

Paris, 1934

Isabelle was prepared for Virginia's reaction
to her grandmother's apartment. Some people
knew about *les demimondaines*—those women
who were the very highest of courtesans in Belle
Époque Paris—but few seemed to understand
how all-encompassing the role really was.

No one seemed to realize that her grandmother
had lived every single aspect of her life as someone other than herself. Yes, she had performed
in the most famous dance halls in Paris. Yes, she
had entertained the most distinguished of men at
the most elegant of places. But this meant that
she could never go back to the person she had
been before she became the famous "Marthe de
Florian," and that she could never get away from
the forgery she had made of herself—not even,
and especially not, at home.

Even though she was in her seventies, Marthe
had let go of precisely nothing that had been given
to her during her time as a courtesan. Her entire
apartment was a perfectly preserved remnant
from the Belle Époque. Was she afraid that if

she sold one piece of furniture, one fading, gilt-edged gift—if she burned one decades-old love letter or disposed of even one of her fabulously dated evening dresses—that her carefully curated persona would crumble? Did she believe that, like Cinderella, she would return home from the ball with her clothes in tatters? Would she simply be Mathilde Heloise Beaugiron once again?

Marthe insisted on not only keeping but also using *that* chaise longue. Even Isabelle knew that the singular piece of furniture had been the subject of an infinite number of whispered conversations at dinner tables during the 1890s.

A stuffed ostrich greeted visitors on their arrival in the salon. Countless sets of elaborate crystal vases and glasses filled every cupboard in the room, while the silverware on display in cabinets was grand enough for royalty. Hundreds of delicate creations in the finest porcelain had been given to Marthe by her illustrious clients—apparently they had competed with each other both for the beautiful young woman's attention and in spoiling her. Only part of the collection was on display on the walls in her sitting room. The rest of the pieces were crammed onto side tables, mantelpieces, anywhere they could be seen, and more importantly, where Marthe's admirers could see their own gifts on display. It was the way that Marthe secured these men's loyalty and made use of their pride.

Isabelle watched as Virginia walked into the salon. She looked dumbstruck by it all. Virginia stood by the window, where she took off her gloves, handing them to Marthe's maid, Camille. Then she unpinned her hat with one hand and ran the other over the gauzy green curtains that hung to the floor.

After a while, Isabelle took her friend to see the rest of the apartment. Virginia seemed entranced with Marthe's sitting room. She clutched at Isabelle's hand, exclaiming at the French wallpaper covered in tiny pink and green roses, their leaves intertwined like so many lovers dancing in pretty patterns on the wall. She appeared to want to touch everything. The silky black grand piano was covered not with family photographs, as one would have found in most people's homes, but with the most perfect of tiny gifts, engraved cigarette cases, and an entire lady's travel set made of silver and glass, with a golden handle. The silver brushes that sat nearby were engraved with the initials *MdeF*. There were silk purses on display and embroidered handkerchiefs, old perfume bottles, and silver jewelry cases, now empty of their wares. Marthe kept her many precious jewels locked away in a safe in the depths of her dressing room.

Isabelle led Virginia into Marthe's bedroom. The room was fit for a princess. The four-poster bed—its cover an ostentatious deep red—was bedecked with a mountain of pillows and soft cushions in amber, gold, and deep mahogany. On either side of the enormous bed, ornate fringed lamps sat atop fantastical bedside tables—their feet fashioned into the shape of some imaginary animal's paws. These tables also held Marthe's collection of exquisite silver bells from the very best silversmiths in Europe.

But Isabelle knew what was going to elicit the sharpest reaction from her friend. She waited in silence until Virginia's eyes alighted on the portrait of Marthe as a young woman that hung on the wall opposite her bed. The painting was by some famous artist or another—Marthe would never say whether he had been one of her many lovers. Marthe's head was turned to the side, one hand on her décolletage, her fingers resting lightly on that part of her that so many men had touched.

If Isabelle hadn't known her friend as well as she did, she could have mistaken her silence for disapproval. But Isabelle knew better. She simply kept her fingers entwined in Virginia's and moved on to the next room.

"It's too much," Virginia gasped.

She stopped dead at the entrance to the pretty, delicate dressing room. This was where Marthe had prepared herself before meeting her clientele in the salon. Through her friend's eyes, Isabelle was reminded once again of Marthe's extraordinary past. Marthe had been warm and genuine and loving with her always, while manipulating men and seeming so resolutely alone in the world.

Marthe had assured Isabelle that none of the men had been allowed to enter her bedroom. But Isabelle wondered whether any of the men had come to understand Marthe, or more to the point, whether Marthe had ever fallen for any of her lovers.

Isabelle opened the next door, taking Virginia into another room, a room that had been decorated only fourteen years earlier, when a confused little girl had arrived at her grandmother's house. She had suffered the loss of both her parents to the Spanish flu epidemic that had swept through Europe.

Camille was unpacking Isabelle and Virginia's suitcases when they entered the room. She had their summer dresses arranged on the two single beds, working quietly, smoothing the items out and hanging them with great care on padded hangers. Next she would put away the hats, gloves, and soft chiffon tops that went with the girls' fashionable high-waisted skirts.

There was some comfort for Isabelle in returning to her own room, to her own space. She had always felt at peace here.

"I think it is time for tea." Isabelle smiled.

They were in Paris. They would eat patisseries.

Marthe was already sitting in one of the Louis XV chairs that were arranged in the salon, pouring the coffee that Camille had laid out before attending to her unpacking duties.

"You are part of a pilgrimage of Americans to Paris, Virginia," Marthe said. She handed the girls a gilt-edged plate of delicate patisseries—from milky creations that wobbled, gelatinous, on the plate, to tiny chocolate gateaux and lush, deep-purple berry tarts. "Their presence here should make you feel quite at home."

Virginia took a miniature tarte tatin and placed it on her plate.

After half an hour, Isabelle put her coffee cup down in its saucer. "Virginia, I think we shall go for a walk," she said, leaning across and kissing her grandmother, who was clearly tired after the journey home.

"You never told me how much there was," Virginia said, once they had put on their hats and were trotting down the stairs to the entrance lobby.

"I never know how much to say." Isabelle shrugged.

Virginia took Isabelle's arm and gazed at the elegant facade of Marthe's building. Gleaming ironwork fanned out over the front door, and the curved windows were polished to a sheen.

Isabelle led her friend down Rue Blanche,

turning onto Rue Saint-Lazare. Even to her, the bustle after Lake Geneva was something of a shock. A sandwich seller, who removed his cap in an effort to draw them in, immediately accosted the girls.

"No, thank you," Isabelle said, dragging Virginia down the street.

But the noise stopped them from conducting much conversation. The air was filled with the sounds of one-man bands, the swish of a fire breather, and conjurers calling out for audiences to watch their tricks. Others begged anyone to buy their shoelaces or their ties, and some people even had displays in upturned umbrellas. Isabelle dodged a sword swallower while Virginia simply turned and stared.

When the sound of a procession filled the air, Isabelle rolled her eyes and pulled Virginia out of the way. "Students," she said. "From the Latin Quarter. Letting off steam."

"Oh, my," Virginia said. Isabelle watched her friend meet the gaze of a handsome young student. Virginia grinned at the boy, completely unashamed.

"That's more like it," Isabelle giggled.

"Oh, it's not this that's floored me," Virginia said. "It's that darned apartment." They walked a little farther, toward the Seine, arms linked.

"I know," Isabelle said. "Do you mind if we don't talk about it?"

Virginia stopped. "Surely you are not ashamed?"

"No, but I am resigned. It's just that I am restricted by it. It has controlled my life, how I am perceived, where I am accepted, who will talk to me, acknowledge me, and accept me because of my name. You understand?"

"So she really was as famous as you say?"

"Yes," Isabelle said. "One of the most celebrated in all of Paris."

While it was clear that a smile had formed on Virginia's lips, her grip on Isabelle's arm tightened. "But you still haven't told Max."

"No." Isabelle felt her mood sink. "I haven't told Max."

"How delicious," Virginia said. "I can't wait to see what his family makes of it." But then she stopped again, looked straight into Isabelle's eyes. "If there are any problems, they will have to deal with me, you know."

Isabelle shook her head. How much had Max told his parents about her? "Excellent," she muttered, and she tugged her friend right on down the street.

Germany, 2010

Wil Jager's mood seemed quite the opposite of what it had been the day before. He didn't meet

Anna's eye when she arrived in the lobby of his office building, and he was quiet as he ushered her into a car that was parked right outside the front doors of his swish building.

Anna fought every instinct that she had in order to remain silent herself—she wanted to ask questions and find out what he knew about Schloss Siegel. Why had the owners left it to ruin? Did they have plans for its future? If so, what were they?

The early-morning traffic had subsided, and it didn't take long until they were on the Berliner Ring road and heading toward Siegel.

After they passed through two bigger towns, the land opened up into flat fields, replete with deep-green crops, and then gave way to thick forest. The road wound through several villages. When they passed a set of elaborate gates, their black iron curling in delicate patterns, Anna craned her neck to catch a glimpse of a turreted roofline—another Schloss, set in a flat, wooded landscape that was reminiscent of fairy tales. Anna could only hope that her ancestral home might have its own happy ending one day.

"I'm sorry, Anna. I've got a lot on my mind. You must think I'm terribly rude. How is your grandfather today?"

"He's going to have an operation on his shoulder. I had a brief conversation with him early this morning. He didn't sound too . . . down.

In fact, he tried to divert the conversation away from himself. Typical Max." Anna smiled. "He was all about reassuring me that he wanted me here in Germany, that I was in the right place."

She glanced over at Wil. He kept his eyes on the road, but she saw a smile pass across his features.

"He sounds like he's very special to you."

"He is." She had so many memories of her times with Max. Often, he would take her out after school for milkshakes. He had loved to chat with her about goings-on with her girl-friends, everything that was happening at school. And Anna had opened up to him as she had to no one else—she had been able to talk with him about the death of her mother, her distant father's decision to start a new life in Canada with his second wife, and Anna's decision to stay in San Francisco with her grandparents. Now Anna realized how hard it must have been for Max to swallow his past, never to talk about it, having left all of this behind. Would he ever tell her why?

Wil slowed down as they approached the Schloss, and Anna felt grateful they were nearly at their destination. The countryside was only sending further worrisome thoughts about Max into her tired mind. She had hardly slept the night before due to thinking about him.

When Wil stopped at the first set of gates that

Anna had found and climbed out of the car, Anna followed him.

"Would you like a hand?" she asked, glad to get out of the car.

"Thank you," Wil said, but he appeared to have retreated into himself even further. He unlocked the padlock that held the wrought iron together.

Anna pushed one of the heavy gates open while he took the other side. The gate stuck to the ground in places as she heaved it open. Once they were back in the car, they bumped along the potholed driveway.

As Wil continued along the main driveway that led to the palace, Anna gasped. The other end of the building from the one she had glimpsed the other day was visible, and to the right, the forest opened up into a vast park, studded with grand old trees.

"I'm taking you for a drive around the whole house," Wil said. "The main entrance is on the other side of the Schloss. It was designed so that the formal living areas open up off the terrace that overlooks the lake."

Anna feasted on everything outside the car window, in her own methodical way. First, there was the park to the right of the car. Remnants of an old garden were visible near the house. Ancient rose bushes still lined what looked like the remains of an ornamental garden. The old plants' stems were gnarled, and the fat, apple-like rosehips still sat valiantly in place. Beyond this, trees dotted the vast lawn.

There were glimpses of an old path that wound down to the lake, which was fringed with reeds. Water lilies mooned about on the surface of the water. Anna found her imagination conjuring parties on the lake's edge—women dressed in white, parasols, champagne. A venerable old ruin sat on the far side of the lake, covered in ivy, and a small jetty leaned into the water, balancing on rickety legs. An island sat right in the middle of the lake.

Wil stopped the car. "Would you like to stop here and have a proper look?" His voice was unexpectedly soft now.

Anna nodded. She focused on the garden for a moment longer before turning to look at the Schloss.

When she did turn to look at the palace, there was such a welling of something—love, perhaps—inside her that she felt paralyzed. There were so many hangovers from desperate times. Bullet holes dotted the building's old walls, some of them opening up into deep gashes. Anna reassured herself that they could be fixed. But she couldn't help feeling that seeing the Schloss in this state was akin to seeing one of her ancestor's graves, crumbling beyond repair.

The windows were not boarded up, but many of them appeared to be covered in newspaper, and they seemed to reach from floor to ceiling all the way along the front of the building before the terrace.

Anna turned to face Wil. "Shall we?"

Wil nodded. He turned on the car engine and drove around to the main entrance on the other side of the building.

Schloss Siegel, December 1934

Isabelle would never forget the day she arrived at the fairy-tale Schloss for the Christmas that she had arranged to spend with Max and his family. When she stepped out of the sled onto the frozen driveway, she did not know where to look first. The ride from the train station through the snow-covered village had been one of the most romantic experiences of her life. Max had described his home to her in the many letters he had sent since they left Switzerland, but nothing he had said could have prepared her for this first glimpse of Schloss Siegel. Now all she could do was gape at the gorgeous building in front of her.

A Christmas wreath laden with bright berries and ivy hung on the double-leafed white front door. The grand entrance had a black-and-white tiled front porch and was flanked with two white pillars. On either side of the door, leadlight glass allowed glimpses of yellow light to filter to the darkness outside.

Isabelle placed her gloved hand in Max's as she climbed the front steps. She turned at the top, running her eyes over the wonderland in front of the Schloss. The snow-covered grounds stretched all the way to the stone wall that surrounded the park. Every tree was weighed down with icicles; hints of dark wood were barely visible through the sea of white.

Max's valet, Hans, was on hand, supervising the footmen who had appeared as if by magic to unload the sleigh. He gave instructions in German and nodded at Isabelle, looking her up and down in a way that was not exactly disrespectful but made her wonder if he knew what was going on between her and Max. Perhaps he was Max's confidant—who knew?

One of the footmen threw the front doors open with a flourish, sending light flooding out to the semidark afternoon, highlighting the servants as they bustled about on the porch.

Max, having kissed Isabelle on the cheek, having clasped her hand in his, stepped aside for Isabelle and Virginia to enter. Though accustomed to her grandmother's distinctive form of glamour, Isabelle found herself simply awed by the grandeur that greeted her here. Gray-and-white checkered marble floors stretched across the vast entrance hall, anchored by a gilt-edged marble table embellished with a bouquet of resplendent hothouse flowers.

A maid appeared and knelt down at Isabelle and Virginia's feet, removing the fur-lined overshoes that they had been given for the sleigh ride.

"We call them elephant trotters," Max smiled as Isabelle looked up at him. "No need for them inside, obviously."

While the uniformed maid removed the warm shoe coverings, Isabelle took the opportunity to feast her eyes. Opposite her, two enormous urns flanked a second set of double doors that mirrored those at the entrance to the Schloss. These white doors were thrown open, and through them, there was a glimpse of a room of the most elegant proportions. Isabelle knew that this was the music salon. Max had described his home in his letters over the past months, while she had pined away in Paris.

To the left of the double doors, a grand staircase wound its way up to the top floors of the Schloss. Suddenly Isabelle stopped and stared.

Her eyes had caught those of the woman who stood on the stairs, but it was not Nadja's face that held Isabelle's attention—it was what she wore. Her blood-red dress was the latest fashion, and it clung to Nadja's slender body like a kid glove. The woman's blond hair was swept up into an elaborate French chignon; a strand of pearls hung across her slender throat.

Something awkward, cold, lingered between her and Max's only sister. It had been there since the first time they had met. Isabelle had tried chatting with her, but Nadja always brushed her aside. Every time Isabelle encountered Nadja, it seemed as if the girl was either in deep thought or in intense conversation with someone else.

Isabelle turned away, distracted by the arrival of another sleigh outside.

"Vati and Mutti," Max said. He guided Isabelle back toward the front door.

The servants disappeared outside in order to meet Max's parents' sleigh.

"They'll love you," Max murmured into Isabelle's ear.

Isabelle braced herself, silently praying that Max's mother had not made inquiries into her family's background. And how much did they know about her relationship with Max? She hadn't felt comfortable asking him such a thing in her letters. What would they think of her?

When Max's mother arrived, her fur coat sweeping behind her, everyone seemed to hurtle to attention—all except Didi and Jo, who leaned against the banisters like a pair of beautiful Adonises. Isabelle sensed their eyes running over her before they turned their appraisals to Virginia. In three months, the boyishness appeared to have gone. They were louche with the sort of arrogance that only youth can pull off.

Virginia was undeniably calm. She moved over to Max's mother, her hand held out—a gorgeous smile lighting up her classic features.

"It's delightful to meet you, Frau Albrecht," Virginia said. "Max has told us so much about you."

Isabelle marveled at Virginia's ability to hold sway over a situation with the use of flattery that was, in fact, genuine.

Max's mother removed her fur hat. A maid took off the elegant blond woman's coat. This one action seemed to transform Frau Albrecht into someone quite different—the swish was gone, and the woman who stood in front of Isabelle suddenly looked far less intimidating. Isabelle knew that of all the relationships in the world, the one between a man's partner and his mother could be the most tenuous. She felt her shoulders relax.

Max's mother took Virginia's hand and murmured something welcoming to her. When she turned to Isabelle, she smiled. There was no calculation in her looks, no tightening of her cheeks into a false smile, and there was absolutely no reaction to the name de Florian.

After a few moments, Max's voice came from behind, and Isabelle turned to smile at him. "My father is talking with his valet outside, but he is so keen to meet you," he said.

Isabelle took in the hint of dark amusement in

his voice as he watched Virginia go over to say hello to Didi and Jo, who both stood at least a head taller than her and seemed to be able to cope with her forward manners with far more aplomb than they had a few months earlier during their expeditions on the lake.

Max's father struck Isabelle as a man with purpose. He handed his hat to his valet, removed his leather gloves, and shrugged off his coat with the ease of a man who was used to having people on hand to catch whatever he chose to discard.

"Vati," Max said, "this is Isabelle de Florian."

The sound of Virginia's laughter rang through the room.

"Isabelle," Max's father said, "it is a pleasure to meet you." He spoke English with no trace of an accent. "I want you to feel quite at home here. We will look forward to talking more tonight at dinner."

Isabelle smiled up into his eyes, which were blue, just like Max's.

"Pleased to meet you," Isabelle said, sticking to English while her thoughts whirled in French.

"Isabelle and Virginia will want to go upstairs and freshen up," Frau Albrecht said. "Berthe will show you to your rooms."

A young maid stepped forward. She held out a hand to indicate that the guests should make their way upstairs.

Isabelle felt Virginia link her arm through her

own. "Come on, darling," she said. "I just cannot wait to see this place. Imagine the fun we are going to have!"

Schloss Siegel, 2010

Anna's boots crunched on the caked dirt in front of the entrance to the Schloss. As she placed her foot on the first tread-worn step, her nose screwed up at the sight of the utilitarian handrail that had been affixed beside the stairs. It looked, like so many other postwar remnants, as if it had been dumped there like an ugly afterthought. Only a scattering of tiles remained intact on the entrance porch floor—the stubborn ones that had survived successions of troops, officials, and other blow-ins over the decades. The remaining tiles were split and cracked, and in some spots only the outline of a pattern remained etched in the cement.

Anna picked her way toward the front door, its white paint dull and faded. Giant cracks split the wood in places, and dirty marks scuffed the plain steel handles. The shape of the old handles was still indented into the paint, and there was a round mark where once a doorknocker must have been.

Wil was close behind her. He had the key in his hand.

"Brace yourself. This might be a shock," Wil said.

Anna nodded.

He turned the key in the lock and pushed the old door open. Then he stepped aside and allowed Anna to go in first.

As she stood inside the vast entrance hall, her eyes darting here and there like a couple of searchlights in the dark, things seemed, in an odd way, right. She sensed that what surrounded her was the product of every year that had passed, of every person who had stepped inside this magnificent old place.

And what had survived? Its essence—that was still alive.

No army general, no politician, no administrator for those twentieth-century political regimes who had hurtled in and out during the struggle to find solutions to every possible social ill in the world had been able to destroy the original architect's vision of this beautiful home.

The past was in the air. It didn't matter that the floor in the echoing entrance hall was hidden under a layer of standard-issue linoleum, clotted with dust and stray leaves that were scattered like debris on a beach. Anna could see past the mouse droppings and the solitary light bulb that swung, almost insolently, in the breeze that scurried in through the open front door.

She walked over to the closed set of doors

that she knew led to what had been the music salon.

Wil was behind her.

She turned to him before she placed her hand on yet another cheap set of brushed steel door handles. "Do you mind if I take a look around before going straight upstairs . . . ?" Her words trailed off.

"Go for it, Anna," he said. "I know it's hard. Don't rush. Take your time."

She nodded and turned to open the doors.

Schloss Siegel, December 1934

As Berthe moved swiftly up Schloss Siegel's grand staircase, Isabelle found herself wanting to turn and stare at the entrance hall below. Virginia had removed her hat and gloves and was climbing the stairs as if she had been born to live in such a place as this. When they arrived at the top of the staircase, there was a large landing with what looked like endless corridors leading to the left and right. The walls were painted duck-egg blue. Deep Persian rugs warmed the floor, and the walls were hung with beautiful paintings.

Berthe turned right, past the central section of the house, past several closed doors, until the hallway narrowed a little, leading to another long stretch.

As Berthe led them down the long hallway, Virginia whispered to Isabelle, "They seem like the most divine parents."

"I'm sure they are." Isabelle smiled. Max had seemed at ease with them this afternoon.

"Max's father has so much, I don't know—chutzpah!" Virginia laughed. "He just looks the part of a handsome aristocrat in a Hollywood film, while she is so stunning that you could put her in a fashion magazine right now and she'd raise a storm. And yet, she seems sweet too."

"Oh, Virginia," Isabelle laughed too. "You are so funny."

"This is your room, Fräulein," the maid said, stepping aside.

Isabelle went in with the eagerness of a child at a fair. Her home while she was here was heavenly—a four-poster bed, piled with pale blue silk cushions, a polished dressing table, an armoire, a delicate rug on the polished wooden floorboards. She glanced at the elaborate blue-and-white tiled stove in the corner.

"This is a *kachelofen*," Berthe said. "It warms your room beautifully—and here, we put a jug of water to stop the room from feeling dry." The maid spoke in halting but understandable English.

Berthe pulled open an ornamental door at the front of the stove. "Here we will put hotties at night for you, so that you can have them in your bed to warm you up."

"Oh, how delicious," Virginia said.

Isabelle went to stand by the window and looked out at the white landscape outside. The picture window was framed with cream velvet curtains that hung to the floor. Her view was of the frozen lake. From this height, she could see beyond it to the forest—dense yet bare.

"Your room is this way, Fräulein." Berthe opened a door into the next room for Virginia.

Isabelle stared out the window for a few moments longer.

She felt that she had, at last, come home.

Schloss Siegel, 2010

Anna stood at a window on the upper floor of the Schloss, staring out at the park. Max's old bedroom was next door, and she was intensely aware that Wil would have to return to work soon. She was not going to reward his kindness by holding him up. She had moved through the decayed and torn rooms of the Schloss as fast as she could, snapping photographs, reining in any upset with the expert firmness that she had honed for years.

What plagued her now was what on earth she would tell Max.

Every room seemed to be a carbon copy of the one before. Linoleum had been stuck fast to every floor except for the hallways, whose floorboards were bare and dusty and rotted through in places. Traces of what had once been elaborate, beautifully designed light surrounds dangled from the ceilings. Every window, whether patched with newspaper or not, was bare of any curtains or blinds. The light shone in where it could, floating through the dust, scattering dotted patterns onto the patched walls.

Anna found it impossible to stop her mind from wandering—wandering to the past, thinking about what these rooms must have once been like. Had Max destroyed all of his photographs of Schloss Siegel too?

It was Anna's American grandmother, the ever-practical Jean, who had told her that when the family had fled before the Russians came, they had taken only the old village school cart, filling the wagon with anything they could grab.

Anna walked into Max's old bedroom. A boarded-up fireplace was built into the right wall of the empty room. Try as she might, Anna found it impossible to feel any sense of Max here.

But she had to focus on the task at hand. She had to find Max's ring. But after breaking three fingernails tugging at the linoleum, she was growing irritated. She was going to have to ask Wil if he had any idea how to remove a box from under the floorboards.

He'd installed himself with his laptop at an old wooden table in the entrance hall. Wil looked up and closed his laptop when Anna hovered on the bottom step.

"No luck?" he asked. Anna saw his eyes run down to her empty hands.

She shook her head, suddenly shy. What had she been thinking? How on earth had she expected to pry up floorboards with her own bare hands?

"I don't suppose you have a toolbox in your car?"

Wil smiled. "Do I look like the sort of man to carry a toolbox? I should have thought of it, though. It's a good point."

"I'm a bit stuck. The floor is kind of—stuck."

"What color's the floor in that room?"

"Chicken manure."

"Nice."

Anna pressed her lips together.

"We'd have to ask the owner's permission before removing the linoleum," Wil pointed out.

"Would they care?"

Wil chuckled. "Oh, yes. She'd care."

"She? I thought a company owned the Schloss."

Something twitched in Wil's cheek. "A

businesswoman bought it. It's simply an investment. She owns a large company and Siegel is
just part of her estate."

"But why is she leaving everything to rot?"

"We're not here to talk about that, Anna.
There's nothing you can do about it."

Anna sighed. She must stay focused on Max's
ring.

"Hang on," she said.

"Yes?"

"Your client doesn't own most of the village
too, does she?"

Wil started walking up the stairs.

Anna followed him into Max's room.

"I can't discuss my client's other interests with
you, Anna."

Anna turned to face him and shook her head.
A bird called through the trees in the park, its
solitary note hanging in the air. Suddenly she
was aware of the silence in the empty house.

It was wrong.

"But this is my family's past," Anna said,
turning to him. "And it deserves a future."

Wil stood where he was. He shrugged, as if to
himself.

What did that shrug mean, exactly? Acceptance? A lack of willingness to fight?

Anna moved toward the window, allowing her
eyes to roam over the park. If she wanted Wil to
help . . .

He tugged at the linoleum. "It won't budge," he said.

"Is there any chance you could ask this—owner—about Max's ring? Is there any chance that she might understand?"

"Let's not go down this path again, Anna." He was quiet for a moment, as if deliberating. "I am so sorry, but I have to get back to work soon. Turns out that a client has to see me."

"Of course," Anna murmured.

"Tonight—" Wil was saying.

How was she supposed to convince everyone that this all had to be fixed? "What?"

He shook his head and suddenly that grin that she had seen when she first met him reappeared. "You were off with the pixies."

"What a funny expression." In spite of herself, Anna was smiling.

"Didn't want to interrupt you." He still looked amused.

Anna hid her own smile.

"So, what do you think?" he asked.

"About what?"

He chuckled. "Thought so. About what I just said."

Anna allowed the silence that followed to drift about for a moment. "So, what . . . ?"

"Did I just say?"

She chuckled. "Yes!"

"Well, what I said was, could I pick you up

about eight tonight, and maybe we can work out another way of doing this over dinner? Sorry. I really do have to get back to Berlin now."

Anna's jaw dropped. She had been expecting him to tell her that there was nothing more he could do to help.

"Oh," she said. Dinner? She could hear Cass's voice in her ear. Why not? Why on earth not? But then, that was all it would be—just dinner. No matter how attractive this man was. For goodness' sake, all he wanted to do was talk about Max's ring. He was offering to help her. She had no other avenue to follow for Max.

"Anna." His voice came out of the fog again. "Do you always overanalyze everything?"

"What?"

"I could almost see the thoughts in your head."

"No, no."

"I have to go." He turned to leave the room.

"Okay."

He stopped, looked at her. "Okay?"

"Yes, thank you. It would be great if we could come up with some more ideas on how to find this ring. And tonight is fine. Thanks."

"Excellent. Could you text me your mobile number and the address of your hotel?" He handed her a business card.

"Sure." Anna's voice came out a little husky as she took the card.

"Good. Let's get back."

"Okay. Thank you," Anna said. As she followed him down the once-beautiful stairs, she understood why Max had never been able to talk about the Schloss. The loss was simply too great.

CHAPTER SEVEN

Schloss Siegel, December 1934

Didi and Jo had taken Virginia sledding with them on the local village slope for the afternoon. It seemed the boys were going to adopt Isabelle's friend, and Virginia seemed happy to charm them right back.

Isabelle was in the library with Max. He had organized afternoon tea for them both. Snow fluttered outside the tall windows overlooking the park. The terrace outside was carpeted in a thick white layer, and the urns that were dotted along its edge were draped in black coverings, protecting them against the harsh winter.

"I can only imagine what it must have been like to grow up surrounded by such beauty," Isabelle said. She turned from where she stood in the window to face Max, who leaned against a heavy leather armchair in front of the floor-to-ceiling bookshelves.

He came to stand next to her. "I wish I felt confident that I could preserve it, that it would be safe."

Isabelle turned to face him.

A maid appeared with a trolley just then and began to set out thin slices of cake, strudel, slices of rich fruitcake, and doughnuts.

When she left, Isabelle poured coffee.

"You have to try one of these," Max said, picking up a doughnut. "It is filled with *Pflaumenmus*."

"What?" Isabelle laughed as he placed the sugar-covered treat onto a plate.

"*Pflaumenmus*." Max grinned.

"And what on earth is that?"

"Plum jam," he said, keeping eye contact with her the entire time.

Isabelle kept her eyes on him as she took a bite. The doughnut was delicious, melting in a swirl of sugar and soft dough and sweet jam on her tongue.

"Please tell me that there is no chance that anything will happen to the estate," Isabelle said.

"I don't know. We have to be able to support the village. We must provide work." Max turned the spoon in his cup. He looked thoughtful for a moment. "Nuremberg was strange."

"I wanted to ask you about that," Isabelle said. He had not mentioned it in his letters. But the topic hung between them.

"It was almost mystical," Max said. "The pageantry, the color. There were thirty thousand people in the Luitpold Hall."

"And what did you make of it?" She had read

up on Nazism over the fall. If Max was going to support the party, then she worried that she should take a stand too. All her instincts pointed toward one word—no.

But Max sounded far away. "The 'Badenweiler Marsch' played when Hitler made his entry. He strode down the aisle while we all had to salute. The lighting was atmospheric. The orchestra played Beethoven, the *Egmont Overture*. Hitler's speech was almost like word from on high."

Isabelle stayed quiet.

"Hitler encouraged us to go home and spread the word—his word."

Isabelle's sense of unease grew stronger. She had read that the government was Nazifying schools, that there was going to be only one religion permitted in Germany.

Max stood up. "Hitler still insists that if war comes to Europe, it will only be because of Communist chaos. And yet at the same time, he is building up Germany's strength by staging mock battles using weapons that are allowed by the Versailles Treaty."

"Your young people are marching the goose step." Isabelle kept her voice gentle, but the pictures she had seen in the papers had sickened her. What did Max really feel? Apart from duty, honor, family, and his country, what did he want?

Isabelle knew how hard it was for him to

separate himself from those things. Where did they end, and where did he begin?

He smiled at her. "My parents are insisting that I support our government. What choice do I have? I cannot abandon everything that I care about; on the contrary, I have to do everything that I can to protect it."

She stood up, moved toward him.

He lifted his hand to her face, traced his fingers, gently, across her lips. "I adore you, no matter what," he said.

Isabelle took in a sharp breath. What did that mean?

But his eyes caught hers, and she was lost, again.

Berlin, 2010

There was a frisson among the reception staff at Anna's hotel when Wil walked into the lobby that evening. But Anna was having none of it. She gave herself a stern reminder that this was a business relationship, nothing more, and that she was going out for dinner with Wil only to help Max.

Wil strolled over to her, seemingly oblivious to anyone who might be staring at him. "Hi there, Anna," he said. "Let's go."

He didn't appear to notice what she was

wearing—a classic black dress and heels with her favorite black silk trench coat—nor did he seem interested in even looking at her, which was a relief. Wasn't it? She was aiming for a professional look. They were simply working together, after all. On her case. That was it.

Wil seemed to be as focused as she was. He opened her car door for her and waited while she climbed into the front seat.

When he was sitting next to her, the interior of the car felt a little close, for some reason, more than it had earlier that day. Maybe because it was dark outside and the only light in the car was the pool cast by the lights in the street. Anna took a deep breath and ignored whatever it was she was feeling. It was annoying, but it would pass. She had not had this feeling for years, and she would not let it bother her now.

"So," she said, keeping her voice bright.

"I want to take you somewhere that's out of Berlin," Wil said, starting the engine. "I hope that's okay."

Anna gazed out the window. The sidewalks were bustling with people going out for dinner, window-shopping, bundled up in warm coats. "Sure," she said. "I don't suppose someone in your position can afford to be charged with murder, so why not?"

"I had every opportunity to murder you this morning, just decided not to," Wil said.

Anna sensed her lips forming a smile, but she kept staring out the window.

Wil reached forward for the car radio as they followed the same road out of the city that they had taken that morning. "What sort of music do you like?" he asked.

"Tend to have eclectic taste," she said. "Jazz, classical, modern."

He chuckled. "Helpful. Thanks." He turned on some soft jazz. It was exactly the style that Anna favored. She sat back and let the mellow sounds of the double bass drift through her.

Wil didn't talk for most of the journey. He seemed content to just drive, and this suited Anna fine. After around forty-five minutes, he drove through an elaborate set of gates and moved along a wide, well-lit driveway lined with bare-limbed trees.

"Another Schloss?" Anna asked. It would be interesting to know how many of the old palaces had been left to decay like Schloss Siegel. Perhaps she could do some research. Then she caught herself. Numbers again. They were such a good retreat for her troubled mind.

"Yes, another Schloss," Wil said.

But now, Ann found her thoughts skittering about—what were they going to talk about over dinner? It had been easy enough today, because they had a focus. But what if the conversation dried up once they had worked out a plan for

Max's ring? Anna shook her head. This was unlike her. It was ridiculous. She could always ask Wil about his career. That was a good topic.

When the driveway opened out, Anna laughed. "It couldn't be more different from Schloss Siegel if it tried," she said.

Wil stayed quiet as she took in the sight before her. Floodlights shone on the expansive facade, highlighting this grand Schloss's pristine, pale yellow walls. Lines of gleaming cars were parked right in front of the entrance. Anna took in the rows and rows of windows, most of which cast light into the dark country night. Their panes were lined with curtains, tucked into neat tie-backs.

Wil pulled into the parking lot at the right of the building.

"Well," Anna said. "This seems to be an example of what can be done."

Wil's eyes caught hers, and his voice was soft when he finally spoke. "This was my family's Schloss, Anna."

Schloss Siegel, December 1934

Drinks were at eight in the salon every evening, and tonight, guests had been invited to the Schloss for dinner. Isabelle sat before the mirror in her bedroom. Rain fell outside, but it was

155

cozy in her private room, which was lit with soft lamps. Virginia was perched on the edge of her bed while Berthe added the finishing touches to Isabelle's hair.

Once Isabelle was satisfied with her appearance, she collected the lower half of her floor-length evening dress in one hand and followed Virginia to the staircase. The sounds of conversation drifted up from the music salon, mingling with the chamber music that was being provided by a small group of musicians from the Berlin Philharmonic.

"Schubert," Isabelle mused, almost to herself.

"I wouldn't know," Virginia said, gathering her own gold gown into one hand and placing the other on the top of the banister. "I have fallen in love with this entire lifestyle here already, though," she said.

Isabelle hesitated at the top of the stairs. It was so tempting to raise Max's political dilemmas with Virginia. But now was not the time to enter into a complex discussion. Isabelle followed her friend down the staircase and into the warm salon, where the guests stood about in front of the three large arched French windows. The terrace outside was lit up, its beauty both stark and wondrous.

Young officers chatted in groups, along with the family and other dinner guests. The young men were from Eberswalde, where there was a regimental headquarters. Some of them had returned after their visit during the summer months. Several young women—daughters of family friends, no doubt—were among the guests, but everyone turned when Isabelle and Virginia entered.

Max was at Isabelle's side straightaway. He placed a hand on the small of her back, and a footman appeared and offered the young ladies drinks. Two officers followed them as they made their way into the room, seeming to realize that Isabelle was with Max, while Virginia was on her own.

Having seen that Virginia was perfectly capable of taking care of herself, Max led Isabelle over to stand near the windows.

"I'm afraid this is all rather formal tonight," he said.

Isabelle gazed around the room. "It's beautiful." She smiled. She didn't hide the twinkle in her eye.

"Mutti cultivates people, you see. Otherwise, she finds the countryside dull."

At half past eight, the butler stood in the double doorway and announced dinner. Max smiled at Isabelle and held out his arm for her. As he did so, Isabelle noticed his quick glance back toward Virginia, checking, no doubt, that she had a partner to walk her into dinner. Isabelle smiled to herself at his thoughtfulness. If she wasn't already completely in love, she knew that she was falling in deeper every day.

Max led her through the next room, its wallpaper decorated with bright birds against a background of dark foliage. Lamps cast a soft glow in here too, and the long white candles that sat in silver holders on the table in the middle of the room were lit.

"This is such an intimate room," Isabelle said. "I can't help thinking that my grandmother would love this."

"The small dining room is one of my favorite rooms in Siegel," Max said. "I hope that your grandmother will visit us here soon."

Isabelle chewed on her lip as they moved toward the next set of open double doors and the big dining room. The thought of Marthe coming to Schloss Siegel caused Isabelle the sharpest of confusion. She couldn't continue much longer without telling Max the truth—and it was not fair to Marthe to withhold who she really was either. But the longer Isabelle left it, the harder it seemed.

At dinner, Isabelle chatted nervously with the officers who sat on either side of her, both of them able to carry on a conversation of sorts in English. She picked at the food in front of her— dumplings in white sauce, followed by rump steak with fried onions, and then pancakes with blueberries and elderberry soup with egg-white islands. Two hours after dinner began, she found herself relieved to be dancing in Max's arms in the salon.

After several turns around the room, Isabelle spotted Virginia making faces at her from where she was surrounded by a group of young men. Isabelle recognized Virginia's expression, and she told Max that she needed to talk to her friend.

"Virginia, I am so sorry to interrupt. I need you for a moment," Isabelle said, putting on her brightest smile.

"Oh really, darling?" Virginia said, in her best Southern imitation.

"Yes, you see, I have this dreadful problem." Isabelle had to force herself to stop a grin.

The young men looked devastated, as only young men who think they have a fighting chance with a girl can look.

"Maybe we can help," one of them said in broken English. He had a particularly eager face and disposition. "Why don't you both stay here? We can chat?"

"We really should go," Virginia said. "You boys will be just fine without us for a while."

"But you'll be back, won't you?" another one groaned.

Virginia patted him with her elegant gloved hand. "Oh, of course we will," she reassured him. She reached up, placing her hand in Isabelle's.

"Thank goodness you came to my rescue," Virginia said when they were out of earshot.

"This way," Virginia said once they reached the entrance hall. "Come on." She headed past the stairs, down a corridor they had never been in before.

Isabelle pulled back. "We can't go down here," she said.

"Oh, for goodness' sake, let's explore. Don't be so boring."

Isabelle stopped. "I am not," she said, "boring." She was used to Virginia's ways, used to her boldness, but her friend had never called her boring before.

"No, of course you aren't, darling," Virginia said, sounding as if she were talking to a child who needed to be soothed. But she was looking at Isabelle with a challenge in her eyes.

"All right then," Isabelle said, casting one last glance back at the salon. "Let's go."

When a servant appeared at the other end of the hall, Virginia pulled Isabelle into the nearest room. Dainty sofas were arranged opposite French-style armchairs, and porcelain sets were displayed in cabinets that lined the walls.

"I heard that Max went to the government rally in Nuremberg," Virginia said, once the servant had passed.

"Yes," Isabelle said.

"What did he say?"

"Not a lot."

"Well, it is all that the officers would discuss. I trust that Max is not too in sympathy with Hitler's cause. Have you thought about that?"

Isabelle folded her arms. Somehow, the delicate room felt close. Were they the only ones in this wing of the Schloss? "He just wants to do the right thing."

"What do you mean?"

"It's not as straightforward as it seems. He has to consider his family, the estate, his workers—he is aware of all the jobs and pride and economic stability that the Nazis are bringing to the village and his country."

"The officers say that he is not as involved as he should be."

Isabelle looked down at the patterns on the wooden floor. She ran the toe of her heeled shoe across the edge of the pale pink rug on the floor. "We shouldn't be in here," she said.

"Rot," Virginia said. "You can't ignore this. It won't fix it. This is real."

"I'm not ignoring it." Isabelle felt something unfamiliar and uncomfortable stir inside her. She had never argued with Virginia before. "I think he is just trying to get informed. He thinks they might bring much-needed change to his country."

"They might want you too, if they think they've got Max," Virginia said.

Isabelle forced herself to laugh. "Max would

never place me in any danger. And in any case, I'm French."

Virginia reached out a hand. "If they suspect you of anything untoward, of influencing Max away from them, then you could be in danger. Remember, there is no freedom of speech and there are ears everywhere in this country. From what I've read."

"I don't think Max is in any danger," Isabelle said. "His first priority is to his family, to the people he employs, and he has a conscience about the future of his country, that's all. He wouldn't get involved in anything questionable."

Virginia had her head tilted to one side. "I see. But the point is, will he stand by while . . . things happen?"

"He says there are only rumors."

Virginia shook her head. "The officers seemed relieved that he was going to some ball in Berlin."

Isabelle chewed on her lip. He had invited her to go with him. "Yes," she said.

"Organized by—"

"The Nazis," Isabelle whispered the word. "It's just a ball," she added.

"Oh, dear goodness." Virginia stroked Isabelle's arm. "I don't like it."

Isabelle looked in her friend's eyes. "Don't worry. I am sure of one thing. He won't do anything to put anyone he cares about in danger."

Virginia's head was on one side again.

"Let's go back. Max will wonder where I've gone," Isabelle said. She took Virginia's hand this time. It had been a good thing to voice her views. If she felt something, it was, surprisingly, more confidence than ever in Max.

Virginia stopped just before they entered the well-lit entrance hall again. She seemed to have read Isabelle's mind. "You might be confident in Max," she whispered, "but are you confident in Hitler?"

CHAPTER EIGHT

Germany, 2010

Anna watched Wil as they climbed the steps to this other Schloss—one that had clearly been restored recently. A frown darkened his features. But when he reached the top of the stairs he stopped, turned to her, smiled that extraordinary, boyish, classically handsome smile of his, and stood aside for her to go inside. As usual, she was struck by his impeccable manners.

The entrance to this Schloss was elaborate—a grand portico sat atop the marble steps.

"Welcome to Schloss Beringer," Wil said.

"Thank you," she said, keeping her own voice even.

"It's a two-hundred-room hotel," Wil said, "with three restaurants and a conservatory. They specialize in weddings. But tonight, I thought I'd just bring you here for dinner." His words were cheerful enough, but Anna detected something darker in his tone.

Anna stopped short as she entered the opulent entrance hall, dazzled by the scale of the room, its imposing staircase, the gleaming marble floors, and the flowers cascading out of oversized urns.

"It's . . ." Anna didn't know what to say. Beautiful as it was, there was something odd about the atmosphere. Artificiality? She couldn't help feeling that the place was simply on show. In some ways, while it was ridiculous, Anna preferred Siegel.

"I know," Wil said. He closed the front door, quietly. The sound of people talking came from the restaurant. "When I look at the facade, I can imagine the past, in spite of the Ferraris and the international flags on the front lawn. But in here . . . it's all lost . . ." His voice trailed off.

"I'm so sorry," Anna said.

"The restaurant's this way. And Anna, I didn't bring you for the food. So, please, don't hate me for it."

With its drab, dark carpet, vivid flowers on pedestals, and stuffy white-linen tables, the restaurant looked like something out of another era again.

"It's very . . ."

Wil broke into that boyish grin again. "Okay, Anna. Let's be honest here. It's tasteless. Hideous. Foul."

Anna caught his smile and returned it. But at the same time her imagination was busy. How beautiful this room could be—imagine if the floorboards were sanded back, the décor less pretentious. Because what it lacked was charm.

Halfway through dinner, she kept the thought to herself that she had been right. There was nothing wrong with her roast fillet of perch, but there was nothing creative about it.

She didn't push Wil to talk about his past, his family, or how the Schloss had ended up as it had, because she sensed that his feelings, like hers, ran deep. Perhaps, one day, he would raise the topic himself. She was certainly interested— but it likely depended on whether they were going to be friends. But why was she thinking like that? After all, the likelihood of her seeing him again once she returned home was nil. She shook her head at her own thoughts.

"I would never bring anyone here on a date, Anna," Wil joked.

"Lucky this isn't a date then." She declined the offer of dessert.

They ordered coffee, and Wil sat back in his seat when it arrived. "I wanted to show it to you, though," he said.

"What, to prove to me that things could be worse?" Anna laughed.

He raised a brow. "Well, there is that. But there's another reason. I want to show you something. Although, first, I have a question for you."

Anna looked up.

"What is it that you do back in the US?"

Anna smiled. "My partner, Cass, and I own an Italian deli in San Francisco."

"Do you cook?"

Anna nodded.

"Double apologies then."

"For what?"

"For bringing you here! I would never have subjected you to such a dull meal if I'd known."

"It was interesting," Anna laughed. "I'm always up for research."

"You know, the worst thing about this place is that the curtains clash with the carpet and the flowers look like they belong in a funeral parlor. And don't get me started on the staff." Wil did a perfect imitation of the unfashionably formal waitstaff.

Anna let out a giggle. "Well, now if I had this place—"

"Oh, do tell." He leaned forward and that wicked smile appeared again.

"Well, I'd sack everybody, of course."

"Of course."

"Next, I'd throw the carpet in a river."

"Excellent plan," Wil chuckled. "I'd have a bonfire."

"Maybe we could reduce it all back to the way Siegel is and cut open the floorboards searching for long-lost rings," Anna said.

Wil put his coffee cup back in its saucer. "I've

arranged for contractors to be at Siegel in the morning," he said. "I'm going to tell them that there's a problem with the floor—that will do as an explanation. They'll pull up the linoleum for us, then I'll get them to leave."

"Once they've established there's nothing wrong with the floor," Anna said.

"Mmm hmm," Wil said.

"Thank you." Anna sat back in her seat.

When the waiter came to take their payment, Wil had a conversation with him in German. The young man nodded and soon another, older man appeared. Wil introduced him to Anna, and then, after apologizing to her, Wil had another conversation in German with him.

When the man had left the table, having slapped Wil on the back several times, Wil leaned in a bit closer to Anna. "We're in luck," he said. "Come with me."

As Wil led her upstairs, Anna stayed quiet about the unsuitable modern iron banisters, the dark navy carpet flecked with ugly gold insignias, a hideous brass chandelier.

Wil stopped at the first room and opened it with a key that Anna hadn't noticed until now. He held the door open.

The room had clearly once been grand, but now it was heavy with pretension—gaudy fake flowers, a veneer coffee table, an ugly wooden desk, and an oversize hotel bed.

Wil pulled an envelope out of his coat pocket and handed it to her. Anna turned it over wordlessly, slipping her fingers underneath the seal. She couldn't take her eyes off the old photograph that was inside.

This room had been a woman's room once.

In the photograph, an easel littered with paint sat to the left of the picture windows. A half-finished picture of a tree with a swing hanging from one of its branches decorated the canvas, and a chaise longue sat next to the easel. A piece of lingerie was thrown across the chaise longue, almost as if it had been placed there for artful effect.

A canopied bed sat in the foreground, scattered with a multitude of cushions. Several pairs of shoes were loose on the floor. A delicate, patterned rug—quite unlike the heavy carpet that was under their feet now—covered the floor.

Anna turned to face Wil. She didn't have to talk. The question was in her eyes and she felt that he understood it.

"It was my grandmother's room," he said. His eyes held hers for a moment, but then he turned away.

"We had the opportunity to buy Schloss Beringer back after the wall came down."

"Yes."

"My grandfather knew your grandfather, Max. They had grown up together. And they had been good friends. While my grandfather was a busy surgeon in Berlin, he knew that Max had done exceedingly well with his own business in America. Grandfather needed someone to help him here who was as passionate as he was about the villages, the people, and the palaces—someone who had inside knowledge, who cared. Max could have helped to raise funds, inject them into both villages, and bring both houses back to life. Your grandfather could have sold Siegel to a family if he had not wanted to keep it once it was done. But Max, unfortunately, refused flat out. He didn't want to be involved with Germany again."

He paused. "Just like I'm helping you now, Anna. Sometimes you need someone who cares—someone who has the same passions as you, someone who you know wants to do what's right, someone from the past. My grandfather felt let down by Max. It was about far more than just the homes they grew up in. It was about who he thought Max was. It was about the friend he thought he had."

"But couldn't your grandfather have found other investors?"

"The company that bought Siegel was making aggressive offers to the government, just like the hotel chain that bought this Schloss. My grandfather didn't have time on his side—apart from the matter of the funds."

Anna inhaled sharply.

"Max was the rightful heir to Siegel," Wil went on. "I guess my grandfather and the villagers couldn't understand why that meant nothing to him."

Anna turned to face to the window. Why had Max abandoned his past, Germany, everything he held most dear? Would she ever know the answer?

"But what if it meant everything to him," she said, her voice quiet. "So much that he couldn't even bring himself to speak about it?"

"I can't see how that's the case."

"What's that supposed to mean?"

"What do you think it means?"

"Please don't play word games with me."

"I'm not."

Anna turned to face him. "Don't you think he may have had his reasons? Even if we don't know what they are?"

There was a silence.

"If Max had come here, even once—if he'd talked to my grandfather and explained his reasoning—it would have shown that Max cared. As it was, my grandfather spent his final years doing everything he could to try to stop this"— he waved a hand around the room—"from happening. On his own. Until it was too late. It broke his heart."

Anna took in a breath. "I understand. And I feel

for your grandfather and how difficult that must have been. But I also know Max. He must have had his reasons." She heard her voice cracking.

"I hope they were bloody good."

A knot formed in Anna's stomach. Max had avoided talking about the past so deftly, but he seemed like such a loyal person to her—he had been her most steadfast relative. It seemed so out of character for him to ignore his oldest friend when he was in need. There had to be more to this story—but how would she find out what it was?

"I just wanted you to understand. That's all," Wil said. He opened the door for her and stood aside.

She walked past him, her arms folded tight to her sides. "I appreciate your help very much."

Then Anna handed Wil's photograph back to him. He took it, but he stayed silent, waiting for her to walk ahead of him down the staircase.

At midmorning the following day, Anna stood on the bare floorboards in Max's bedroom at Schloss Siegel. When Wil came back into the room after seeing the workmen out, Anna was scouring the floor for any cuts in the wood that might indicate a hiding place. Wil leaned against the door for a moment.

"How's your grandfather today?" he asked.

Anna wiped her dirty hands on the old blue

jeans that she had paired with a black polo sweater.

"The operation went well, I think," she said. "He was groggy with drugs when I spoke to him last but he didn't complain of any pain."

Wil stood for a moment, his head tilted to one side. "He does sound as if he isn't selfish, Anna. Not needy."

"Oh, no," Anna chuckled. "You've hit the right button there. That's why I—" She stopped. There was no point getting into another character analysis now.

"So, where do we start?" Wil asked.

Anna frowned at the uneven old floorboards. "You know, I have absolutely no idea."

Schloss Siegel, Christmas 1934

The household was awake early on Christmas Eve at Schloss Siegel. Isabelle hated to think what time the servants must have begun their day. When she walked into the dining room for breakfast, she was greeted with one of the loveliest sights of her life. On the giant mahogany table was an entire village of gingerbread houses studded with brightly colored sweets. Thick strands of holly and ivy wound around gorgeous silver platters of food.

Isabelle had lain awake a great deal of the

previous night, her mind a swirl of thoughts about German politics. Max. Nazism. Did he really believe in Hitler's policies? Or was he just trying to do what was best for his country? What would she do if he were to become irrevocably involved—in all aspects of it?

Now she moved toward the stack of plates on the sideboard. The family's Christmas porcelain was decorated with exotic red and green patterns, swirling flowers, and dancing red ribbons. Her shoulder brushed against the arm of Max's valet, Hans. He apologized in German and stood aside for her to pass. But Isabelle insisted that he go first. He nodded, his blue eyes falling to the floor as he moved on.

This was one of the days of the year on which the servants were given special privileges. The household staff was chatting informally with the family and other guests, and each of them had been given a personal gift, along with a box of gingerbread and a bag of sweets and chocolates. The atmosphere was convivial, even relaxed; it was as if the normal formalities of the house had flown away, if only for a few hours.

"You have to try one of these." Max appeared behind Isabelle and handed her a plate of chocolates, exquisitely decorated and formed into tiny handmade wreaths, perfect little Christmas stockings, even a miniature Christmas gift, complete with a bow. Isabelle took this one and held it for a moment.

"It seems a little indulgent for breakfast." She smiled.

"How so?" Virginia said, sweeping into the conversation in a green silk dress that hugged her perfect figure. "Chocolate is always a good idea."

Isabelle chuckled and popped the delicacy into her mouth. She took Max's hand and led him across the room, toward the double doors that opened into the small dining room.

"You know, I think this is my favorite thing in the entire house," she said, leaning in toward a tiny triptych on the small sideboard. The decorated panels illustrated the Christmas story, and the triptych was lit by a single candle in front of it.

"Wait until you see the church later today," Max said. He leaned down and kissed her on the cheek, the backs of his fingers lingering on her face for a moment.

Later that afternoon, everyone had changed into their festive clothes, layered with fur coats and mittens, hats, and scarves against the freezing cold. A path through the snow had been cleared along the curved road so that the family and all the servants could walk to the village church. Isabelle had her gloved hand tucked warmly into Max's. On her other side, Virginia chatted away with Didi and Jo, their high-spirited conversation ringing through the crisp, otherwise silent air.

"My parents are so happy that I've met you," Max said, keeping his voice quiet against the other loud chatter.

Isabelle felt a warmth spread through her body. It didn't matter how cold it was in the snow. She leaned in to rest her head on his shoulder and sensed that they were smiling at the same time.

Siegel's main square was crowded with villagers. Darkness had fallen—it was nearly four o'clock—and some of them held lanterns. The villagers shook hands with Max, and when he introduced them to Isabelle, she understood the warmth behind their greetings perfectly well—even though they were speaking German and she could not decipher a word.

Max held Isabelle's hand through the church service. She had to force herself to stop gazing around in awe. Lights blazed in the chapel. Christmas trees taken from the forests that very day decorated the little church. Pine scented the air, and a multitude of candles flickered and danced. The Christmas story was read aloud by a group of village children, who stood in front of the wooden Nativity scene.

Isabelle began to relax. Everything seemed to be perfect. Out here in the countryside, it was hard to imagine the soaring unemployment rates, the desperation of the people, their need to turn to someone like Hitler for strength. There wasn't any hint of that right here, right now, and it was hard to marry the new Germany with these proud folk and their traditions of old. Isabelle forced herself to push these troubling thoughts aside, just for one day.

Once the service had ended and easy conversations had been exchanged between the locals and Max's family, it was time to walk back to the Schloss.

"This is the best part of the day," Max said. "When I was a child, it was magical."

Every window in Schloss Siegel shone out into the darkness. The porch was lit up. The front door had been opened wide, and the servants were gathered in the entrance hall.

"Watch," Max said. His eyes followed his father, who was making his way to the double doors that led to the salon. These were closed, and a hush fell over the crowd in the entrance hall.

Max's father made a short speech in German. Isabelle looked up at Max, and he smiled at her, his eyes crinkling in that way that she loved.

There was a pause before the sound of hand bells pealed through the closed doors of the salon. The notes flew up and down as if in delicious anticipation of the next wave of magic that was about to envelope this day. Everyone stayed silent. When the rendition had finished, Max's father stood still for a moment, then turned and threw open the double doors. Everyone was quiet for a second before gasps of delight took over, and the family and their guests entered the gorgeous room.

A magnificent Christmas tree glittered before them. Elsa, Max's mother, had spent the afternoon with Nadja decorating the handsome spruce that nearly touched the tall ceiling. Cascades of silver hung from its branches, catching the light of the numerous white candles. Angels danced between gold, silver, red, and blue balls, their wings appearing to float in the candlelight. A star sat atop all of this.

Max's mother went to the grand piano. A hush fell over the room as Elsa started to play "Stille Nacht," and the guests sang along.

Then the chandeliers were turned on. The big table at the foot of the tree groaned with gifts. Two new bicycles were propped against the table, a shining sled stood at one end, and a pair of brand-new skis leaned against it.

A few hours later, Isabelle was not sure that she had ever had such a perfect evening in her life—let alone a Christmas like this one. The men had removed to the smoking room, and she found herself sitting next to Nadja in the salon. The other girl was staring at the tree, her brow furrowed.

Nadja did not seem to be the sort to place herself anywhere unless she had a purpose—and they had formed an uneasy truce in the last few days. Nadja, almost grudgingly, appeared to have accepted Isabelle. They had not had any long conversations, or even much talk, but at dinner the other night, Nadja had smiled at a comment Isabelle had made about Max. That had been enough. Isabelle had smiled back straightaway— and Nadja had not frowned.

"You know," Nadja said, "I can't understand Max."

"Oh?"

"No. If Max is going to support Hitler, then why not just do it?"

"It's not as simple as that, surely," Isabelle said.

Nadja sat up. "Yes, it is."

"But—" Were things so black and white?

"He's scared," Nadja insisted.

"I think he's just been getting informed." Isabelle chose her words with care.

Nadja looked at her with a new expression. "Maybe, but I think that fear and doubt are not helpful companions when one is facing inevitable change. You need to tackle it, head-on. He'll have to take a stand."

But when it came to Nazism, wasn't doubt a useful companion? "Surely there are some exceptions to your rule."

"Do you hold such principles in relation to Max? Do you hold back, Isabelle? Are you scared?" Nadja asked, her voice deadly quiet.

"It is hardly the same thing," Isabelle said. She felt rattled. Max's sister had gotten under her skin. Again. But she would hold her ground.

"I think, I do hope . . ." Her thoughts trailed off. What was she saying? She had to be careful. "I have faith that Max will do the right thing by his country," she said in the end. She sounded too vague. It hadn't been what she wanted to say. Suddenly Isabelle felt the enormity of the situation in which the German people found themselves.

"You are not clear, either," Nadja said, but she sounded more matter-of-fact than anything else.

Something changed in Isabelle's perception of Nadja. Perhaps her cold, clinical exterior masked real passion. Isabelle thought before she spoke.

"I know he wants to help make things better, Nadja. I know that he hates to see people suffering, and I know how much he wants prosperity for his country. But surely you can see that how this is achieved is the most important thing. There are ways of doing things that are not harmful."

"Sometimes sacrifices have to be made," Nadja said, her voice tinged with anger.

So Isabelle's instincts had been right about Max's sister. While Max thought things through, Nadja saw things in black and white.

"But don't you think despicable acts are wrong under any circumstances?" Isabelle kept her voice so low that even were they the only two in the room, Nadja might still have had trouble hearing her.

But the other girl was listening. "It is impossible for you to understand. You are not German," Nadja said.

Isabelle took in a breath. "Okay. I grant you that," she said. "But I love your brother."

Nadja flinched next to her. "Then you had best advise him to be careful," Nadja said, her voice cold. "If anything were to happen to him, it would be insupportable for the family and the village."

Suddenly Isabelle felt faint. And the room was too warm.

Virginia was sitting with a lively group of guests near the Christmas tree. Isabelle patted Nadja on the arm, told her that she was going to get something cool to drink, and headed across the room toward her friend.

Virginia seemed to take in Isabelle's white face in one glance. She stood up. "Tired, darling?"

"I think I need to go upstairs," Isabelle managed.

She had to sleep tonight.

When she placed her foot on the first step, the men came out of the smoking room, Max in the lead.

"Isabelle?" he called. "Darling?" But his voice became lost in a fog. Isabelle allowed Virginia to guide her.

"She's tired," Virginia said. The way she spoke English with an American accent sounded reassuring, confident. "It's been a charming day. Thank you."

"Go and rest, darling," Max said, his voice intimate, close, in the way she loved.

"One step at a time, honey." Virginia's voice now. "None of us knows what's going to happen, and the scary thing is that none of us can do a thing about it."

Isabelle followed Virginia along the heated hallway to her bedroom. She'd tried so hard to keep the harsh realities of the world at bay today, but the world had a way of rushing in at the most inopportune moments—and she couldn't help thinking about the countless people in this country whose hearts and minds must be torn apart by it all.

CHAPTER NINE

Schloss Siegel, 2010

Anna had two options, neither of them very promising. The first was to call Max and ask him if he could remember the exact location of his ring. Option two was to pull up the floorboards in his bedroom. Calling Max was out of the question; he would be asleep. For the millionth time, Anna kicked herself for not having pressed him for more details as to the precise hiding spot of the ring. As for option two—the house was not hers to destroy. It would take hours to remove a floor; doing so was clearly beyond her capabilities, anyway, and probably Wil's too.

Wil was sifting through a cardboard box that he had brought back with him after the workmen had departed, having removed the layer of old linoleum, inspected the bare floor, and informed Wil and Anna that there was nothing wrong with it at all.

"Okay, Anna," he said. "This is where we get professional."

Anna looked up. "Oh?" she asked, unable to stop the smile that was forming on her lips. Wil looked so funny, frowning at tools as he pulled them out one by one. Anna had to bite her bottom lip to stop herself from giggling.

"I borrowed some things from a friend," he said.

"Handy," Anna quipped.

Wil pulled out a pair of protective gloves, a claw hammer, and a small black box.

"Scanner," Wil said, looking impressed with his own words.

"What are you scanning?"

"We run it along the floor to check for pipes and cables, of course." He grinned.

"Sorry. Of course we do."

He brandished the claw hammer. "And this."

"Right."

"A utility bar," Wil said, pulling one out of the box.

"I can see that you're quite at home with this . . . stuff." Anna's lips twitched.

Wil stopped and looked at her. "I'm not entirely incompetent with a saw."

Anna chuckled. "Of course you're not, handyman. Where do we start?"

"Clearly you can see that I've brought all the tools, Anna. You have to be the brains."

Anna had no idea. She scanned the floor. The boards offered no hint of where to start.

"Well," she said. "If Max didn't cut an obvious square out of the floor, which clearly he didn't, then he would have hidden the ring at the easiest access point."

"Brilliant," Wil said. "You see, this is why you are here." He leaned against the window, where he was framed against the curious old newspaper cuttings that half-covered the glass. The light from the top half highlighted his stunning features.

"So," Anna said, trying to ignore his pose. He was hardly standing in such an alluring posture for her amusement, was he? They had work to do. Anna moved across the floor, her eyes scanning the boards. "We should begin with one of the shorter boards. See," she said, stopping in the middle of the room. "Some of the boards are cut in half. You'd think Max would have chosen one of these."

"You'd also think that the room would have been covered with a rug across its center. Let's start with a floorboard near the edge of the room."

Wil ran the scanner over the area around the short floorboard closest to where he stood. No sound came from the machine.

"I guess that means we can start. It does seem a shame to cut these beautiful wooden boards away, though." Anna said. "And one more thing."

Wil stopped, poised with the utility bar over the floorboards. "Just one?" he asked, his eyes looking wicked now.

Anna walked over to the window. What was

going to happen once they found the ring—if they found it? Finding it might make Max feel better, but its discovery would not fix any of the problems in the village. The state of the place was not sitting well with her. But what could she do?

"Tell me," he said.

"Perhaps it's just because Max is in the hospital. Maybe that's making it worse," Anna said, half talking to herself. "Just go ahead. Sorry I stopped you."

"No. Come on."

Anna shook her head.

"What is it?"

Anna stared out at the forgotten garden. "It's just that everything is so wrong. The Schloss can't just stay here like this forever. It will decay. It won't just be abandoned, it'll become a . . ."

"Ruin," Wil said, sounding close.

Anna nodded. "It's not too late to save it now, but in a few years' time, it might well be. And in a few years, Max probably won't be here either. So . . ."

"Okay." He put the utility bar down. "First, I know this is hard, but I wouldn't advise you to waste your time trying to save the past—there's nothing you can do. If anything could be done, my grandfather has already done it and failed. I saw it eat away at him. I don't want that to happen to you."

Anna let out a sigh. "I don't think I can stand it."

"Anna," he said, "how about we just find this ring today? I'll talk to you about the Schloss, if you like, later—but—you have to be realistic."

Anna folded her arms around her body. What was there to say? Realistic was her middle name. What had gotten into her? She accepted things. That was what she did. And then she got on with her work. Why was she so agitated here, now? It wasn't as if she hadn't dealt with significant blows before in her life.

"Oh, I don't know. I'm just letting it get to me, that's all," she managed.

Wil caught her eye, then looked back at the floor. He levered the short floorboard up with the utility bar—it came away easily. Anna walked over to stand next to him. As she peered down at the dusty area under the floor, something strange happened. For some reason, another thought, another feeling, just as strong as the last one, flew into her mind.

This had been Max's room.

How many secrets, how many memories lurked in the dusty narrow space under the floorboards? And how often had Max closed his eyes and dreamed about this very room in the last seventy years? He would never come back. Never see it again. He had lost his chance. The life he had planned and the life he had lived could hardly have been more different. And he had chosen not to come back. He had made that choice. Why? What, exactly, were his regrets?

How suddenly Max's childhood life had disappeared. And yet look at all this! Look at this Schloss, steeped in history, a witness to it all. What could possibly have caused him to want to leave and never return, making him turn away from everything and everyone he knew? What had happened—and why?

"Are you okay?"

"Fine," Anna said quietly. She turned back to face the room.

"I think we should just keep going." Wil moved to another spot in the room, ran the scanner over the floor.

After he had done this several times, he sat back on his heels as if he were waiting for her to tell him what they should do next. One thing was for certain—she didn't want to leave today without Max's ring. But she was also aware that she was taking up Wil's precious time.

"I don't want to steal your entire day," she said. Her words came out softer than she had intended—almost seeming to linger in the eerie space. It was the silence, the stillness, that seemed to catch things out in this old palace. Past sensations and feelings drifted like forgotten ghosts in the silent atmosphere.

Was it because Schloss Siegel was surrounded

by whispering forest? Was it because the entire place was abandoned that there was this sense of something brewing in the air?

Anna couldn't help but feel the old palace was waiting.

She had a terrible sense that the someone it waited for was her.

"You're not taking up my time," Wil said, shaking his head. "Let's keep going."

Anna nodded. "Okay, and thanks."

"Oh, I'm in my element." Wil grinned, pulling out his scanner yet again. Soon they were halfway around the room. They had set up a routine. He would open up a section of floor, and she would investigate what was underneath, looking for anything that might be hidden there.

The time seemed to whisk by. When the sun moved, it seemed to do so suddenly—causing shadows to stretch across the floor. Anna had become so absorbed in the task at hand, so involved, that nothing else seemed to matter. Fortunately, Wil seemed equally focused. He had not once complained about the time or the fact that it was looking more and more likely that either Max's ring was so well hidden that they would never find it or someone had removed it already.

It was just after four o'clock in the afternoon when he sat back on his heels. "Anna," he said softly.

She was crouched over the last place they had looked. Something had caught her eye as she was about to put the floorboards back in place, and she had begun poking around in the dirt. She had become used to the tingling hope that her fingers might hit upon something, maybe a little box, but once again, her hands clutched at nothing except gray dust.

Anna looked up when he spoke. She walked over to him without a word.

"You do this, Anna," he said, moving away slightly so that she could lean in over the latest spot where he had removed the floor.

And there it was. A velvet box—velvet that must once have been a deep navy blue but was now faded with age and dust. The fabric was worn in places, threadbare down to the pale yet valiant old wood.

Anna reached in. Though her hands were steady, her insides shook, dancing to some old song that had nothing to do with her, but everything to do with Max and the girl he had loved.

Schloss Siegel, Christmas 1934

Max stood next to Isabelle the morning after Christmas as they served themselves from the silverware that held breakfast.

"What are your plans for today?" he asked.

Isabelle smiled. "Plans? Why, I think I'm free," she laughed.

"What happened last night?" Max was so close that if she leaned her head a few inches it would rest on his shoulder.

She couldn't tell him the truth about her unsettling conversation with Nadja. "Too much excitement, I suspect," she said.

Max was quiet, and Isabelle knew that she hadn't fooled him, but he changed the subject. "I've been thinking," he said. "I've been far too self-absorbed while you've been here. Sorry about that."

"Oh, don't be ridiculous," Isabelle laughed. "I'm having a wonderful time."

"I want to take you out on a sleigh ride this morning. Just the two of us. Sound all right?"

Isabelle felt as if he had offered to fly her to the French Riviera for cocktails. "Yes, sounds all right," she said, not bothering to keep the smile from her lips.

An hour later, a maid helped her put those elephant trotters on her feet again, and she found herself clasping Max as they made their way out the front door to the sleigh that waited at the bottom of the front steps. It was silent outside, and the sun shone with a bright clarity that caused the snow-covered garden to gleam.

Once Isabelle was safely in the sleigh, covered

with blankets, her hands warm in mittens, and Max right next to her, she found herself relaxing properly for the first time in days. The frozen white landscape was not only silent, but peaceful as well.

Max drove her through the park, around the frozen lake with its little snow-covered boat moored to a short jetty, past the orangeries, and into the forest, where a sleigh trail covered the path that Max said he walked or rode along in the summer.

It was easy to picture elves and imaginary creatures out here in the woods.

Max laughed out loud when Isabelle told him so. "You are so funny," he said.

"Well, I'm not the first person to think that way, clearly."

"No, I grant you that." He brought the sleigh to a stop in a clearing. "I want to show you something," he said. He helped her out of the sleigh and supported her elbow as he led her a few steps into the trees.

Once they were inside the forest, something became visible that could not be seen from the path. A small building rose up, seeming to grow out of the snow in all sorts of pretty shapes—a turret sat atop a round tower, and a small curved wooden front door with a smart black handle marked the entrance.

"Oh, you are joking," Isabelle said, reaching

her gloved hand out to touch the folly's pale stone. "Now this really could be in the Brothers Grimm."

"My grandfather built it," he said. "For my grandmother, whom he adored all his life. She was English—they met in Paris."

"Oh," Isabelle said, turning to Max.

"And then he brought her back here, the following summer," he said, running a hand across her soft cheek. "And he asked her to marry him, right then, no constraints."

And no Hitler, Isabelle thought, but she pushed the intrusion away as if it weren't real. If only it weren't real, if only that was the thing that was a dream, not this.

Max leaned down then, his lips brushing hers so softly that Isabelle thought she might die if he stopped.

"We'd better get back," he said after a few moments, not breaking the spell.

There would still be the delicious ride to the Schloss with him in the sleigh. The day wasn't over, nor was the week.

"Cook will be ringing the gong for lunch," Max said, pulling the top of her warm hat down so that it was covering her ears. "She gets cranky if anyone is late," he added.

"That is fair enough." Isabelle smiled. "One would hate to keep her waiting."

"Only wish I could," Max murmured, but he

took her hand and led her back to the sleigh. "I wish we could have more time together," he said.

"Well, neither of us is going anywhere for a little while yet," Isabelle said as she climbed back into the sleigh.

Something passed across Max's face, and a shadow from a heavy branch threw a jagged pattern across his body while he climbed back into the seat. But as they began to move, the shadow disappeared, and the light was clear again as they travelled along the well-worn path that led through the quiet forest full of still trees—and ice.

Two days later, Isabelle alighted from Max's town car in Berlin. She had been to more balls than she could count in Paris, even though she had always felt on the outside. Not one of them stood out for her—but here in Berlin's glamorous Hotel Adlon, the scene before her was quite something else. She knew that her feelings were heightened because she was with Max, who had told her that the Adlon was one of Europe's most famous hotels.

Isabelle's pale silk dress was fitted in the bodice and hung in a straight line to her feet. When she removed her fur coat, Max placed a hand on her back. She had never felt so alive in her life.

The crowd consisted of a swirl of dignitaries and foreign press officers, all mingling in a glorious room filled with gilt and flowers. The guests looked utterly at home and sophisticated, and, for the first time, Isabelle had a sense of what Marthe might have felt when she had entered the highest ranks of Parisian society—accepted as one of them and yet right on the edge.

Max was representing his family. Otto Albrecht had been invited as the largest landowner in Prussia, but he had given the invitation to Max instead.

Later in the evening, Max found himself engaged in a discussion with an American journalist who seemed intensely interested in how Max saw his family's future in a country run by Hitler. Max had one hand in Isabelle's as she chatted in French with the man on her other side, a charming newspaper correspondent from Switzerland. She had danced with him after dinner, which had been at a table for two hundred.

But it was later still that Isabelle's heart plummeted to her pink satin dancing shoes. It was at the point that Max became involved in a conversation with a man in uniform that she gained an inkling of what was going to transpire. Max was clearly interested in what the Nazi officer had to say. Isabelle managed to catch his eye, but Max averted his gaze, fast. When Max shook the man's hand at the end, he told the man that he would report for duty the following morning.

Isabelle felt cold. Suddenly, she wanted to go home.

The following morning, all the servants lined up on the curved driveway in front of the house to say farewell to Max. Isabelle wanted to throw her arms around him so very badly, but she could not show her emotions here, and it was taking every ounce of her strength not to burst into tears.

Max had told her on the way home from Berlin in the car in the early hours of the morning that Hitler was planning to restore universal military service. There was talk of a conscripted army, so it was possible he would have been called up soon anyway.

He had had a conversation earlier that day with his parents. They had told him that they expected him to join the army now, that it was his duty, that they knew he would not let them down or fail to do what was right for the future of Germany, their family, the village, their way of life, and its continuing prosperity. Most importantly, they had impressed upon him the fact that their country had to be kept safe—Max would be doing what a long line of his ancestors had done before him, including his father, who had fought in the last war.

Now, Otto Albrecht, the great landowner, was quiet, while Elsa simply laid a hand on her son's shoulder. Then she leaned up and kissed her son's smooth young cheek.

When Max came to say his formal goodbye to Isabelle, he kept things brief. He had caught her after breakfast on the stairs earlier that morning—they had held each other then. Isabelle had not slept the night before, and yet when she had looked in the mirror after her farewell to Max, her eyes had stared back at her, wide. Hideously alert.

He leaned down now, kissed her on the cheek. She took in the familiar scent of his aftershave, held it as close as she could, and closed her eyes.

"I hope it will not be too long, my darling girl," he said.

Isabelle took his hand in hers and ran her fingers over his warm palm for the last time before he went. She nodded. She couldn't find the words. Why was it so hard to be separated from him? She had no sensible answer to this question, or to the question of why she loved him, to the question of what on earth was going to happen next, or to the question of when she would see him again.

Berlin, 2010

Wil stopped the car outside Anna's hotel. The drive back from Schloss Siegel had passed quickly. Anna held the little jewelry box safely in her hands. Wil had kept up light conversation, but everything unsaid had hung between them like the dead light bulb in the main entrance at the Schloss. Turning it on would illuminate everything—throw up all the cracks in their conversations, show all the unswept dirt, highlight the things that seemed to linger every time they met.

People drifted in and out of the revolving glass doors, maps in hand. Tourists in Berlin.

"You have what you came for, I guess," Wil said, his voice shifting down a few notches as he turned off the car's engine. He was quiet for a moment. "Anna, I know you wanted to talk about the Schloss. But I suggest you leave it well alone. Go back to your old life—forget about the past."

"I can't do that." She never would have imagined she could become so invested in the fate of the old palace. She was normally so businesslike—if anything, people accused her of being too practical. Were she to return home, give Max his ring, and try to move on, she would only be lying to herself about what mattered.

Wil seemed to smile back at her with his eyes. "Go and look after your grandfather. You have a life in San Francisco—don't let that fall apart chasing ghosts around here. You can't change anything in Germany."

Anna turned the faded box over in her hand.

She pressed the little silver button that released the clasp, opening the tiny lid to reveal the ring nestled in the frayed silk lining.

The ring remained surprisingly well preserved. It was tarnished with age, of course it was—but seventy years of darkness had not destroyed its inherent beauty. It was the symbol of a dream that had never come to fruition. But why? What had happened? What had stopped Max from being with the woman he loved, caused him to talk of the situation as his greatest regret, caused him to keep the affair a secret for seventy years?

Wil's hand rested on the steering wheel, but his eyes were on the ring. The single, clear diamond was set in a band of white gold. Intricate art deco patterns decorated the band.

"It's like a fairy tale in reverse," Anna whispered.

"Is it?" There was indulgence in his voice.

"Max's story. Happily ever after didn't work out for him for some reason—but then he created his own once-upon-a-time in the New World."

Wil, thankfully, did not laugh.

"I'd better go," Anna said, snapping the box shut, unclipping her seat belt. "Thank you," she said. "I know how much Max will appreciate this."

"It's been a pleasure," Wil said. "Not an ordinary case. It has been interesting."

Anna felt deflated when Wil called it a "case."

But she pushed this aside. "You'll need an address for the account."

"Don't be ridiculous."

Anna turned to him.

His eyes met hers and he ran a hand across the stubble on his chin. "I can't ask you to do that." He shook his head.

But then, something in Anna's being kicked into gear. She couldn't leave it here. She had to say something right now.

"Wil," she said. "I can't go home and leave Siegel as it is. I have to do something. No matter what you say."

"It's a useless business. You won't get anywhere."

"I know that your grandfather tried and—it hurt him greatly. I understand that. But it's going to bother me all my life."

"You'll be wasting your time."

"While we were driving back to Berlin, I came up with a plan."

Wil shook his head, but Anna could see warmth passing into his expression.

"First, I need to find out what happened—why things are the way they are at the Schloss and in the village. Then I'll have to talk to the new owners, see if I can persuade them to do something. I'm not trying to buy the Schloss. It's different from what your grandfather tried to do, but it would be criminal to let it go to ruin."

"But you're not even German. You don't live here. How are you going to go about any of it?"

"I am a quarter German. And this place is in my bones."

Wil leaned on the steering wheel. "I know you've heard this before, but it's impossible for an outsider to understand what has happened here. It's so damned complex. You can't just come in here and . . ."

"Someone has to try!"

"Your involvement will be seen as interference. Someone else owns the Schloss now. It's out of your hands. Sorry to be brutal. You have to move on. Put your head down. Leave it alone."

"How would I feel if I didn't even try?"

A wry expression passed across Wil's face. "Are you sure you're not a covert lawyer, Anna? You know, the art falls in the choosing. You can kill yourself over a project that you know deep down will only destroy you. Like I said . . ."

"As you say, this is a choice. And it's mine to make."

Wil raised a brow.

"First, I'd like to do some more . . . research. Would you mind if I got in touch should I need some help?"

Wil leaned back in his seat. "I've warned you."

Anna felt a flicker of irritation, but she needed Wil if she was ever going to speak to the people who owned Siegel.

"No point starting with a title search," Wil said, sounding almost cheerful. "The Schloss is in the name of a trust, and that name means nothing. It won't tell you anything. Just in case you were wondering."

"I see."

Anna could understand that Wil was not going to stand by and watch another person spend years doing what his grandfather had done. On the other hand, if she could get Wil on her side, he could be of real help. He was just the person she needed—he spoke German, knew the area, knew her family history, represented the new owner.

Anna placed a hand on the door handle.

"Anna—" Wil started.

"Thank you so much for your help today." She would resort to politeness. "I am very appreciative." She reached out her hand for him to shake.

Wil seemed to be stifling a grin. "It's been a pleasure," he said. "No problem at all. Take care. Enjoy San Francisco."

Anna nodded and climbed out of the car.

The first thing she did once she was back in the hotel was to pick up her phone and call Max. She leaned back on her bed as she waited to be put through to him, gazing out the window at the building opposite her hotel—yet another new office block in the old East.

"Oh, my darling girl," Max said when Anna

told him that she had found the ring. She skimmed over the details, only letting him know how it had felt to stand in his old bedroom, how the view over the lake was probably much the same as ever.

"Thank you," he said. "Honestly. You have no idea. Just to see the ring again . . ."

There was a weariness in his voice that worried Anna, though. She decided not to bother him with her plan to find out more about Schloss Siegel just now.

"Grandfather," Anna said when she sensed that Max was really becoming tired. "Would you mind if I stayed just a little longer here in Germany?"

Max chuckled. "I'd be delighted if you did. I'd love for you to enjoy a little break from work."

"Thank you!" She would try not to be too long.

"I'm being cared for perfectly well," Max continued, as if he had seen the threads spinning on their spools in Anna's mind. "Now is the perfect time for you to take a break. You've been looking after me for years. I'm in the hospital. Perfectly well cared for. Surrounded by delightful nurses."

He had a point. Anna could fly home quickly if she needed to.

And her investigations were not just about the past. They were about the future, and heritage, and beauty, and—most importantly—people, about seeing if anything could be done to wake the town of Siegel up again, to entice young people back into the village. It was only an hour away from one of the busiest cities in Europe. Surely, something could be done. If she could find investors, people to help the new owners . . .

"Don't tell me you've got a project." Max's voice slid into her mind.

He had always been able to do that—read her. "No, no," she said, standing up and walking over to the room's funky modern desk. She opened her laptop. "I'm just keen to have a look around—that's all. It's an interesting place."

There was a silence. She doubted she had convinced Max. "Well," he said, finally. "Perhaps you've met someone, darling—"

"Don't be ridiculous," Anna said. She opened her search engine. "Perfectly happy as I am, thank you."

"Oh dear, darling . . ." Max's voice trailed off. He did sound tired. It had been the right thing not to bother him yet with her plans.

She would do whatever she could on her own. Only when she had some real hope would she involve Max.

CHAPTER TEN

Paris, 1936

Paris was always a good distraction. Tonight's entertainment was a private affair at the home of Elsa Maxwell, an American gossip columnist who put on regular parties for her guests. As Isabelle slipped on her long gloves and smoothed down her silky evening dress, she convinced herself for the thousandth time that everything was fine. Isabelle's trumpet sleeves floated behind her as she walked toward the salon. Marthe had done it. Artifice. Pretending. Isabelle could do it too.

It was easy enough being an automaton. Isabelle chatted with people at the ball as if there was no ache in her soul at all. She hid what she felt in her heart with the finesse of a seasoned expert. No one at the party had any idea that she hadn't heard from Max in months. She posed for Man Ray with Virginia while reporters from *Excelsior Modes* and *Harper's Bazaar* spun around the room like ballerinas.

The past few months had taught her that love was a double-edged sword.

When the evening finally ended, Isabelle

chatted away with Virginia in the car as if she were any other carefree young girl out in Paris. She had danced with several young men; she had pretended to be interested in their talk, while saying almost nothing at all.

Back in the apartment, she said good night to Marthe, who had sat up late to wait, and then went to bed with a sense of relief. Virginia was already stuck into one of her American novels. Isabelle went to reach for a book, anything with which she could escape. But when she saw the envelope that had been placed by her bed, her heart skipped. The handwriting was Max's. The letter was postmarked Berlin.

Berlin, 2010

Anna walked around Berlin for hours the morning after her conversation with Max. Around every corner, on every street, grim reminders of the Nazi and Communist eras remained—Checkpoint Charlie, the Brandenburg Gate, the remains of the bombed-out Kaiser Wilhelm Memorial Church, the old sites where the Nazis had held power. Up until now, Anna had not realized that the history of this country was so much a part of her. It was as if something she hadn't known she possessed had opened up within her—a well of feelings, of movement. An abandoned apartment in Paris had sparked it all. What if it had never been found?

Anna wrapped herself tightly in her coat as she wandered through Potsdamer Platz, stopping at a café in the square to buy coffee in a paper cup. As she looked at the fragments of the old wall that were on display, she tried not to picture Max and his family escaping Siegel, their faces surely masking the fear that must have shaken them to their core.

And Max had never taken his mask off. Why not?

While she wanted to learn more about the family's sudden departure from Siegel, about what had happened to Max's other relatives, and about this great love that Max had left behind in Paris, Anna knew that she had to focus on the present too. People were suffering because of Siegel's abandonment—and there was nothing she could do about the past.

It was hard to imagine the villagers opening up to her. They had not seemed pleased to see a member of the Albrecht family back in their midst. Were there family archives somewhere? Anna knew that she couldn't do this on her own, but the problem was that every road led back to Wil. He was the only person who could help. And he was the only person whom she did not want to ask.

Anna paused, throwing her empty coffee cup

in the bin. As she walked back to her hotel, her phone rang.

The American caller sounded at once startlingly close and miles away. The hospital in San Francisco.

The voice did not beat around any bushes.

Max was dead.

Anna stopped on the pavement.

People swarmed past her. She was next to the Jewish Memorial. She was aware of people out of the corner of her eye, shady figures moving between the sculptures that were some of the most poignant tributes to the dead that she had ever seen. The sounds of children calling and playing in the memorial resonated in the Berlin air—the future dancing on the shadows of the past.

The faceless voice on the phone told her that Max had died peacefully. He had eaten his breakfast, and then, when the nursing staff had gone back in to collect his breakfast tray, he was gone. He had seemed calm—even content—during his last few hours.

Anna felt for the tiny faded box that was safe in her coat pocket. Her fingers clasped the threadbare velvet, rubbing at the stuff as if it held some sort of answer. She thanked the nurse, hung up the phone, and sat on a bench.

When the phone rang again, she answered it on the first ring and immediately wished she hadn't.

But the person on the end of the phone was Wil.

"Anna." He sounded matter-of-fact.

Anna's hand seemed to have taken on a life of its own—a shaky one. It was doing its own thing and she couldn't seem to make it stop.

"Anna?" Wil's voice was sharp on the phone. "Is the line bad?"

"No," she said. She felt a choke rising in her throat. Took in a breath.

"I've been thinking . . ."

"Mm." It came out like a grunt, but Anna nodded.

"I don't want to see someone else get hurt by our history. Not you," Wil said. Anna heard the telltale sound of footsteps on a hard floor. She pictured him pacing in his office.

Another picture came into focus—Max's body being covered, sent to the mortuary. Anna closed her eyes.

"Does that make sense?" Wil asked.

Anna breathed, hard.

More footsteps. "But I'm also only too happy to hear what you've got to say. Would that help?"

"I don't know what to say right now." Anna stood up, then slumped back down on the bench.

"Look," Wil said. A pause. "How about I pick you up from your hotel at eight? If you're going to do this, and I suspect you are, then . . ."

"Max just died," Anna said. She had to stand

up. She had to move. So she began to walk. Walking was good. "The hospital called a minute ago."

"Where are you?" Wil's voice suddenly sounded close, urgent.

"Brandenburg Gate," she managed, looking up at it. "But I'm fine. You must have loads of work to catch up on."

"Stay there," he said. "Don't move."

"You don't have to—you must be busy."

"It can wait. I'm walking out of the building now." There was the sound of a door closing.

"I can go back to the hotel." She should have been with Max when he died. He had been alone. How awful.

Wil's voice was even. "We need to get you on a flight home. I'm on my way. I'll be there as soon as I can. And don't hang up."

Anna looked at the phone as if it had taken on a life of its own.

A young family appeared at the base of the Brandenburg Gate. The woman had a guidebook in her hand, and her two children were listening to her, pointing and asking questions. They both wore orange hats. There was a father too. They all looked . . . happy, functional. Was it real? Did anyone have that sort of a life? Probably. But would she have changed anything about hers?

Pictures of Max came to mind. She wouldn't

swap what he had meant to her for anything—
he had been both father and mother to her since
she was twelve.

Wil was suddenly striding toward her. He wore
a dark overcoat. He looked serious. "Come on.
You must be freezing. Let's get you moving."

"Okay." Anna nodded.

She let Wil tuck her arm into his. "Let's go,"
he said.

Yes, Anna thought. Where to now?

Wil guided her to the beautiful Tiergarten,
Berlin's most famous park. As they passed
secluded benches, tucked away from the paths
among the trees and early spring flowers, Anna
didn't know whether she wanted to sit down,
keep walking, collapse, be stoic, or simply stare
into space. It was so unlike her—she always had
a game plan, total control over whatever came
her way.

If it hadn't been for Wil's ability to keep the
conversation flowing when she wanted to talk
and to stay quiet when it was all too much, then
she didn't know how she would have held things
together.

"There's a café overlooking the lake, if you'd
like to sit down," he said, after about half an
hour. "Perhaps you could do with a coffee?"

"Coffee would be good, thanks." Anna felt
a ghostlike smile form on her lips—in spite of

everything. The park was soothing. It was the perfect place to be. The history of the place seemed to wrap itself around her in some sort of protective embrace. This was Max's home. His parting gift to her had been to kindle her connection to his past—and in doing so, to her own. He had given her a hint of what she needed to know, and it was clear to her now that she needed to know everything.

Anna managed to eat some of the cake that Wil ordered for her. After that, she was able to walk back to the hotel and pack, while Wil booked her on a flight home. It wasn't until she was on the plane, having accepted Wil's offer of a lift to the airport, having shaken his hand and said goodbye, that she sat back, closed her eyes, and allowed the full effect of what had happened to sink into her.

Three days later, Anna stood at Max's grave in San Francisco. A sea of people surrounded the coffin, and yet somehow Anna felt cocooned in her own grief—safe somehow, firmly convinced that Max would always be with her, no matter what. Her father, Peter, stood by her side. His new family—three children and a young wife—provided something of a distraction.

And then there were the flowers. Anna's house was resplendent with them. Max had been well liked. He had had a long life and people wanted to pay tribute. But none of them really knew him. No one had an inkling about his past except Anna. Somehow she wanted to protect that, not for herself, but for him.

Once the final rites were read, and those who were closest to Max had each placed a rose on his coffin, many of the guests came back to Anna's house.

People chatted, laughed even, while Anna moved about in slow motion, helping her staff from the Italian Café as they served all the guests. Although she talked to various people who had known Max, she was only going through the motions. She felt apart from it all, as if she were talking about someone else, not the Max she knew.

And she continued to think about Schloss Siegel. She had to do something. She could not allow it to rot. She knew Max wouldn't want it to be left as it was. It was clear now—the discovery of the apartment in Paris had reignited all the broken dreams that he had pushed aside for decades. He had seemed so focused on finding his ring right before he died, and Anna suspected that this was only the first step in a longer journey that he had wanted to take. So now her work on Schloss Siegel was for him. It was up to her to continue the journey for Max.

Once the guests had departed, Anna decided

it was time for a well-earned rest. As she turned down the hallway toward her bedroom, she found a woman standing there.

She had her back to Anna, but Anna could see what she held in her hand: Anna's favorite photo of Max. The woman stood still. She was a little shorter than Anna. Her hair was secured in a neat French knot, and she wore a navy suit with a green silk scarf around her neck. When she turned, Anna caught her breath, though she did not understand why.

"Hello," the woman said.

It was a perfectly reasonable thing to say.

"You've caught me." The woman had to be in her sixties. Her eyes were blue, and a few stray locks of her still-fair hair framed her face. Anna hadn't noticed the woman earlier in the day—or at the funeral. But then there had been over three hundred people at the service, and a hundred had crowded into Anna's house, so this was hardly a surprise.

"Can I help you?" she asked.

The woman put the photo back down on Anna's hall table. The click of the frame on the wood seemed to punctuate the older woman's precise movements. Not for the first time that day, Anna wished that Max were around.

The woman ran a hand through her hair. "Okay," she said. "Very well."

Anna felt a jolt of shock run through her.

The accent. German.

"Wil Jager told me Max had died," the woman said.

"Wil?" Anna knew her voice sounded odd.

"He has told me about your interest in . . ."

"Schloss Siegel." A dead certainty had arrived in her head.

"That is correct." The woman's accent was crisp.

Anna nodded. Her mind raced ahead. She was having trouble making it stop.

"My name is Ingrid Hermann." The woman held out a perfectly manicured hand. Her fingers were covered with serious rings.

Anna held out her own bare fingers in return. "Anna Young," she said.

"I know."

"Can I offer you a cup of coffee?" Anna asked.

Ingrid shook her head. "I have already had your excellent coffee," she said. "I just have one thing I want to say. Then I will leave."

"Come into the living room," Anna said, moving out of the hallway, hoping Ingrid would follow.

Ingrid clasped her small patent leather handbag tight in her hands and stayed where she was.

"I must go," Ingrid said from behind Anna. "But I have a reason to be here. I am your cousin. But that is not all. I am also the owner of Schloss Siegel. Please do not go there again."

Anna spun around. The woman standing in her hallway stared straight at her. Her eyes were not warm.

Anna, most unusually, was speechless.

CHAPTER ELEVEN

Paris, 1936

Marthe was pacing in her bedroom—albeit slowly. Her knees were bothering her, and she'd started using a cane in the last few months. While Marthe's declining strength was worrisome, at the moment Isabelle felt more concerned about the way she was waving the cane in the air like a conductor's baton.

"This," Marthe said, "is what bothers me, Isabelle. You have the opportunity to be taken out by a decent young man and yet you sit here, your head in the veritable ether most of the time, thinking about heaven knows what. This fine gentleman turns up at our very *doorstep* to profess his feelings for you—which is just the sort of romantic overture I thought you'd always wanted—and you refuse him! I do not understand."

Isabelle sank onto Marthe's four-poster bed. She grabbed one of the deep red cushions and held it close to her chest. She stared at the portrait of Marthe on the wall opposite the bed. Surely as a young woman Marthe had understood how important it was to make one's own choices. So why was Marthe bullying her now?

The last thing Isabelle wanted to do was go out with the vapid young man on whom Marthe seemed so keen. He was just another swain—no interesting conversation, and no ability to see anything in her beyond the way she looked.

Isabelle knew exactly what she wanted: a family, love, and stability. Just not with someone she did not care a jot for. She was over that. She had known something better.

"I don't understand you," Marthe went on. "Virginia is out at this very moment with a charming young man."

"She means nothing by it," Isabelle said. "She is only stringing him along."

"That may be the case." Marthe's hand flew up to her forehead. "But couldn't you possibly do some stringing yourself? Wouldn't it be better than sitting here moping? You might surprise yourself. I am not suggesting that you fall in love. But I am suggesting that you try to enjoy yourself, properly, instead of simply pretending to do so—I can see you are not happy. You must have a life. Take control of yourself, Isabelle."

"I am not moping," Isabelle began. She hadn't told Marthe about the extent of her feelings for Max. A part of her worried that if she did so, Marthe would, in turn, worry about Isabelle moving to Germany, which would make it difficult for Marthe to see Isabelle at all. Maybe ever. Marthe had made clear her opinion about Hitler's occupation of the Rhineland and the fact that France was not marching into battle.

In the same way, Isabelle had put off telling Max, and potentially his family, about Marthe's past and who she really was.

She was juggling two separate lives, and their eventual collision could wreck her chances of acceptance with the Albrechts, or leave Marthe alone in her old age. How much longer could she keep the two people whom she loved most in the world apart?

Isabelle had a telegram from Max tucked into the pocket of her dress.

Marthe stopped in the doorway. Isabelle met her grandmother's hard stare with a tentative smile. Marthe raised her cane again, shook her head, and walked out.

"Camille!" Isabelle heard her grandmother call. "For goodness' sake, it is time for my luncheon."

A few hours later, Isabelle stepped into the garden of the Hotel Ritz. She had changed outfits several times before finally deciding on a pale blue tea dress that Camille assured her brought out the color in her olive skin. Isabelle had imagined this moment countless times. She was about to see Max. He had come to Paris during his two-day break to see her. Why did something feel wrong?

221

A waiter led her to a wicker chair. Plants on pedestals vied for position with the statues that were dotted about the garden. Waiters slipped in and out of the French doors that opened out onto the gorgeous scenery.

"You fit in perfectly in these surroundings." Max's voice came from behind her chair. He rested a hand on her shoulder for a moment, and she brought her hand up to rest in his before he sat down.

But when he sat down, he glanced around the place like a nervous cat.

"I don't think anyone's going to attack us here," Isabelle laughed.

"I have to tell you something," he said. "I'm going to be . . . travelling for some time and I may not be able to contact you much, if at all, for a while."

Isabelle sipped at her coffee and eyed the patisseries that were arranged on the table between them. Suddenly, she felt that she could not eat a thing.

"And I have something to take care of this afternoon, here in Paris," he said, still looking around, but with one hand resting in hers.

"You have things to take care of in Paris?" Isabelle almost whispered the words.

He nodded and again looked around the room.

Isabelle almost did the same thing, because her

heart was pounding in her chest. Nazi business? In Paris? Isabelle knew enough to realize that he wasn't talking about buying his mother jewelry at Van Cleef & Arpels.

Isabelle knew that Hitler had emphasized his desire for a friendship with France—but Max's nervousness worried her more than she cared to admit to herself. He could have something completely different on his mind—his family, the villagers. It might not be Nazism. Isabelle was not going to allow herself to panic, no matter how well she knew him, no matter how much she cared.

"Shall we meet tonight, say at nine?" Max asked suddenly. "How about La Coupole? Can you catch a taxi and meet me? I might be tied up until then."

"Of course I can," Isabelle said. "Shall I bring Virginia?"

"Of course." He stood up, waited for her, but his eyes roamed toward the exit.

"Very well," Isabelle said, putting on her white gloves. She adjusted the angle of her hat.

Max seemed anxious to leave. He waited for her to walk out first, but when she stole a glance back to look at him, his gaze was once again darting around the room.

La Coupole didn't help. Virginia had brought along a party of friends, and as the evening was warm, they all sat outside on the crowded terrace.

Every now and then, a couple from their table would stand up to go dance inside.

"Isn't this fabulous," Isabelle said. "I adore Paris in the summer." She tried to catch Max's eye.

"Fabulous." Max seemed fascinated by everything but her.

His hand still rested in hers, but he seemed so distracted that Isabelle didn't know what to think.

"Max—" she started, keeping her voice low.

Virginia was out of earshot, chatting with a young Frenchman she had met earlier in the day.

"Don't worry, please," Max said. But he didn't meet her eye.

Virginia appeared at the table then. Her face was flushed as she sat down, fanning herself with a napkin. "Oh, it's just gorgeous out there. Such fun." Virginia grabbed hold of Isabelle's arm. "You have to come and dance."

"Max," Isabelle said, her head tilted to one side, "are you going to ask me to dance, or will I have to ask you?"

"Go and dance with Virginia, darling," he said. "I'll stay here."

Virginia was up again in a trifle, taking Isabelle's arm, pulling her toward the curved white staircase past the crowds. Cigarette smoke hovered in the air, sending a haze over the entire place.

Isabelle stopped at the top of the stairs, stood

on the balcony, and took a look back down over the room. La Coupole was an unmissable part of any night out in Paris. Anyone who was anyone was here. Max couldn't be bored with the place. And he didn't seem entirely cold to her, just distracted. What on earth did it mean?

Virginia pulled Isabelle toward the dance floor on the upper floor and began doing the shimmy. Isabelle was starting to think like a young girl in a panic. She would not overanalyze his behavior and think the worst. The band was all female. Isabelle concentrated on the dance.

"Who needs men?" Virginia called into Isabelle's ear.

In spite of it all, Isabelle smiled. Virginia could always be relied upon to say the right thing. She would not think about politics, not for a few minutes. Instead, she began moving to the chirpy sounds of jazz.

Max stood up when they arrived back at the table. "I have to go," he said, leaning in close to Isabelle's ear.

She felt a small stab in her stomach. "So soon?" she asked, looking him straight in the eye.

"Sorry," he said. "It's not something to bother you with."

He had one hand around her waist, and as he leaned down, his lips brushed her forehead for a moment. Then he pulled back.

"Goodbye," he said.

His tone was still odd. He nodded at her and left.

"Everything all right?" Virginia appeared at her side the moment Max had gone.

Isabelle watched his retreating back. He hadn't said anything about seeing her again.

"You know, I'm just not sure if it is," she said. "I don't know."

"Oh, darling." Virginia linked her arm through Isabelle's. "For goodness' sake come and dance again. It does you no end of good."

But Isabelle shook her head and sat down. Where was Max going? What could he be doing? Had he said one kind word to her all day? Did she want to ignore what this might mean? Or not?

The incessant singing and the noise and the smoke all mingled together into a haze of sound and smell and light. But Isabelle didn't want to get up and dance again. Confusion swamped her and she felt naïve all of a sudden and out of place. She tried to push away the sense that she was dealing with a force far greater than anything she could control. She only hoped it was not controlling Max.

San Francisco, 2010

Anna stood in Max's empty apartment. She had packed everything up over the last month, and his home was about to be sold. The furniture had gone to auction, but she had kept anything precious that she wanted to save. There had been nothing left of Max's past. None of the clues that she was so desperate to find—about his relationship with the owner of the abandoned apartment in Paris, or about what had happened to the rest of his family.

After Ingrid had left—rushing out right after her dramatic announcement—Anna had been completely confused. Ingrid was only in San Francisco for business. Did not want any further discussion. Had repeated several times that all she wanted was for Anna to keep well away from the Schloss. The past was the past. Ingrid had everything under control.

Well, no, she certainly did not.

For the first few days after the funeral, Anna had been in a zombielike state—unable to sleep much, yet exhausted, not wanting to eat, yet forcing herself to get something down. She went into work but was unable to focus on a thing. During her free time she sorted out Max's affairs—but she was on autopilot.

And now, there was nothing for it but to go back to her old life and simply get on with her work. It would be the sensible thing to do.

She tried just going into work as she always used to and coming home at night—although the gap that existed where she used to visit Max every evening loomed larger and larger each day. She hadn't realized what an anchor her visits to him had been. She had thought the visits were for his sake, but now she realized that she had truly been going for her own. Now, going home to a silent house on her own only caused her mind to wander straight back to Germany.

So she tried keeping busy in the evening—tidying, rearranging things, going to the movies with her girlfriends. Cass threw a dinner party one night—supplying a veritable fleet of eligible men. But nothing worked. Anna was simply distracted and at sea.

She tried to relax, but whenever she stood in the shower, lay in her bed, turned on the television, or opened a book, she was lost.

It was as if she were haunted. The Schloss, Max's past, her family—dare she admit it, Wil—all spun around in her head.

Anna's life was here in San Francisco. Thinking of Wil was ridiculous. She had met him only a few times. Why was her mind drawn to him? She was meant to be grieving! This was supposed to be entirely about Max, not Wil. What was wrong with her?

Germany was bouncing around in her head like a pinball. The blindingly obvious thing to do was to call Wil and tell him that she had met Ingrid. She could not simply leave it alone. No matter what Ingrid said. No matter how unlikely it was that Wil would help her. No matter, even, that Max was gone.

Wil would be loyal to his client—of course he would. But still, her mind wouldn't leave it alone.

She turned on her bedside lamp and picked up her phone. She looked at it, wondered if she were going completely insane, and decided to make the call. It was eleven o'clock in the morning in Berlin.

Wil answered on the first ring.

"Anna," he said, "what are you doing awake?"

"Hello."

"Hi. I hope you are doing all right."

Anna was a pro at answering that. She got up and paced out into the hallway. "Oh, you know. Everything's done."

"Yes, but how are you?"

"Okay." Anna picked up the photo of Max. Bad move. She frowned and padded off to the kitchen.

"Take it easy for a while." He sounded kind.

Anna was getting sick of kind. She sighed.

"You sound a bit . . . ," he started.

"Fine. No. I'm fine." Anna paced toward the fridge. Opened it. It had become a comfort thing. She would check that she had enough food in the fridge. She always did, but nevertheless.

"Mmm hmm." But Wil's words ended with an upswing, and he sounded closer now, intimate almost.

Anna shut the fridge and slumped down in a kitchen chair. "You see, I met—"

"Ingrid? Yes."

There was a silence.

"I couldn't tell you who she was. She had to be the one to do that." He sounded closer again.

Anna resorted to practicalities. This conversation was making her feel like a truck on a bumpy track, and it didn't feel good. "Can you tell me anything at all?"

"Before she met you, she asked me why I had to pull up floorboards." Wil paused for a moment. "I couldn't lie. So I told her the truth."

Anna moved back to her bed and sat on it, cross-legged. "Do you have any idea what her plans are?"

"I can tell you that she tends to buy up property, then leave it. Does nothing with it. Just lets it rot."

"Why would she do that?"

"She's bought old factories, estates, and whole villages. She shuts down the businesses, sits on the buildings, and sits on the land. She watches their value rise, spends nothing on the assets, and sells them at a profit after a certain period of time—depending on the investment."

"But why would she do that with her own family's past?"

"You tell me." Wil sounded as if he were about to walk in the door.

Anna was drawn in too, and she hardly dared to notice that she liked it. "That's not the only question I have."

"Like I said, you should have been a lawyer."

Anna felt the hint of a smile on her lips, but she plowed on. "I just can't stop thinking about my grandfather and this . . . woman he loved in Paris. Who was she? Could she still be alive? What if she knows something? And I have more questions. Does Ingrid see any of my family? Because now that Max is gone, I really have no one left except my father, and I hardly ever see him. And shouldn't I at least talk to Ingrid about the Schloss? See if I can convince her to change her position on this one, special place?"

"That's quite a list of questions." Wil sounded amused.

Anna only felt relief fan through her system. She had gotten it all out. Well, most of it, a smart voice inside her head seemed to jeer. She pushed that thought away. It was no use at all.

"What time is it there?"

"Two a.m."

"Oh, God, Anna. I knew it was late. You should get some sleep. Is this happening every night? Is someone looking after you?"

"There's more," she went on. His questions were too raw. "Why did Max cut himself off from all his relatives? Why did he never ever

231

talk about it? What went wrong? Because I'm wondering if once I've got to the bottom of that, then I could try to talk to Ingrid—make her understand his perspective. If she understood him—if I could figure out what happened—she might be willing to do something with Schloss Siegel and the village. Once I can convince people that Max is not the person to blame, maybe everyone can move on. It seems things are downright stuck—not to mention all wrong."

There was another silence.

"Listen, Anna," Wil said.

"Sure." Anna stood up again. Perhaps she would make herself a warm drink. He hadn't laughed, or told her she was mad. She walked into the kitchen.

When Wil spoke she stopped dead. "I didn't want to interrupt you with all this while you were grieving, but I think you should talk to Ingrid, and soon." He was quiet for a moment. "It would be better for you to come to Berlin to do that. Meet her in person. I don't think a phone call would do it. I'm happy to help. If you don't mind me saying this, I did talk to Ingrid about it myself. I asked her if she'd talk with you when you were ready. She said she would, but I had to convince her. I can be there if you want me to, or not. It's up to you."

Anna ran a hand through her hair. Suddenly, a smile spread over her face. That had been kind of Wil. He hadn't had to do that. He was being a good friend to her.

So.

She opened the fridge again with her free hand. She shut the door again. Walked out into the living room.

"If you don't come over and follow this up I think it's going to bother you. You need to do this, and soon." Wil's voice softened. "It sounds as if Max was unsettled for the rest of his life, not following things through," he said.

"Yes."

"Would you like me to call Ingrid, see when she's free? Once we know, we can get you on a flight to Berlin. You can sit down with her, talk about it properly, and work out a way forward."

Anna nodded. "Okay. And thank you."

"Pleasure."

Another silence. He would need to get back to work.

"Wil?" she asked.

"Yes?"

"Don't get me wrong, but I'm wondering what made you—" Why had he changed his mind?

"Anna." Wil sounded firm now. "I'm sorry. I'm late for a meeting. I have to go." A pause. "What made me think about this is the fact that something doesn't seem quite right—the beloved and loyal grandfather you describe doesn't match up with the man who abandoned his entire family. If

I can help set the record straight, then that would be good. I'll talk to Ingrid. Then I'll get back to you. Okay?"

Anna nodded. "Okay," she said. "And thanks again." There was something unfamiliar about relying on someone else—a lack of surety. Was she doing the right thing? She had been her own best friend for years now.

"Anna." Wil's voice cut into her thoughts.

"Yes?"

"You should get some sleep now. We'll work it out."

Anna nodded. "Thank you." Her instincts were, of course, to push Wil away. Just like she had always done with any man who had ever been kind to her. Why was that? And yet, here he was offering to help. He was asking nothing in return. She sighed.

He said goodbye and hung up the phone.

Anna wandered back to bed. With her thoughts all aswirl, she doubted she was going to get any sleep. But when she woke up five hours later, refreshed after a deep, dreamless sleep, she climbed out of bed with a mind that was clearer than it had been for weeks.

CHAPTER TWELVE

Three days later Anna woke up in the hotel that Wil had chosen for her in the old West Berlin. It was near his house, apparently. The boutique inn was infinitely more charming than the last place she had stayed in the city. Anna stretched, letting her eyes wander over the attractive room. A funky chandelier hung above the retro-looking brass bed, and the bathroom was all indulgence; a claw-footed bath sat in a sea of marble. In the corner of her room, Anna had draped the clothes that she had worn on her long flight the day before across a Louis XV chair covered in leopard spots.

Wil was going to meet her for breakfast at nine o'clock. Instinctively, she reached for her phone. There was a text from Wil that made her smile—he had thought hard about where to take a café expert for breakfast. In the end, he had decided that she had to try *Streuselschnecke*, a local specialty that he hoped was new to her. He suggested a bakery that was famous for the treats.

It was hard to know what to think about meeting Ingrid again. What sort of magic had

Wil worked in order to change her mind after their cold exchange last time?

The *Bäckerei* that Wil had chosen was set between a bookshop and a fresh produce market. As soon as Anna walked in, she knew that this was her sort of place. It took her two seconds to sniff out the fact that the coffee smelled fabulous. Artisan breads were displayed in wicker baskets behind the counter, and sugar-topped squares of butter cake, fresh apple fritters, and quark cheesecake sat in sparkling glass cabinets. The baristas looked like they knew what they were doing, and the lines were similar to those in the Italian Café.

Wil had chosen a table in the middle of the room. He looked up when Anna walked in. When his eyes caught hers, they lit up with a genuine warmth that made her feel more relaxed than she had in a long while. Anna smiled back and headed over to the table.

"Good news and bad news," Wil said, sitting back down after greeting her with a hug.

Anna looked at him and waited.

"I thought we might go out to the Schloss today. Have a look around. I've got us a picnic." He looked almost shy.

Anna bit her lip, but smiled back at him.

"That was the good news," he said. "The bad news, I'm afraid, is that Ingrid had to fly out to Singapore all of a sudden—but she'll be back tonight. She wants to meet with us in the morning for coffee. I thought that might work better for you, anyway. You'll be a little less jet-lagged by then."

Wil ordered *Streuselschnecke* for them both, which turned out to be warm little buns covered in sugar. Once she sipped the excellent coffee, Anna forgot all about her jet lag. But that was not the thing that surprised her. As she chatted with Wil—asking him about his work, about what he had been doing—something happened, right then, right there, that she had not been expecting. Was it a thought? An instinct? A feeling? Afterward she was not exactly sure.

All she knew was that that was the moment she decided to enjoy herself. Not so long ago, she would have turned Wil down out of hand, closed herself off from the very idea of spending a full day alone with him. But now, she was actually having a good time with a kind man, and she was going to allow herself to do so.

So instead of telling Wil, no, she couldn't possibly go for a picnic with him on this beautiful day, she told him, yes, she would love to.

Anna licked the last of the *Streuselschnecke*'s sugar off her fingers and let it melt on her tongue. When had she last had fun?

"A picnic," Anna said, "sounds perfect."

Wil's eyes were warm. "Good. I don't think being at Siegel will cure you of your desire to save it—in fact, it will probably make things worse—but I thought you might like to have a look around. We could explore the park."

Anna met Wil's gaze. There was something more relaxed about him today. His striped shirt was open at the collar, hanging loose over his chinos. He looked as if he hadn't shaved that morning, but the effect made him even more attractive than the last time she had seen him. Those warm green eyes looked right back at her, and his boyish grin kicked in. He averted his gaze first, picked up the tab, and went to pay at the counter.

Anna had offered to contribute to the check, but he had refused. Now she sat back in her seat. The sun shone on the sidewalk outside, and people stopped in the street to chat with one another. She could hear peals of laughter. If only the same atmosphere could prevail in Siegel. Surely she could do something to save it.

She sensed Max urging her on.

The drive to the old Schloss was quick. Wil joked around and was good company. Anna found herself laughing for the first time since Max's funeral. The landscape seemed familiar now—endearing, even. Every tree was resplendent with verdant leaves, and when they approached the Schloss gates and Anna rolled her window down, she heard birdcalls coming from the park.

She climbed out, telling Wil that she would open the gates on her own. He handed her the key, his eyes crinkling in the way that she had come to like.

Anna pushed open the gates and leaned in the window of the car as Wil drove through them.

"I'll walk from here," she said.

"Sure," Wil said, waving at her.

After tugging the ornate gates shut, Anna stood for a moment, breathing in the crisp, clean country air. A breeze stirred the tall trees in the park, as though welcoming her, telling her that this was where she belonged. This was her home.

She heard Wil's car engine stop. She was keen to explore the area around the lake.

Anna stretched her arms high above her head and rolled her neck after the car journey. She was going to savor every moment of this beautiful day because she knew that Max would want her to do so.

Paris, 1938

Isabelle sat down to read a letter from Max. She had waited to open the envelope until Marthe had decided to take her afternoon nap. Virginia was out and Isabelle did not want to be disturbed while she read. It was the first time she had heard anything in months.

But before she opened the thin pages to reveal Max's solid handwriting, Isabelle sat back on the chair in her bedroom and waited for another few moments. This letter could tell her what she did not want to hear. She had tried so hard to move on from Max and failed. She had questioned what he felt for her after his last visit. He had confused her, but no matter how many young men she and Virginia met, her thoughts always turned back to Max.

He filled her head.

When Isabelle finally opened the letter, it was full of Hitler's plans. Max wrote that the prohibition against Austria joining Germany that was laid down in the Treaty of Versailles was resented by many Germans. That the *anschluss* had been managed without warfare and that relief was felt by many Germans after weeks of tension and agitation over the outcome of the plan. He wrote that he had been able to listen to the broadcast newsreel of Hitler driving into Linz and Vienna.

But Isabelle had read in the newspapers that Hitler had demanded that Austria appoint Nazis to the cabinet, and that he had also demanded that the Nazi party's rights be fully restored or he would invade Austria. The *London Times* had called it "the end of Austria."

This had been followed by reports of Germany's plans to protect all the Germans living outside its borders. It was becoming icily clear what that would mean.

Isabelle put Max's letter down and went to stand at the window.

She wished she could look him in the eye and understand what he was really thinking. She wasn't sure what to write back, and she hated not knowing when she would see him again. Had they promised to wait for each other—or not?

Then, one morning in late September, she had a completely different letter from Max. Occasionally—but only very occasionally—there was the hint of something personal in his words. She could glimpse a sign of what she thought of as the real Max. She suspected that this happened when he was tired, when he was a little emotional—maybe even confused.

But this time, his tone was new. He sounded urgent. Isabelle read his letter in the privacy of her bedroom.

Once Isabelle had finished reading, she bolted to find Virginia. Her friend was seated at the piano.

"We have to go to London," she whispered in her friend's ear.

"Really, darling?" Virginia turned from Claude Debussy.

"Don't you see? You simply have to come with me."

Virginia stood up from the piano stool, took Isabelle by the arm, walked her back into their shared bedroom, and closed the door.

"I take it Max wants to meet you in London?"

Isabelle did not meet her friend's eye. "He has leave."

"But last time, he was so . . . odd." Virginia whispered the words. "He upset you."

Isabelle sat down at her dressing table and started to play with her hair. "I need to know what's really going on with him."

"Are you sure you should just drop everything and go?" Virginia asked.

Was she sure? If her mind and her heart had anything to do with it, then, yes, she was certain. She knew now that politics could never come between her and her feelings for Max. And she needed to know for sure whether he felt the same way.

Isabelle stood up again and walked over to the window. A line had formed outside the theater across the road. People chatted underneath the trees, whose leaves were tinged with the first rusty stains of autumn. Isabelle did know one thing. She needed to feel his arms around her, know that he still cared about her as much as before, discuss their plans for the future.

"Yes," she said. "I'm one hundred percent sure." She turned back to look at her reflection in the mirror. "But I want you to come with me."

Virginia stayed quiet. Isabelle could see her friend's reflection behind her in the mirror.

Virginia was frowning. "I suppose the only way to fix it is to bring it to a head."

"You know," Isabelle said, "you are not simply the party girl that everyone thinks you are."

Something rueful passed across her friend's face. "Well," she said, "there are two things I do know. One, you're never going to settle for one of those vacuous young men here, and two, you're in love with Max. And that, perhaps, is all that matters."

Isabelle leaned forward and put her arms around her friend.

Who knew what the future held for any of them—for her, for Virginia, for Max, for Germany, or for Paris?—but one thing was certain. If there was any chance that she could be happy, even a tiny spit of an opportunity, then she was going to take it. Now.

Schloss Siegel, 2010

This time, Anna didn't take in the decrepit state of the driveway, and she didn't focus on the bullet holes in the walls. It felt right being here at the old Schloss. It felt almost as if Max were here too—as if his spirit had settled in this place. He had gone full circle—sending Anna back to where everything had begun for him. But why had his life gone so wrong?

Wil parked the car in front of the terrace overlooking the park. He climbed out of the car and stood looking at the old garden.

"Would you like to go for a walk first?" Wil asked.

"I'd love to," Anna said. "Thank you for this. Exploring the park is just what I want to do right now." She opened the car door and changed into the sturdier shoes that she had grabbed when she dashed back to her hotel to freshen up after breakfast.

There was an ornamental garden in front of the lake—it was sunken, in the French style. Old plinths were all that were left of the statues that must have once graced the garden paths. An ugly park bench was stuck in one of the natural alcoves that lined the path. Once, there would have been something beautiful there.

When they arrived at the lake, Anna became entranced with the building that sat on its far side. It was partially hidden from view by a bank of willow trees that lined the still water.

"It was the orangery," Wil said. He had stayed mostly quiet, but Anna enjoyed the way he smiled when it was clear that she had fallen in love with another aspect of the Schloss. She was grateful to be here with a person who seemed to share her feelings toward her ancestral home.

Anna stared through the old glass panes into the empty, dust-filled orangery.

"I'd like to walk around the lake," she said, turning to Wil.

"I think it's important you do that."

She turned around, took the old path back toward the still water, lined with trees.

"Imagine growing up here," Anna said, turning to Wil, who was close behind her.

"I know," he said. He stopped then. "Look," he went on, leaning in a little closer.

A little farther on, the path widened, leading to a grassy embankment. There was a small bridge. Incredibly, a little rowboat was tied to the bridge. Its oars had been left neatly folded in place, as if they were ready for someone—Max perhaps—to return again, one day.

Wil approached the water's edge, and Anna shaded her eyes, watching him inspect the boat.

"The bridge isn't safe," he called back to her. "But the boat looks fine. Would you like to row out to the island?"

Anna felt herself smiling. "Well, yes. Would you like me to row?"

He grinned back at her. "I can row, Anna. It's one thing I am able to do."

It seemed Wil was able to do many things, but Anna wasn't going to say that just then. She followed him down to the edge of the lake while he untethered the boat from its moorings.

The oars were tied fast together with thick rope, tucked inside the two metal rings that sat on either side of the little dinghy.

"It's the perfect weather for a spin," Wil said. He seemed to be checking the boat over again, and Anna cast her eye over it too. While a swim back to the bank might be amusing, they were an hour from a change of clothes, and the water didn't look inviting.

"It's fine," Wil said. He climbed aboard and stood upright in the small craft. He reached a hand out to Anna.

She felt a little shy taking hold of his hand, but she stepped aboard and sat down as soon as she was able to.

"Shall we take a trip around the lake first?" Wil asked.

Anna leaned back in the sun, allowing its warmth to play on her face. She had forgotten about being jet-lagged, with all the excitement of being here. But now that she had sat down, a wave of exhaustion washed over her. She closed her eyes for a moment.

Wil stayed quiet, and she enjoyed the soothing sound of the water lapping against the boat.

When Anna opened her eyes again, they were heading toward the driveway and the main gates.

"It's like a hidden paradise in here," Anna said, "a little haven in a vast estate."

"The Schloss lands stretched for miles to the

east," Wil said. "The estate once owned huge amounts of farmland and forest, but then it all became part of a cooperative during the Soviet era."

"And now, most of the land has been sold off, I guess?"

"Ingrid bought back a good deal of it."

When they rounded the lake and the Schloss came into view, Anna pulled out her camera and took some shots of its impossibly romantic facade.

Once they had done a circuit of the lake, Wil rowed toward the island.

"Would you like to have a look at the island?" he asked. He indicated his backpack. "You must be starving."

"Oh, those streuselly things did a pretty good job of filling me up," Anna laughed.

"Those streuselly things were ages ago." Wil started to row again.

Once they had moored the dinghy and walked the entire circuit of the island, Wil put his backpack down at the foot of a horse chestnut tree. Its dappled leaves provided welcome shade from the sun. The day had become thick with heat, sending a haze over the lake. A dragonfly hovered above the rushes at the water's edge. Wil leaned against the base of the tree, while Anna sat nearby on a rug he had brought.

There was a cold pack with baguettes, cheeses,

tomatoes, and cucumbers, and a lemon cake that oozed with syrup for after lunch. And coffee, as well as lemonade.

"Pink lemonade." Anna smiled, sipping out of the small glass bottle. "I don't think I've ever had that before."

"I bet they used to have it, you know, right here, years ago," Wil said, sounding a little lazy now.

"I bet they did," Anna laughed, "and pink gins and caviar . . ."

"Anna?"

"Yes."

"I'm surprised that you haven't asked about—"

"Ingrid?"

"Yes."

"Well." Anna rolled onto her back, stared up through the floating leaves at the blue sky. "She is your client. I didn't want to pry."

"Sensitive of you."

"Maybe I'm just going to grill her when I meet her—perhaps I'm saving it up."

"Come on. You must have a few questions."

"Why did she agree to see me again?"

There was a silence for a while. "I don't know. Maybe it was the funeral, the realization that Max has gone."

Anna nodded. She felt almost too tired to ask anything more, and she hardly dared hope to get any real information from Ingrid, but she would certainly try. She felt so lazy now, lying on the rug, and at peace.

"I have some questions," Wil said.

"I can't guarantee I'll answer."

But something had shifted. He didn't laugh back, didn't take the bait she had cast into the easy banter realm.

"I'm curious. About you."

Anna felt something quiver in the spot between her ribs. "Oh, there's not much to be curious about," she said.

"I understand why you'd want to drop everything to come here—but apart from your business, was there anything else—any person—that you had to leave?"

The quiver in Anna's chest had turned to a beat. When she tried to speak, it seemed that her words were stuck.

"I, look, I—"

"Tell me."

Anna propped herself up on one elbow. "There's not much to say."

"I bet there is. No, I can see there is." His voice was drawing her in. Anna felt lazier still, almost as if she were with a snake charmer—and something seemed different. Perhaps it was all the stress of the past few weeks. Perhaps it would be a good idea to talk, and she was confident that she could trust Wil.

"Well," she said, then stopped again.

"Try me."

But then, perhaps she shouldn't open up. Because she was having feelings about Wil that were unsettling her. If she were honest, she had never felt so drawn to a man in her life. No one had interested her in this way. But he lived in Germany. It was impossible. She shouldn't allow herself to get carried away. "Do your parents live near Siegel still?" She kept her voice firm.

"They live in Hamburg. My father is retired but my mother still works as a doctor. They are happy. I guess they sort of have it right."

Anna nodded. Getting it right. Why was that so hard? Some people seemed to make an art form of it.

"If you want to talk, I'm happy to listen. Nothing goes any further, you know. Unless it makes you uncomfortable—but I think things are better out than in."

Anna sat up then. Annoyingly, tears bit at the back of her eyes. She focused hard on the haze above the lake.

"Okay," she said finally. It seemed that she had reached a crossroads. If she opened up about her personal life to Wil, she would be taking a risk that she hadn't allowed herself to take for a long time; she would be going down a path that she had avoided, adeptly, for years. And yet, a part of her urged her forward. But while she felt safer talking to Wil than she did with anyone else on the planet right now, she also felt confused and panicked and in danger and excited and exhilarated all at the same time.

If she didn't look at him, it was also easier to talk. She had noticed that when she had been with him before. And why was that? Why? Because something else was happening. She couldn't avoid it. Something bigger than anything that she had felt for years, no matter how she looked at it. And that something else was life—it was the will to embrace life in all its gloriousness. She realized that Max had not dared to live his life to the fullest ever again, and that she had allowed herself to have only meaningless, risk-free relationships with men. For the first time since her mother's death and her father's departure, Anna felt alive.

CHAPTER THIRTEEN

London, 1938

Isabelle felt like royalty as she walked into the lobby of the Dorchester. Any doubts that she had about coming to London were dispelled when the doorman called her by name and the bellboys took not only her luggage but her coat, hat, and gloves. The reception staff told her that Max would meet her for the famous Dorchester afternoon tea in an hour. Virginia had rushed off to meet an old friend for some shopping.

The entire place was heaven. The suite of rooms that she was going to share with Virginia was full of the prettiest things. Antiques had been placed in the sitting room, and the entire suite felt more like private rooms in a grand country house than any hotel. Lamps were dotted about the room, and there was a bottle of champagne on ice on one of the cedar side tables, along with a bowl of white roses and a selection of petits fours.

Forty-five minutes later, Isabelle had washed, changed, and redone her makeup. She was ready to meet Max. Stemming her anticipation and her nervousness was impossible, because she knew that this was a turning point. This was where she would find out how Max felt about her. She simply had to know.

A short while later, she made her way down to the hotel's Promenade in the cherry-red Coco Chanel suit that Marthe had insisted on buying for her last spring.

A charming young waiter escorted her to her table. Isabelle couldn't resist staring at the ever-so-plush Promenade. Shapely vases filled with spectacular but tasteful blooms decorated nearly every table in the center of the room.

A pianist played Chopin in the background, and when Isabelle sat down, she tugged at the pearls around her neck. Did she look all right? She had hardly slept the night before.

Isabelle sensed Max's arrival well before she saw him, but she kept her eyes focused on the menu until Max kissed her on the cheek.

"Isabelle," he said, sliding into the banquette opposite her.

She knew that if she looked into his eyes she would have her answer, but something held her back—not wanting to know, not just yet? Giving up hope was the last thing she wanted to do.

They placed their order and a silver platter soon arrived, containing layer upon layer of delicate savory finger sandwiches on fresh-baked brown and white breads, filled with smoked salmon, chicken, egg, and cucumber.

"How are you?" he asked.

"Fine. Well. I'm well."

"You look well."

Still, she was not able to meet his eye.

"And your grandmother?"

"Yes, fine. Although—she's been a bit unwell lately. Coughing. Spending more time at home."

"I'm sorry."

When a plate of scones arrived along with a selection of delicate macaroons, Isabelle didn't know if she could manage another bite. But she forced herself to take something in order to be polite.

"Shall we take a stroll through Hyde Park?" Max asked, his voice still coming from some disembodied place.

Isabelle nodded. She stood up and strolled out to the park with him, just like any fashionable young couple out for the afternoon. Dogs scuttled about among the trees, and children accompanied by chattering nannies played timeless games. They rounded a bend in the path. Max was quiet, but it felt as if a river of things unspoken ran between them.

Finally, when the path narrowed and they were in a secluded spot, Isabelle stopped.

"I have to tell you something about Marthe," she said. "I am so sorry. I should have told you before."

Max lifted her chin to his face. "Look at me.

You haven't met my eye since we met."

She shook her head. "I don't know how to say this, and I don't know whether I should. Perhaps, it might make things . . . well . . . I don't know." What did she mean? Easier? If she told him about Marthe's past, would it make it simpler for him to end things with her? Justify his decision to let her go? She shook her head again. Her thoughts were more in turmoil than a wasp trapped in a bottle. But she had to tell him.

Either way, he had to know.

"Grandmother has a past," she said, her voice sounding rough. But she couldn't control it. "I was embarrassed, and it has stopped me from being accepted anywhere, by anyone's family in Paris. People talk to me, men dance with me, but their mothers won't touch me with the tips of their parasols."

"Well then, they are stupid," Max growled. "What in goodness' name did she do? Murder someone? Throw herself in front of a building site? Whatever it is—"

"She was a courtesan," Isabelle blurted out. Tears nipped at her eyes. "She was born to a lowly family, became a seamstress. Marthe de Florian isn't even her name."

"I don't care what her name was." Max leaned forward and brushed his lips against hers.

Isabelle closed her eyes but then opened them, pulling away slightly. "No. I have to tell you.

She worked as a dancer at the Folies Bergère after she was discovered in the garment district when she was twenty. She had two babies—boys—to two different fathers by then. And after she was discovered, she worked her way to the top. She was a demimondaine. A fashion leader, and everything in our home in Paris was given to her by . . . men." Isabelle was determined to go on. "By her clients. She was a high-class prostitute."

"Stop." Max had his arms around her. "For pity's sake, stop. I don't care if she had an affair with the Pope. It's irrelevant. Isabelle, I adore you. I am so sorry for what I've put you through in these past years. The thought of you, the idea of you, the real you, has kept me going. If I lose every material possession I own, if this damned Hitler loses another bloody war for Germany, it won't matter because all I want is you. Please would you marry me?" He took her hands, kissing her forehead, moving down with butterfly touches to her lips. "After this is over, whatever the outcome's going to be?"

Isabelle reached up to him, her hands stroking his cheeks. "I love you," she said. "I always have. Yes."

"I have something to tell you, though," he said, his words coming out clearer, harder now. "My parents insist that I fight for Germany. My parents insist that Hitler is doing the right thing

257

for our country. God help me if they are wrong, because I am seriously starting to doubt. Last time I saw you in Paris, it was all going on. My parents, the army, seeing you. I didn't know whether I was on this earth or wanting to jump off it and go somewhere else. But I'm in the damned army. And everything that my parents say is going right is going as wrong as a wrecking ball in my head."

Isabelle leaned her head against his chest.

Max leaned in closer and whispered in her ear. "If I don't stay in the army, everyone I know, my parents, my younger brothers, my sister, will be under threat. The Nazis have eyes everywhere. It's terrifying. I just have to get through it. And the only thing I have to keep me going is you."

Isabelle choked back the sob that rose in her throat. She hugged Max, held him like she suspected every woman who has loved a man going to war has held him. And she never, ever wanted to let go.

Schloss Siegel, 2010

Anna had made her decision. She decided to talk to Wil. No matter where this conversation was going, no matter what happened in the end, if she didn't start to live her life, she would regret it, just as Max had done, just as she was beginning to realize she had regrets of her own too. Her steadfast reliance on work had been enough for a long time, but now, she had to move on.

"Are you with anyone, Anna?" Wil's voice still held some sort of magic. Anna had no idea why, but she took a breath and went with it.

"I haven't been with anyone for years," she said. "I had a relationship that ended badly six years ago. He turned out to be not so nice. Cheated on me after almost convincing me to let him buy into the Italian Café. Unfortunately, he did manage to charm me into thinking that he was right for me for a while—until I saw his true colors. I haven't met anyone who has interested me since." Until now, she added to herself.

"Ah ha."

"He had all these grand ideas for the business, and for me. He was very enthusiastic."

"I've met the type," Wil said.

Anna took in a breath. "You must think I was naïve."

Wil sounded closer now. "Nope. Sounds like he wasn't up to the mark."

Anna sat up. She hadn't thought of it that way.

She let her eyes wander over the lake, but she wasn't really taking it in. She closed her eyes and shook her head.

"I'm just wondering," Wil said, sounding thoughtful now, "why you chose someone who wasn't worthy of you."

What? Anna's body seemed to jolt to attention. "What do you mean?"

Wil leaned forward a bit. "What I mean is, why not go for someone who is worthy of you? Who is up to the mark? It can be that simple, you know. It's all you need to do."

"But I haven't met anyone like that." Anna was almost smiling now. Why had she just said that? Someone who was worthy of her was sitting right here, right now, someone who was clearly kind, who was attractive—and who lived in a country thousands of miles away from home, she reminded herself. And who was probably just using his skills to help her. It wasn't the first time he'd done that. He probably had a gorgeous girlfriend back home, anyway. She slumped back down on the grass.

"My role models were . . . interesting. My parents were always fighting," Anna said. "When my mother died of cancer, I was twelve. My father just up and left a year later. It was as if he shrugged his shoulders after she died and moved on straightaway. She was my mother! When he announced he was leaving San Francisco, I absolutely refused to leave my friends, my school, my grandfather, any of it. I was thirteen, and pretty stubborn."

"Really," Wil said. "I'd say that was strong."

"Or mad." Anna chuckled. "In any case, Max offered to let me stay with him and my grandmother during school, and I would go to my father for school holidays. But I used to hate those visits. A few weeks after my mother died, my father rushed into a dysfunctional relationship with my stepmother, who thought of me as some sort of aberration—in the way of her social life. My father is an architect. He's always done well. Financially, that is. It's just that he views his partners as he would a painting or an investment. My mother was so unhappy."

"Okay," Wil said. "I get it."

"Added to that, Max had withdrawn from his relationship with my grandmother. They led separate lives. So I guess I just assumed that . . ."

"There was nothing better out there for you," Wil said. "That it wasn't worth trying. Better to rely on yourself. It would never happen for you either."

"And I didn't know what the fuss was about love," Anna said.

"Didn't?" Wil's voiced dropped a couple of octaves. The word seemed to hang in the heat.

"Well, at least I'm independent," Anna said, trying to sound cheerful. "I've learned what I can do."

"You have," Wil said. "But have you thought about letting go and just seeing what might happen? You don't know what the future could hold. Anything could happen."

"Nothing to let go of—everything went when I was twelve."

"I know. But I think you tried to hang onto it. You haven't let it go. You haven't opened yourself up to possibilities. It's time to do that now."

Anna was still.

"Come with me," Wil said, standing up. He held out a hand, and instinctively, without thinking about it, Anna took it.

He led her toward the water, then leaned down and picked up a smooth stone. "Let's say that this rock is your past."

"My past?" Half the time she felt like bursting into giggles when she was with Wil, and half the time she felt as if their conversation were strung up more tightly than a set of choker pearls.

"Can't you see that clearly this is a stone sitting in your heart?"

"Do you talk like this with all your clients?" Anna couldn't help it. She was laughing out loud now.

"Only the clients who I'm really trying to impress," Wil said. "Only special ones."

Anna looked down at her feet.

"So." He was standing behind her now. He handed her the small stone, reaching around her arms and putting it in her fingers. Then he wrapped his fingers around hers, and closed the stone—still warm from the sun and his hands—tight in her fist.

Anna felt her breathing quicken. But she focused hard on the water, not on the feeling of Wil so close to her, not on the sensations that were starting to stretch their dormant selves as if telling her that finally, finally, she was giving them a chance to wake up.

"Now," he said, sounding ever so close and gentle. "Throw it."

"This is so funny," Anna murmured. "But it's kind of—"

"Therapeutic. And no one can see except me."

"That's true."

"Go for it."

Anna lifted her arm and hurled the sharp little stone as far as she could. It skipped several times, almost as if in defiance, almost as if it were trying to have a last life or some sort of final say. Anna folded her arms and watched it disappear.

"The past is never coming back again, by the way," Wil said.

Anna turned to face him.

He had his head tilted to one side.

Anna turned her head to take one last look back at the lake.

But Wil took her chin in his hands.

"You should remember the good stuff. Think about what made you smile. Keep the times you had with Max with you, always. You weren't responsible for your parents' fighting, or Max's broken-down marriage. You won't get hoodwinked again like you did six years ago, because you are strong now. Trust your own instincts and be true to yourself. That's all you need to do."

She caught his eye, which was almost too much, so she looked down again.

"And to think I almost didn't come on this picnic today with you," she said.

"Why ever not?"

"I don't know." Suddenly she felt something shift again. She was embarrassed now. Why had she said that?

And he was on to her. "Hang on, right there," he said, taking his hand away.

She should have known.

"What put you off today?"

Anna closed her eyes.

"Sorry, I'm just a bit raw—it's so soon after Max's death." She moved toward the wooden boat.

But Wil was right behind her. "It's only been a few weeks," he said. "It's natural that you'd be in turmoil. Just take it step-by-step, Anna."

Anna kept walking, but she nodded.

"The sun," she said. Her voice was bright. "Look at the way it's shining on the Schloss." She had reached the top of the island, which afforded the most stunning view of the entire old palace that she had seen so far. Somehow, being up on a slight rise made all the difference.

"It's beautiful out here," he said, close behind

her. He moved toward the boat. "We'd better get you back." Wil climbed aboard and held out a hand for Anna.

She glanced across at the Schloss. It was tinged with pink light now.

They were both standing in the boat, face-to-face.

"Let yourself grieve for him."

She had been fighting tears on the way back to the boat. How Max would have loved to be here now! But Wil was making her want to laugh again, and as he said, she would focus on the good times she had been lucky enough to have.

She had to get past Wil to get to the wooden seat on the boat. As she did so, she slipped a little, almost toppling over. Surprisingly, the little boat didn't move too much. It was clearly stronger than it looked. Wil caught her arm and held her up. Anna caught her breath.

"That was close," Wil said. He didn't let go of her arm. "Are you okay now?"

Anna nodded. "I'm fine. Thank you, Wil."

He rowed in silence back to the shore of the lake.

Anna stared out at the exquisite landscape that surrounded her forebear's old home.

CHAPTER FOURTEEN

Paris, November 1939

The trees that lined the footpath in the cemetery at Montmartre were bare of leaves. Isabelle avoided looking at the tumbled mass of graves that had been there since the cemetery's opening in 1825. While her thoughts ran inevitably to questions—*who were these people buried here? What had their lives been like?*—there was only one person here who mattered—Marthe. That one constant in her life was gone now.

The old woman had not fought death. She had not raged against its slow grip on her deteriorating frame, had not complained about the pneumonia that had gripped her chest, sending her into coughing spasms that had rent the apartment at night. Isabelle had sat with her grandmother during those long, cold hours, sponging her forehead, holding her ragingly hot hand, but she didn't know what she would have done without Camille. The girl's silent practicality, her acceptance of things, were blessings that taught Isabelle there was only so much she could control.

Camille had not talked when Isabelle wanted silence. The maid's quiet presence had been an utter balm to the wretchedness that Isabelle had felt at the thought of losing her grandmother.

Camille had kept everything in the apartment in order, and that in itself had helped. She had patiently dusted all Marthe's precious things, had kept the silver sparkling and the porcelain shining and clean. She had not once complained of exhaustion nor asked for anything extra for all the long hours she was putting in.

Isabelle, in turn, had made sure that Camille had her evenings off. Isabelle knew that Camille was friends with the young girls whom she had met at secretarial school. And Isabelle knew that Camille had given up her hopes of working away from domestic service because of loyalty to her and to Marthe.

When Marthe had closed her eyes for the very last time, she had thanked Isabelle. She had thanked her for bringing such joy into the second half of her life. She had thanked her for all that she had done to bring life back into the apartment on Rue Blanche.

Virginia had been called home to Boston the following week. With Nazism spreading its talons throughout Europe, her parents had insisted that she return to America. Isabelle had accepted this too with a new practicality—a sense that there were forces in the world right then that were far stronger than those of idealistic youth.

And now, as Isabelle stood at Marthe's grave, her eyes running over the inscription on the tomb, she tried to let go of the swirl of thoughts that raged constantly in her head these days. Where should she go? What would become of her?

Max's last letter still sat by her bedside table. It had been there three months now. It had arrived, just as its counterparts had, bound up with sticky tape that didn't even attempt to hide the unmistakable diagonal slashes across the envelope.

Max had been on leave in Siegel for a few days in August, and he had written, among other things, of the lakes and woods around the Schloss where he had sailed and walked. Isabelle had read his words over and over, picturing it all in her mind—the forest, the folly hidden away in the trees, the lake, everything.

Max had also told her in his letter that his father had been called up. Now Germany and Poland were at war, and Isabelle had no idea where Max was, where his Vati was. German troops had entered Poland in September, driving the Polish in front of them, taking prisoners. Warsaw had been bombed, encircled, then taken.

She had not heard from Max since he had been called up again, and two things kept her awake at night—her terror that Max would be killed or was dead, and the circular question that she could never answer: What was the point of this war?

Isabelle brushed a few stray sticks from Marthe's grave.

It all seemed so useless. Power? Money? Conquering others? What was the use of those things to anyone? What about freedom, tolerance, respect, and opportunity?

When another letter arrived a few weeks later, Isabelle had just returned home from one of her walks around Paris. She combined these with errands to ground herself, but the simple act of just walking around the city was the only thing that seemed to soothe her these days. When the letter arrived, she tore into her room, collapsing on her bed to indulge in every word.

Max wrote that his father was in a military training camp. His grandfather had been called up too, offered a position as a colonel—and Polish prisoners of war had started to arrive at the estate, taking up the work that young Germans had always done.

People had lost their cars—Max's father's luxurious six-seater had been taken for the conveyance of army personnel. Max's car was gone too. Riding horses were requisitioned by the army, and fuel for farm tractors was severely rationed.

All the young men in Siegel had been drafted, friends of Adolf Hitler or not.

Mutti was working for the Red Cross and covered meetings, inspections, and rallies of the troops. Nadja was training as an air-raid warden. Resident guards ran Schloss Siegel now, taking over for Max's father—and Max.

Everyone on the whole in Germany had returned to horses and bicycles for their means of getting around. Food was rationed because money had to go to the war effort—bread, butter, margarine, milk, cheese, sugar, eggs, jam, flour, beans, meat, coffee, and even soap.

The Schloss had increased its fruit and vegetable production to try to supplement people's diets. To get any rationed food you had to produce your ration card, and the relevant amount would be snipped off. Luxury items had given out, and no more were being produced. No chocolate, no sweets. Clothes and shoes were another casualty. Production in factories was practically all used for the armed forces, and the severest shortage was, of course, manpower. The women ran everything now, from farms to factories.

Hitler was beyond everyone's control.

But Max also wanted to know how Isabelle was doing. He told her he would come to get her one day. One day in the not-too-distant future, he hoped. He hoped when it was all over he could bring her home with him to Siegel for good.

Having read the letter three times, indulging in

every word, Isabelle tucked it into the pocket of one of her winter coats and went back out into the salon.

The radio had become the most important feature of the room. Every day, she listened along with Camille to the bulletins as the war ground on, feeling desperately unable to help, while worrying constantly about Max.

It was so hard to imagine all those young men she had met that Christmas at Siegel participating in the skirmishes, as weeks turned into months and the New Year relentlessly rolled in.

When a German cargo ship slipped past a British blockade in the neutral waters of Norway in the spring of 1940, the British navy got wind of it and sent a destroyer on the attack, killing a number of German sailors. These small victories caused Camille to look at Isabelle in hope while they listened to the droning, professional voice on the wireless. Isabelle pretended to return Camille's smile, but she started to feel ill.

Her need to hear bulletins became more frantic. All the time her ears were pricked for any sliver of information about the German army. What was she hoping to hear? A daily announcement that one man, Max, was safe? A reassurance from that bodiless voice on the radio that he would survive and return to her?

As the calendar turned to June, Isabelle came

to understand that she was going to have to leave Paris, and fast.

Berlin, 2010

Wil turned back into Berlin's old West, stopping at the first set of traffic lights on Kurfürstendamm. He seemed to be thinking for a moment.

"What have you got planned for tonight?" he finally asked, turning to her.

Anna exhaled. Well, what did she have planned? Nothing? Surprisingly, jet lag was not bothering her at all.

She shrugged. "I might go for a walk around Berlin."

"Would you like to come over to my house?"

Anna bit her bottom lip.

"I have some friends coming over for dinner," he said.

The traffic started to inch forward.

"You might like to meet some fellow Germans," he went on, keeping his voice light. They were close to Anna's hotel.

The idea was appealing. "Great. Thank you. I'd like that," she said.

"I'll pick you up from your hotel at around eight. It's very casual."

Anna nodded. She turned to him. She had to, in order to say goodbye, even though it was becoming a little uncomfortable to look straight at him. Those feelings that had stirred down by the lake were evolving into something that was taking over every moment she was with him. Here Wil was, a sophisticated man, being kind, listening to her, cheering her up, helping her with her family's past. That was all it was. Anything else in her head was there only because she had not encountered a man like this for a very long time.

"Excellent," she said. "Thank you."

Wil looked amused. "Excellent to you too," he said. "And, by the way, Ingrid wants to meet us at Schloss Beringer tomorrow at ten. She's rented out a private room there so that we can talk. Interesting choice, I must say."

"Oh," Anna said. "Is she always so dramatic?"

"I couldn't comment." That wicked smile again.

Anna smiled back and climbed out of the car.

Anna was ready just before eight. She had chosen to wear a pair of jeans, a black polo sweater, and a scarf. She layered on a few of her favorite bracelets, put on her black boots over the jeans, and left her long hair loose. A few sprays of Van Cleef & Arpels First and she was done.

She had been businesslike getting ready— had forced herself to focus on the task at hand. There was no point getting carried away thinking about what might happen, though her mind had wandered a little when she stood in the shower. Eventually she had shaken away any unbidden thoughts and given herself a stern talking-to in the elevator down to the hotel lobby.

Wil was only five minutes late.

"Sorry," he said, appearing like some sort of ridiculously handsome god.

"That's fine." Anna smiled. "You're only five minutes late."

"Don't like being late." He grinned. He leaned down and kissed her on the cheek.

So that was friendly. If he had feelings that went beyond friendship, then he would not have kissed her on the cheek, Anna rationalized. Then she kicked herself again. What was she thinking? It was highly likely that his guests were going to include a girlfriend.

"Anna?" Wil said. "You're on another planet. It's quite cute, actually, and I don't want to interrupt you, but the others will be arriving in the next half hour, so . . ."

"Sorry." Anna shook her head. She had to get herself in line. Was she so starved of male company that her mind went into a spin as soon as some came along?

She was not in a spin! She hit her head with the palm of her hand.

"Anna!" Wil was laughing now. "Do we need

to take you to the hospital or are you just in need of one of our gorgeous German wines?"

Or a gorgeous German man, Anna thought.

"I was just thinking about Siegel," she said as she followed him out the sliding doors. His car was parked around the corner.

"Mmm hmm," he said. "You could have a break from thinking about that tonight, if you wanted to. But if you want to talk about it, I'm happy to do that too."

Once they were in the car, Anna looked out the window as he drove toward his house. That was the spot to focus. When Wil turned into his street a little farther into the old West a few minutes later, Anna couldn't help but stare.

"This was an old suburb of Berlin," Wil said, slowing the car down a little.

Graceful houses sat behind immaculate front gardens. The car's headlights threw shapely trees and handsome old dwellings into focus.

"What I like about my house," Wil said, "is that my great-grandparents owned it and used it as their city base."

"Really?"

"They built it," Wil said, "but sold it soon after the war. I was looking to buy a house a few years ago, just after my grandfather died. He used to drive me past this place when I was a child to show it to me. Told me of all his memories here. They always came for the concert season in the winter. The restaurants, the theater, and the social life were all in full swing that time of year."

"Sounds idyllic," Anna said.

"It was—for them." Wil sounded wry now. "I approached the owners, made them a fair offer, and—"

"That was too easy." Anna snapped her seatbelt open when the car came to a stop. Picked up her bag.

Wil looked at her curiously. "You know, you almost sounded European then—if I didn't know better I'd say I heard a bit of an accent."

"You couldn't have," Anna said. She felt slightly irritated now—who knew why? Honestly, she hardly seemed herself lately.

Wil's front garden was in shadow, but the semicircular driveway leading up to the front door was well lit. Large trees were dotted about on the lawn.

Anna turned to the house. It was ornate—art nouveau details decorated the window tops—and yet his home had a relaxed, welcoming feel. Garden beds softened the exterior, and a climbing rose made its way up one part of the front wall.

Wil opened the gleaming black front door and stood aside to let her through. Black-and-white tiles continued from the verandah into the entrance hall, and a curved staircase rose to the upper floors. It was grand, in a way, but it was also charming. Wil led her into a cozy sitting room that had warm, polished floorboards and Oriental rugs. A grand piano sat against the window, and there were a pair of sofas opposite a fireplace, where a fire was crackling away.

"Would you like a glass of wine?" Wil asked. "Make yourself at home."

Anna sat down on one of the sofas. She could hear Wil opening cupboards in the kitchen. Judging from the smell, something delicious was cooking in there.

When he came back out with two glasses, Anna said, "This is gorgeous. It's very you."

"Interesting—what's me?" he asked, handing her the glass.

"Oh, I didn't mean anything by it."

But someone was at the front door.

"Excuse me," he said.

She could hear a speedy conversation in German coming from the entrance hall. Any tension that Anna had felt dissipated when a little girl, probably around six years old, came running into the room. She was wearing her pajamas and she came straight up to Anna and settled down right next to her.

"I am Sasha," she said in English, raising a pair of chocolate eyes to Anna's face.

"And I am Anna." Anna smiled.

The little girl held up a book. "I am allowed to read this, then I have to go to sleep," she said. "Would you read it to me? My parents talk to me in English and German at home, and they said you would be here and I could practice."

Anna took the book and started to read. She was soon so enthralled by the story that she hardly noticed Wil and four other people enter the room. When she was done, she looked up. Sasha had nestled herself on Anna's lap. Wil was looking down at her with a smile on his face. If she had had to describe the expression in his eyes, Anna would have said he looked indulgent—and she reveled in his warm gaze. But he probably didn't mean anything by it.

"Anna, these are my good friends, Petra and Andreas and Eva and Stephan."

An hour later, Anna felt as if she had known everyone for years. They had all continued to speak English for her benefit. Petra was dark, attractive, with an avant-garde fashion sense that intrigued Anna. Some women knew how to wear a scarf, and Petra was one of them. Anna would have loved to see where she lived. Her partner, Andreas, one of Wil's oldest friends, was as fair as Petra was dark and bewitching. They were both so obviously in their element together, making them excellent company for a dinner party. The other couple, Sasha's parents, were Eva and Stephan. They were warm with their little girl. She spent the drinks part of the evening on her father's lap before going to bed.

Wil took charge of everyone when it was

time for dinner. He was in fine form. The wine flowed, his conversation was easy and amusing, and he had produced a perfect meal of pasta with a succulent ragout, along with a green salad and rustic bread.

"He throws himself into his work," Eva said when he was in the kitchen with the other two men. "There are plenty of women who would love to go out with him, but his career is the thing. It's all about that."

Anna stayed quiet.

Petra chuckled then. "He had an on-and-off relationship with someone a few years back, but they were never committed, and when she moved to Munich for her work, Wil stayed here."

"I think that was about the convenience more than anything else," Eva said.

Anna nodded. So what was he protecting himself from then? Was his work an insurance policy against collateral damage? Or had he simply not met the right girl? She was about to say something when Wil appeared at the door.

"Coffee is in the living room, if you'd like to come through," he said.

"Sure," Eva replied, standing up.

Anna noticed the glance exchanged between the other two women. Had Wil overheard their conversation? Please, no.

The fire threw flickering patterns across the room, dancing on people's faces as everyone told stories about their years together at university. Anna found herself curled up in the corner of one of Wil's huge sofas, cradling her excellent coffee and wishing the evening would never end.

It was good to meet new people with whom she felt utterly at home. As the others got up to leave, Anna realized how long it had been since she had had an evening like this. Somehow, between running her own business and looking after Max, she had forgotten how to enjoy life.

Wil leaned against the doorframe once he had said goodbye to his friends. The evening air that filtered in from the front garden was mild.

"Would you like to take a walk with me, Anna?" he said, all of a sudden.

"A walk?"

"There's something I'd like you to see."

Anna was intrigued. The neighborhood was beautiful. It was hard to reconcile this timeless area with Berlin's fractured, disturbing past. Anna was aware that farther east, there were still rows and rows of stark Communist flats.

"I think it will be good for you to see this," Wil said as he put her coat over her shoulders.

A few minutes later, Wil stopped outside a set of curling iron gates. A dark garden sat beyond them, but when Anna looked down the long paved driveway, she could see the hint of a prosperous-looking house. Its roof was steeply pitched, with a row of dormer windows tucked into its gables. A Labrador retriever shuffled up to the gate.

Wil stayed quiet.

Anna turned to him.

"I thought you should see it," he said. "They used to come here regularly. Your great-grandmother gave fabulous parties, apparently."

Anna took a step closer to the gates and peered past them in an attempt to drink in every last vestige that she could.

"The current owners have four children. They've done a good job with it. I could introduce you to them if you like. They would love to meet you. It's a happy house again."

"That's good," Anna said. She stared at it a little longer. It looked as if it were how it was meant to be.

Wil reached out, then drew his hand back. "It's getting cold," he said. "I should get you back to your hotel."

Anna nodded. She suddenly thought of tomorrow and what the next day would bring. She had to talk to her cousin tomorrow. She had to learn what had happened. Then she would have to work out what she could do to put things right.

As they walked back to Wil's house, he talked if she wanted to talk, and he stayed quiet when she was quiet. Was it possible that he understood not only that she had to know about her family's past and whether there was any future for Siegel, but also that until she had done all she could, she couldn't move on with her own life?

When they arrived back at his house, they both stopped for a moment on the driveway. Anna focused on the surroundings—the garden, the lights on the veranda. Anything but Wil standing there.

After a few seconds she heard the clink of his car keys. She didn't know whether she was pleased to hear them or not. She followed him to his car and they both climbed in silently, but Anna was aware, so aware again of that something unspoken that was passing between them every time they met. Nerves twinged and flickered inside her, but she wasn't able to say anything.

She looked out the window of the car at the silhouettes of the old houses that were in shadow now—they weren't illuminated anymore.

Anna's thoughts ran to the future while Wil drove. His quiet presence next to her was like a balm and a bonfire at the same time. She knew she hadn't felt this way about anyone before. She knew she had never found anyone quite so— right. Or was she vulnerable, simply trying to replace Max?

After Wil pulled up outside her hotel, he was out and opening her car door before she had time to gather her thoughts. She climbed out onto the sidewalk, and he didn't move for a moment from where he held the open car door.

She looked at him and she saw something flicker in his eyes. Something that for some reason gave her more hope than she had felt in ages. She smiled then, felt something whimsical pass across her lips.

He touched her arm.

"I'll be here at nine," he said, his voice intimate. "I'll come into the lobby. Not sure where I'll manage to park."

"Thanks," Anna said. Practicalities, they were good. But she was more caught up in the mood than the facts, and this was odd for her. Because she didn't want to break it. She didn't want it to end. If she were honest with herself, she wanted everything to begin.

The next morning, as they drove to Schloss Beringer, it struck Anna that she was becoming familiar not only with the physical landscape around Berlin, but with the way it made her feel. The woods, the soft pastures, the sleepy villages, a mysterious Schloss—all those other stories buried deep in their labyrinthine German past—stirred up a strange yearning, almost a physical ache for something deeper, something she could not quite express.

Anna could see why Ingrid had not wanted to meet them at Siegel—that was clear. But why

Schloss Beringer? Was Ingrid demonstrating what should not be done to Siegel by meeting them at Wil's ancestral home? Or worse, was she about to tell them that she had similar grand plans for Siegel?

They turned into the Schloss's curved driveway and were now headed to the parking lots, where there was an array of prosperous-looking European cars, their hoods still glimmering with droplets of morning dew.

Did Wil view these hotel guests as intruders at his old family home? And then the thought struck Anna that the past must be dealt with on one's own terms. Max had pretended that the past didn't exist until his life was almost at an end. That was how he had done it. She couldn't help feeling that his reaching out to her in his final weeks was, if not a cry for help, then perhaps an acknowledgment that she had the right to know.

As for Wil—it was clear that he felt deeply about Schloss Beringer and was conflicted about his grandfather's fruitless efforts. Perhaps the answer was that the past never went away. Old Brandenburg and Prussia would always overshadow Berlin and its surrounds like a ghostly grandparent—hinted at in magnificent baroque buildings; whispering forests; flat lands and their hovering mists; magical, fairy-tale palaces; the people and their stories.

The past and Schloss Siegel were taking Anna

on a circuitous journey. It did not conform to the linear, orderly way she had led her life to date. She felt out of her element. It was unnerving, but part of her wanted to grab at it with both hands.

"Tell me something," she asked as Wil turned off the car engine. Wil stayed looking straight ahead. "How do you deal with the past, Wil?"

She saw a smile form on his lips. "What do you mean?"

"Your family's legacy, the history, the loss, Germany, the war, all of it?"

Wil was quiet.

"What do you carry with you? What do you leave behind?" Anna asked.

Wil pulled the key out of the ignition and flicked it around in his hand. "Memories on both counts. Then there are stories. But I think it depends on how you choose to look at it. I admit that I've tended to focus on the future. My work has been so flat out—and my grandfather's experiences were hardly encouraging." He turned to her. "But now that I've met you, that's changed. A lot."

"I hope that's a good thing." Anna's voice came out soft. There was something in it that she hadn't heard before.

He didn't turn his gaze away from her, and it struck Anna not for the first time how steady he seemed—how kind and patient—and yet there was something else, something indefinable there that she could not quite grasp. Was it toughness? No. It was strength.

"Time to go in, you know." He opened the car door.

"I'm trying to work you out," Anna said as she undid her seatbelt. She sensed Wil tensing up. "Don't worry," she added, as she climbed out of the car. "I'm not getting anywhere," she lied.

He caught her eye and smiled, then looked down. "Okay," he said. "Good."

Anna smiled back. "Come on," she said. "This is going to be—"

"Enlightening, I hope." Wil grinned.

"Yes." Anna turned. There was something satisfying about the crunch of her shoes on the gravel. She had chosen to wear a black suit today. Something told her that she needed to look formidable for her meeting with Ingrid Hermann.

Paris, June 1940

Paris's inhabitants were attempting to flee. Traffic, buses, and the metro—everything had stopped dead. The city's commercial centers were shut down. Every news report pointed at the same irrevocable truth.

France was on the verge of collapse.

The army was destroyed. Paris had been bombed.

And yet, still Isabelle did not want to leave her home. What would become of all Marthe's treasures?

Visions of the recent bombings in Paris played themselves like stubborn repetitions of the same interminable reel of film in Isabelle's tired head. Ghastly images of tumbledown buildings, fire, sirens, rubble, people running in the streets, and others standing in silent, bewildered shock had caused Isabelle to shrink into the safest place she knew—home. But outside, women and children crouched on street corners, homeless.

People moved in sad packs down Paris streets—the war had draped dusty curtains across the city and it was as if nobody had the strength to fight it. And at the same time, summer rolled on, oblivious to the relentless forces that were about to destroy everything Paris knew.

The city should be at her most beautiful tonight. It was an evening for walks along the Seine, for dancing in the clubs where only a few years ago, the city's youth had kicked up their heels and done exactly what young people on the verge of life should be doing—celebrating.

A family passed underneath the window where Isabelle stood—in the absence of a wagon, they seemed to have procured an old, thin horse. Isabelle turned away. Where would she go? Stories had swept the city—by midnight not a café would be open. The SS would shut everything down. The Gestapo would set up military borders and follow up on everyone who was living in Paris, calling on them systematically. The Third Reich was a place where you did exactly what you were told.

And where was Max? How did he feel about the talons of Nazism spreading all through Europe? Did his parents still expect him to think as they did? Had they changed their minds, turned face? Surely, surely . . . and right now, Camille had rushed off, saying she would be right back.

Isabelle shuddered as a new thought struck her. What if something had happened to Camille?

She walked into Marthe's dressing room. Took in a sharp breath. Closed her eyes for one split second and then opened a drawer.

Isabelle had flurried around all afternoon, grabbing some clothes and getting ready to leave. And now, where on earth was Camille? Isabelle had discussed this with her. Had told her at least two hours ago that they would flee.

She pulled out Marthe's strongbox, unlocking it with the small key that she had pulled from its hiding place. With the determination of a professional, she removed every piece of Marthe's exquisite collection of jewelry. Next, she pulled out two silk purses, whose long woven handles were the perfect length to hang around her and Camille's necks.

Not stopping to even glance at their still-twinkling beauty, Isabelle filled the two bags with all the diamonds, rubies, emeralds, and sapphires that Marthe had been given when she was young.

When Isabelle heard the door latch click, she almost sank onto the padded chair in the corner of the dressing room with relief. The sound of Camille's efficient footsteps echoed through the apartment. The girl was going up to her bedroom above the kitchen.

Isabelle zipped up the purses, but their fabric strained, almost tearing against the thin teeth that bound the little bags together. They would simply have to hold everything in place.

Isabelle ran back into her bedroom and took one last look around. Strangely, she had found it necessary to leave things tidy. If the Nazis were to enter Marthe's old home, they would, Isabelle knew, take the lot.

She marched out through the dressing room, then said goodbye to Marthe's bedroom without turning once. She closed all the curtains and pulled the last set of wooden shutters tight.

Everything was still.

She walked through the salon. It was time to go. She had no choice. Marthe's ostrich seemed to stare at her. It had been such an odd gift, but Marthe would not part with it, like everything else. In a fit of impulsiveness, Isabelle grabbed the shawl that was draped over Marthe's favorite chair—the one she always sat in to have her coffee—and draped the shawl over the poor stuffed bird's back. She took a last glance around her room, her heart, her belly, everything aching with a strange new feeling that had started to develop in the last few weeks.

Camille came into the living room from the kitchen, shutting the door that led to the servants' quarters with a soft click. The girl had her suitcase at her feet. She looked as calm and determined as ever.

"We will have to walk out of the city," Camille said.

Isabelle shook her head. "Surely, there will be a train?" Suddenly, her sense of desolation at leaving her home was replaced with an urgency to get out of Paris.

"No, we should go directly to Honfleur. Then south." Camille was frowning.

Isabelle watched her for a moment. Camille was intelligent—she was also street-smart. Without her, Isabelle did not know what she would do.

"I know which way to go, Mademoiselle," Camille said, her voice low. She had pulled her long dark hair back into a ponytail, and she wore a simple summer dress and sensible shoes.

Isabelle nodded. She would trust Camille.

Isabelle didn't turn around when she locked the apartment's front door. She did not look back at the life she was leaving, at the life that had been ripped away from her in a few short, dreadful months. Maybe she would be back by the fall. Who knew? No one did.

CHAPTER FIFTEEN

Schloss Beringer, 2010

Ingrid was waiting in the conservatory at Beringer with her back to the entrance as Anna and Wil walked in. She was dressed in an elegant suit with a red scarf. When Ingrid turned around and caught Anna's eye, Anna could tell that the woman was distressed, but after a moment, she bustled across the room, clearly trying to hide her emotions. A maid arrived, pushing a cart with the sort of elaborate breakfast that Schloss Beringer probably did to perfection. There were croissants that did not look fresh, fruit platters, white coffee cups, a jug of milk, and a plate of strudel and other pastries.

Anna held out a hand and nodded at Ingrid, who looked more determined now. Back to her usual self. "Thank you for meeting with me, Ingrid."

Anna followed Ingrid's lead and sat down at the polished oval table. Wil sat next to her.

Ingrid poured coffee. "I wanted to meet with you because it seemed important to clarify a few things," Ingrid said. "Your grandfather, Max, is responsible for Schloss Siegel's condition today." Her voice cut like clear crystal through the glass room.

Anna stayed quiet.

Seeing that Anna was not going to protest seemed to spur Ingrid on. "My mother was your great-aunt and Max's older sister. My mother's name was Nadja. There were two younger brothers as well. I assume you do not know about these people?"

"Anna doesn't. No," Wil said softly as he poured coffee.

Anna sat perfectly still.

"Max and Nadja's two younger brothers were known by the family as Didi and Jo," Ingrid spoke with precision. "But their real names were Dieter and Jochim. They were both killed in the war, loyal to Germany until the end."

"I'm sorry," Anna said.

"After the war, Max's mother, Elsa, and my mother, Nadja, tried to contact Max. He was the heir, since my mother, although older than Max, was discounted, being female.

"Their father, Otto, your great-grandfather, was missing at the end of the war, so it was imperative that Max come home and take up his role, but he was nowhere to be found. They thought he might be dead or a prisoner. They did everything they could to track him down.

"On the afternoon my mother and grandmother were told by the Foreign Office to flee the

Schloss, the Soviets were ten kilometers away. There was no German unit nearby. They were told to leave within the hour. With only females in the house, my grandmother knew that they would all be raped if they stayed. They had to get out. Taking the old school coach, some loyal servants, and what food they could to survive, plus one suitcase each, they travelled southwest, away from the Soviets. My mother found work along the way as an agricultural hands-on student. But it took them months to get anywhere.

"They sought refuge where they could— travelling through border towns full of refugees and bombed-out German cities. Their anxiety over my grandfather, Otto, and Max must have been like a knife in their hearts.

"Rations were scarce and they were practically starving. And then they learned that their assets had been frozen in the East. They had lost everything. They had no money at all. There was no way of fighting the system. My mother went to college in Hannover, then eventually found work as a secretary. She had to do what she could to survive."

Ingrid stood up. She walked over to the glass wall and stared out at the tranquil park. How could nature remain so calm in the face of such history?

Anna folded her arms around herself and waited.

"Something else had happened—before they left." Ingrid stopped.

"I want to know. I am family," Anna said.

The sound that came from Ingrid's lips was more of a snort than anything else. "Don't talk to me of family," she said. "There is only work, hard work, and grit, and determination. You can only rely on yourself."

The irony of this hit Anna hard. Was the woman a mirror of herself? She felt a sudden flicker of empathy for Ingrid. She sensed Wil watching her and turned to look at him. He shook his head.

Anna bit her lip.

"So," Ingrid went on. "Here it is, then. My mother, Nadja, had an affair before she left the Schloss."

Anna said nothing.

"My father, you see," Ingrid turned around to face them, "was Max's valet. Hans Kramer. My mother and Hans Kramer were lovers. When Nadja and my grandmother ended up in Hannover, my mother told me it was Hans who came and found them. Not your grandfather. Max did not appear."

Anna took in a sharp breath. She shifted in her seat.

Wil reached out, took her hand underneath the table. She was finding it hard to keep her breathing even. She let her hand rest in his.

"Hans and Nadja resumed their love affair in

Hannover once he had caught up to her. Your great-grandmother, Elsa, did not know about their affair. She was only pleased to see someone connected with the family. But when Nadja became pregnant, and the two of them wanted to marry, Elsa asked Hans to leave. She refused to acknowledge him as a son-in-law. The only person who could have convinced her was—"

"Don't say Max." Anna knew her words sounded like a warning.

"Max's mother adored him—she would have listened to him. If Max had advocated for Nadja, explained my father's—Hans's devotion and steadfastness to Nadja and to the Albrecht family as well, then how different things could have been! The world had changed. My father had grown up with Nadja and Max, and he loved Nadja. My grandmother had not yet adjusted to any such idea."

Anna took a sip of her coffee.

"Life between Nadja and Elsa became impossible after that. Hans left, unable to face the guilt of tearing Nadja away from her mother. But my mother told me that Elsa could never bear to look at her daughter again. She would never understand what Nadja had done." Ingrid turned to face them. Her eyes, which had struck Anna as cold before, seemed to flash with something else now.

"My mother left her mother and went to

Berlin. She gave birth to me in West Berlin. She continued to work as a secretary. We were poor, but we survived. When I was five, my mother met and married my stepfather, who was a successful businessman. She did everything she could to forget Hans. And he left her alone. You see, he was trained as a servant. He was taught to obey his betters—and then he was trained as a Nazi soldier. He had to obey. It is almost impossible for us to understand this mentality. While my mother knew Hans loved her, she knew that he would not return to her. It was not in him to do so. It is hard to explain to your generation. But my mother's anger towards her family, towards Max, towards her mother, and towards Germany as well—it bred in her soul. She had lived a life of privilege, of luxury, and she enjoyed those things. I think her attitude, her odd attitude to life started right back when she was a teenager, because she always told me that when she fell for her brother's valet, she knew that it was going to be impossible. And on top of all this, she was a woman living in a time when the only role she could play was that of wife, sister, mother. She was the eldest in a great German family, Anna, but she was never going to be the heir. She was never going to be the center of her own life. She was never taken seriously, not at all."

Anna chewed on her lip.

"My stepfather was a property developer, and he nurtured my interest in business. I took over his portfolio when he died fifteen years ago, and I have extended it. Things have changed—but we still have a way to go, Anna. So. There we are."

Anna nodded.

"Elsa, my grandmother, died in 1963," Ingrid went on. "She stayed in Hannover until then and never saw my mother again. And as for my grandfather, Otto—it took him three years to find Elsa after the war had finished, but he was ill and did not live long after that. The devastation of losing every one of their children—two to war and two who had left them—certainly contributed to his death. But I only found that out much later."

Wil let go of Anna's hand. He leaned forward, looked thoughtful. "Ingrid, I understand where you are coming from—with regard to your mother's relationship with Hans. Do you know what happened in Max's life immediately after the war? What I am asking is, do you think there could have been some reason for his leaving everything he knew behind? What you are telling us sounds so unlike the man that Anna has described to me."

"Max absconded." Ingrid almost spat out the words. "He left the Nazi party in 1940. He was stationed in Paris until then, but incredibly, with all the mayhem in France, he managed to escape before the Nazis were in total control of Paris. He would have been shot if he'd been found. Furthermore—"

Anna closed her eyes.

"Furthermore, my mother would not mention his name in the house. She said he had always been indecisive. He was torn about Germany's future and what he wanted. So, you see, this is why what I am doing is right. Schloss Siegel is, by rights, my property anyway—my mother should have been the heir—would have been, in any just and sensible place. Not your grandfather. My mother did not run away from everything. She stayed where she belonged and worked hard. I see Siegel as I do my other properties. It is being preserved in its original state. I do not want people there whom I don't know. They will wreck it.

"I am now almost the substantial landowner that my family always was," Ingrid went on. "Everything is as it should be. There is no place for you here, Anna. Max chose to go to America. He left Germany, never to return. You should go back there too. That is where your line of the family belongs now. I only wanted to see you today so that you would know the truth. And so it is. That is all."

Anna's mind raced.

But everything came back to one thing.

Ingrid's story, no matter how convincing she

made it sound, was not a true reflection of Max's character. Anna knew him. She only had to close her eyes and picture any single memory that she had of him. Ingrid's account didn't add up. And now, he was dead. How on earth was she supposed to prove her cousin wrong?

His surviving family's ability to force the blame on him was astounding.

Anna stood up. "Thank you," she said. She would not speak up until she had some proof of what she knew was true. "I need to think," she said, simply. "But I have one thing to say. Please would you consider restoring the Schloss? It is part of your history, as you say, but leaving it to rot is cruel."

"I will run my business interests as I see fit. While I am alive, I don't want the Schloss touched. I cannot live out there alone. I cannot bear the thought of anyone else living there. It is my mother's home, her rightful estate. I bought it, I own it, and I will keep it safe for her until I die."

Anna bit back a response. She couldn't accept that.

"Ingrid. I will talk to you soon," Wil said. "Anna, would you like to think about all this? If you have any more questions for Ingrid, anything you would like to say, I can put you in touch. You have shared a lot of information, Ingrid. Anna has a lot to digest."

Ingrid nodded. She reached out and shook Wil's hand, then Anna's, but Anna felt so distracted that she was almost disembodied, somehow.

Wil was silent all the way back to Berlin in the car. What was he thinking? Was he judging her badly? Anna felt embarrassed to have Max exposed by Ingrid in such a way. She climbed out of the car when they reached the hotel before Wil could even say goodbye.

"Anna—" he called, leaning out through the window.

But Anna shook her head.

He climbed out of the car too, raced to follow her into the hotel.

She turned. "I have to think," she said. After a moment, she had to say something more. "That made no sense."

"I know," he said.

Max had some darned good reason for never going back. She knew him. "I should go," she said. She was going to cry. She did not want Wil to see that.

She had to sort this out herself.

It was what she always did.

"You don't have to do this alone," Wil's voice cut into her thoughts.

But Anna pulled away from him. "This is Max. I can't believe Ingrid's story."

"Just think about it. Go slow," Wil said. "And I'm always here."

She nodded. "Thank you for your help," she said.

And as she walked away from him into the lobby, a question repeated itself like a crow circling around one spot. What on earth was she supposed to do? She was the only person who seemed to believe in Max.

She looked back at Wil's retreating car.

Max was dead. It was going to be impossible to find out the truth about his past.

So. She had a life in San Francisco that she should return to at once, and a tumult of family history that would not go away in her head.

CHAPTER SIXTEEN

Paris, June 1940

Camille had taken everything in hand. The girl seemed to know exactly how to navigate the narrow streets in the Left Bank, while insisting on carrying Isabelle's bags for her, while deftly avoiding any troublesome strangers who crossed their path.

Isabelle did not have to think.

For this, she was grateful.

Her mouth had set into a grim line. Her entire body was rigid with tension. Her mind swirled with worries. Was Max safe? Marthe's things—would they all be stolen by the Nazis? Had she locked everything well enough? Should she have hidden more of Marthe's treasures?

She looked at Camille's steady, strong back in front of her. It was as if the girl were almost scouting the dark streets. She had noticed the way the maid's eyes darted about, checking down alleys before they turned into them. It was as if Paris itself held dark secrets that Isabelle had never glimpsed before. It was as if it were a different city, a strange city. Almost a foreign place.

Isabelle suddenly found herself to be immensely grateful for the loyalty of this strange, dark girl who had waited on her so faithfully without once complaining of her lot. She'd earned so very little and had hardly any life outside the apartment; she'd never experienced any of the fun that Isabelle and Virginia had known. And yet, here Camille was, leading Isabelle now.

And after they reached Camille's hometown of Honfleur, they would travel south toward Spain.

"Mademoiselle?" Camille's voice cut into the warm air.

Isabelle stopped.

"We have two options here." Camille's dark eyes scouted up and down the street.

"Camille. You are ten times wiser than I out here in the streets. I am not sure how I would have fared, doing this alone."

Camille's eyes flared brightly for a moment. Isabelle felt Camille's hand clasp her own.

"This way then," Camille said. And she turned down a cobbled, dark alley. "This will be the quickest, Mademoiselle."

The lane was narrower than Isabelle expected. Its buildings loomed overhead as though forming an arch in the black sky. All was silent. There were no others about.

Camille still held her hand. She stopped all of a sudden. "Stay quiet," she whispered.

They stood stock-still.

Someone was around. There it was—and again—a shuffle, farther up the alleyway. It was slipper soft.

Two men stepped out. They were in uniform. Isabelle gasped before Camille did. She dropped the girl's hand. Was she dreaming? Was it finally all going to be all right? She took a step closer. He was here. Of course he was. He had come to take her away from this nightmare.

She would have known him from any distance. His silhouette, his gait, the shape of his head—everything. Thank heavens. A flood of relief—because he would make sure not only that she was safe, but that her loyal Camille was safe too. She wanted to run to him, to hold him in her arms, to stroke his face. He was here.

He had come for her.

She took another step.

"Camille Paget?" a voice called. A German accent. Not friendly—but then, that didn't necessarily mean anything, did it?

"They know your name?" Isabelle turned to Camille.

"Get away from me," the girl whispered. "They are after me. Go! Run!"

Camille pushed Isabelle away.

"What are you talking about?" Isabelle almost wanted to laugh. She felt tears of relief stinging her eyes. "It will be all right," she whispered. "Max is here."

She took a step toward Max. There was shouting.

When the shot rang out, and her chest exploded with pain, Isabelle choked a little at first. Then she turned to Camille.

"What?" She managed it—but the word hurt. It was too hard to think now. She seemed to be looking up. The sky was there.

"Oh, my God." Camille had her in her arms. "Bastards!" she shouted.

Isabelle looked up at the girl—her loyal friend, for that was what she was. That was what it all amounted to. Friendship, in the end. Her breath came in short little gasps now.

"Run!" she heard. A male voice. Max?

Isabelle tried to lift her head, tried to reach him. If she could reach him, then everything would be all right . . .

CHAPTER SEVENTEEN

Berlin, 2010

The sun, the fearless, shining sun, sent slivers of its own brightness through the gaps in the curtains the morning after the meeting with Ingrid, throwing light onto Anna's brass bed. She sat up after a while, her thoughts dancing around each other in that half state between wakefulness and sleep.

She had to decide what to do now, so she made a list of the facts. She had found Max's ring. The situation with the Schloss seemed hopeless. Anna could hardly take on the largest landowner in Prussia. Nor could Wil, who might be risking his job and everything he had worked so hard for if he were to do so.

So, what now? She should probably leave it alone. Leave Wil to his life, leave the Schloss to Ingrid. Let everyone think what they liked about Max. She knew differently. That was the most important thing.

And she, Anna, should go back to the life she had created for herself, the life that afforded her security and peace of mind.

Things could be far worse.

She was better off without all those feelings that seemed to confuse her here. She would do what she had always done—rely on herself.

Anna climbed out of bed and went into the bathroom. She looked at herself in the elaborate mirror. Who had she been kidding? This was not some fairy tale where she could save her family palace from ruin and run off into the sunset with her gorgeous German knight in shining armor.

Anna hummed a determined little tune to herself as she packed her bags for the flight back to San Francisco. She had been in luck: there were a couple of seats left on a flight later that day.

And now she took one last look at her room before she closed the door behind herself and stood in the corridor of the hotel. Her stomach swirled with nausea. In spite of all her resolution, her thoughts still kept flashing back to what Ingrid had said.

Anna shook her head and dragged her suitcase toward the tiny elevator. One step at a time. One foot after the other.

Two months later, Anna was convinced she had put the matter to rest. She was back in a routine, she was back in her house, and the past was back where it belonged. It was a cool, misty fall morning, and sodden amber leaves blanketed the streets. This suited Anna's mood—things ending, time to let go.

But now a young man stood in front of her at the café and repeated his name after placing his coffee order. As she wrote his name on the cup, her mind started to spin.

Hans. The young man had said he was Hans. That was the name of Ingrid's father. He had been Max's valet. What if he were still alive?

Max had only just died. Hans Kramer had been Nadja's lover. The name had etched itself in Anna's mind.

Hans was far more than a servant.

He would have been Max's right-hand man.

After Anna had finished fixing the coffee, her hands working fast but shaking and stumbling as she fixed the lid on the cup, she called one of her staff to take over and swung off to her office, almost smashing into another employee on the way. She ripped off her black apron and turned on the computer at her desk.

She could ask Wil to contact Ingrid and ask her about her real father, but that could open up a jar of snakes. Or she could google the valet.

Anna chose option two.

She turned up a businessman, an actor, and a university lecturer. If Max was born in 1916, Nadja was older than Max, and the three of them had grown up together, as Ingrid had said, then it was likely that Hans was born in or near Siegel around 1913 or thereabouts. Anna spent half an hour doing research—but there was nothing obvious on the Net. The businessman was only twenty-seven. The actor was thirty-two. And the university lecturer was based in Hong Kong and in his late forties.

Dead ends, no answers—and nothing more to look up.

And then an ad appeared on the screen. Anna shook her head at it in annoyance. What use were those things anyway?

But it didn't go away. It lingered there, and she found her eyes lingering right back on it.

Ancestry.com. Had the computer really been that smart?

An hour later, she was staring at a birth certificate on the screen. He had been born in the village of Siegel in 1914.

When Anna found a photo of him, she had to sit right back in her seat. Blond, handsome, regular features. No wonder Nadja had fallen for him. Anna found his military records. He had served in the German army, yes, yes . . .

She clicked on marriages and deaths. Hans died in 1989. Aged seventy-five.

And he had left one son.

A Gabriel Kramer.

Anna searched Gabriel. Ten minutes later, she picked up the phone. And then put it back down. It was the middle of the night in Amsterdam. But the man she had found had to be Hans's son.

She switched off her computer and picked up her jacket, slinging it over her shoulder and turning off lights as she left the café. It had closed while she was shut away in her office—Cass was away, but her manager had popped her head in the door to say goodnight to Anna a while back.

Anna's mind was still reeling when she went to bed. Unable to sleep after tossing and turning for hours, she got up and went to her computer to read some more. Gabriel owned an art gallery in Amsterdam. He looked like his father and appeared to be around the right age for someone born in 1960. His bio said he had moved to the Netherlands from Berlin in the 1980s. Anna tried not to allow her thoughts to leap too far ahead. Instead, she focused on what she was going to ask him. How on earth was she going to explain what she wanted?

She had a pen in her mouth as she worked, and she sucked on the cold plastic tip. It was a terrible but lifelong habit. She smiled as she thought of Wil flipping his pen when he was thinking.

Wil. Several times, she had seen someone who reminded her of him on the street in San Francisco. A couple of times, she had looked inside BMWs similar to his to see if the driver was in fact him. It had become silly. But time and again, she had forced herself to push away thoughts of how he seemed perfect for her. How he listened, his sense of humor, the way he had helped her, his friends. But he hadn't been in touch. He was done. It had been a couple of months.

Anna turned back to her screen.

It was nearly three a.m. in San Francisco, but the gallery in Amsterdam would be open now. She had rehearsed a speech. She knew what to say. All she had to do was pick up the phone. Now.

"*Met* Gabriel Kramer."

Anna stood up and walked. She had researched this. *Met* meant "with"—you are speaking with. She had to announce herself now.

She stopped at her living room door. "Anna Young," she said. "I am calling from America. Do you speak English?"

"Yes," he said. Sounded casual. Sounded friendly enough.

Thoughts rushed into Anna's mind. He would think she wanted to buy a painting. How ridiculous. But logical. She shook the idea away.

Focus.

"Mr. Kramer—"

"Gabriel."

"Thank you. I. Look. I am calling about a personal matter."

"Oh?" Still he sounded relaxed.

"Okay. I'll introduce myself properly first." She had researched that this was an important part of Dutch etiquette. "My grandfather was Max Albrecht. I understand that your father, Hans Kramer, was his—"

"My father was his valet."

Silence down the phone line.

Anna had to sit down. She slumped into her favorite armchair. "Okay. Well. Look. This is a bit awkward, but I'm researching some family history. No. That's not it. I'm looking into why my grandfather never returned to Siegel after the war. He came to America and never went back. And I've done everything I can possibly think of, but I'm getting nowhere. I know it's a long shot, but I didn't know whether your father, Hans, may have said anything to you about Max. Whether he might have known him . . . well. At the time that he left everything behind. It was in 1940, I'm pretty sure of that."

"Anna," he said. "Look."

Anna could almost sense him thinking.

"I think we need to talk."

"Yes." Anna closed her eyes. The relief. She leaned back on her cushions and waited.

"Look, I think, if you have come this far, if you have found me, then, well. I think we need to talk this through together. I know this might be hard, but do you think you could come to Amsterdam and meet me in person? Are you based in the US?"

"Yes," Anna said again. She was exhausted,

but she would go to Mars if it meant she could put this to rest.

"Yes, you could come here? Because that would be best, I think, Anna," he went on.

"Tell me where you are." Anna stood up and swayed over to her neat kitchen bench. She picked up a pen.

Gabriel spoke quickly, giving her more contact details, and told her he would be available any time.

After Anna hung up, she went straight back to her desk and searched for flight times.

CHAPTER EIGHTEEN

Amsterdam, 2010

Anna had arranged to meet Gabriel on her first afternoon in Amsterdam. With a few hours to spare after she arrived, she decided to walk to pass the time. Each canal seemed to have a flavor all its own—drawing her in. The timeless city was laden with bikes and students and impossibly chic apartments, their uncurtained windows revealing funky designer interiors in charming old buildings that blended with all that was modern.

Anna made her way to Gabriel's gallery in plenty of time. When she pushed open the door to the space, he stood watching her from a desk at the back of the white-painted room. Anna looked around. A series of stunning portraits lined the walls, and the art was lit dramatically, throwing emphasis on certain features in the paintings. If she were here for different reasons, Anna would have loved to browse and have a better look.

"Mr. Kramer?" she asked.

He inclined his head.

"I'm Anna Young. I hope this is still a good time for you."

It was a few moments before he spoke. "I admit I've been thinking about your call ever since I hung up the phone." It struck Anna right now that his accent had a slight American nuance.

He looked almost incredulous to see her—as if she had appeared by magic in his gallery on Prinsengracht and was about to disappear like a rabbit back into a black top hat.

Anna looked openly at him too. She searched for any resemblance to Ingrid. But she couldn't see anything definite. There might have been something in the blue eyes, if Gabriel's were not so much warmer than Ingrid's. His gray hair, which she suspected had been blond once, was cut close to his head, and he wore a faded leather jacket over his black polo sweater.

"I was almost expecting you not to turn up," he said, unlocking a drawer under the counter and pulling out a leather wallet. "Let's go and get coffee. You have to try the best."

"Oh, believe me, I've done well with the coffee already." Anna laughed. "I can see that you Dutch know how to create a good blend."

"Wards off the jet lag?" Gabriel was pleasant, chatty.

Anna felt her shoulders relax. If she were a

betting girl, she would put a wager on Gabriel being a good talker.

"It's the only solution," Anna said.

He called out in Dutch to someone in a back room. A man's voice answered. Anna tried to focus on what she was going to say.

But as she walked with Gabriel along the narrow footpath, she found herself distracted by the late afternoon sun that was throwing pink light on the canal houses, the floating flower market replete with tulips, the mismatched rooftops, and the boats moored picturesquely in the canals.

She followed him as he pushed open a glass door into a café. The walls were lined with shelves stacked with vases and books and even lamps that were turned on, casting a warm glow throughout the room.

Once Gabriel had ordered coffee, he sat down opposite Anna and leaned his head in his hands.

"I'm sorry," Anna started. "Are you okay?"

"Yes, yes," he said. "It is just such a surprise seeing someone connected with my father."

Anna decided not to go into how recently she had learned of her connection. She waited for him to speak.

"Okay then," he said when the coffee arrived, along with two perfect-looking pieces of pie. The pastry was cut in a diamond pattern. "You

319

have to try this—our specialty—*vlaai*," he said. "The cherries in the center are local."

"Have you lived here all your life?" she asked, taking a bite of the sweet pie.

"My father came here after the war. He was looking for a place where he could . . . be himself."

"I see."

"How much do you know?" Gabriel asked.

Anna told him about Max and found out that Gabriel already knew about his half sister, Ingrid, but he had never sought contact with her. Anna told him all she knew about Nadja, and she talked about Ingrid's bitter-sounding views of the past. Anna told him that she didn't believe that this bitterness was entirely justified—that there must be more to the story, that Ingrid's view of Max didn't mesh with her own experience of him. That she wanted a more balanced understanding of what had happened.

Gabriel nodded. "I understand that. My father, Hans, was in and out of psychiatric institutions all his life. He never recovered from what happened in Paris. He was traumatized. I—"

Anna put her fork down and stared. "Paris?" she asked.

"You have come all this way, Anna. There's no point in keeping any of it a secret anymore."

Anna nodded. Finally, finally, was she about to hear the truth?

"It was clear that my father, Hans, was tormented by some secret," Gabriel said. "Eventually, one of the doctors got it out of him."

Anna leaned her chin on her hands.

"My father had worked for the Albrecht family since he was fourteen years old. Your grandfather, Max, and my father got along especially well. So he was promoted early—quite an achievement."

Anna nodded.

"Max was in love with a French girl before and during the war."

"I know. She lived in that apartment in Paris. But I don't know anything else about her."

"You have seen the news articles then?" Gabriel looked up all of a sudden. "Were they the catalyst for your search?"

"Max found them. His reaction to them made me curious. I couldn't rest until I had gotten to the bottom of it."

"Good timing, then."

"In some ways, not in others."

"That is often the way."

Anna waited.

"My father and your grandfather were both part of the German army that was involved in the occupation of Paris. You see, Anna, the Nazis were after the French girl's maid, first and foremost. The Nazis told Max and my father that the maid was a spy. They were ordered to kill the girl. And they were also told to kill Isabelle de Florian—the girl Max was going to marry—because she was harboring a spy."

Anna closed her eyes. She had to put her hands out on the table to steady herself.

"Are you all right?" Gabriel asked.

"Yes, sure."

"It was a test of Nazi loyalty. They knew everything—all about Max's love affair. That was why Max was sent on the mission, not anyone else. My father knew Isabelle too, of course. She had stayed at Schloss Siegel with them one Christmas. She was, he said, regarded as part of the family. Everyone expected Max and Isabelle to marry after the war. My father liked her. The entire situation was beyond anything we can imagine."

"Oh, help," Anna said. "Poor Max."

"Yes. It was, as I said, a test. How far would his loyalty to his country go? What would Max do in the name of Nazism? The expectation was that you pushed your own desires aside. The party came first. Germany came first. Nothing else mattered. You have to understand."

Anna nodded, but she was starting to feel ill. "Go on," she managed.

She was almost biting her bottom lip through.

"Max was ordered to take my father with him on the mission in Paris. It was the eve of the Nazi invasion. Both of them would recognize Isabelle from any distance. The Nazis knew that she had not left her apartment and that she was still in Paris that night. And the fact that the girls had not escaped Paris earlier was telling—it gave the Nazis even more ammunition. Were the maid and Isabelle planning on staying in Paris and making trouble? The Nazis could not tolerate spies. And the maid was a big suspect."

"But how could the maid have been a spy?" Anna had to ask the question.

"They were told she was helping a designated Nazi enemy," Gabriel said. "I imagine that was a convenient way of saying she had a friend who was an illegal immigrant, or Jewish. It happened all the time."

"Of course," Anna sighed.

"So, Max and Hans followed Isabelle and her maid as they dragged their suitcases through Paris on the night of June 11, 1940, when they were finally trying to escape.

"It was not until the girls turned into a quiet lane that they had the opportunity to kill them."

"But my grandfather . . ."

"Anna." Gabriel leaned forward. "Max had papers ready for Isabelle's escape."

Anna felt her breathing quicken. She looked up at the man sitting opposite her. Suddenly, he seemed weary—looked every one of his years, and more.

"It was my father who carried out the deed. It was Hans, the luckless valet, who shot Isabelle de Florian dead. My father had always been ambitious, had always tried to prove his worth. My father's loyalty to the Albrecht family was unwavering. It was his duty to protect Max, even if it meant acting against Max's will. My father felt Isabelle would be the death of Max, and were anything to happen to Max then he would have failed in his duty to protect him, and they'd both be shot for insubordination. No matter how much he admired Isabelle, he had to be loyal to Max. But I cannot tell you how tormented he was for the rest of his life."

Anna stayed silent, but her heart was beating loud enough to wake the dead.

"So. My father carried out the order. He shot Isabelle first, because she stepped out and called for Max. She had seen him. And it was that shout that stayed with my father forever."

"No."

Gabriel reached a hand out across the table. He rested it just near Anna's own.

"Max ran to Isabelle. He transferred the papers to Camille as they leaned over Isabelle's dying body. Hans had to hold off firing now that Max was in front of the maid. He couldn't get a clear shot without risking killing Max instead."

Anna nodded, but her breathing was shaky now.

"My father felt the most terrible guilt for years. It eroded him. Guilt can do that. He had killed an innocent young woman, a woman whom his employer loved, and whom he had liked, and for what? Isabelle de Florian probably did not even know of her maid's activities. The poor girl was probably only trying to escape. She was nothing but sweet, he said."

"God." Anna hardly heard her own voice.

"Max clearly couldn't trust Hans after what he had done. He couldn't take a chance on staying. He had no choice but to disappear. Max abandoned his uniform, which was found nearby. My father never knew where he went at the time.

"My father did say, though, that Max's parents pushed him into the Nazi party. They insisted he join to save the estate—to keep everyone safe. Max confided in my father about his terrible conflict at having to join the Nazis at all. They were close. Max had such grave doubts.

"Essentially, his family put him into a compromising position, which brought about the death of his true love. Perhaps he could never forgive them. Or perhaps he could simply never go back. I suspect the latter was the case. It was probably just all too much, and the years passed, making things harder. He probably knew that his parents were dead, and that his younger brothers had been killed. So there was only Nadja and my father, and my father had killed Isabelle."

Anna patted his hand where it rested on the table. The café had quieted. She needed some time to think.

"Thank you," she said. "Thank you so much, Gabriel."

"If you have anything you'd like to talk about, just let me know," Gabriel said. "I'm always here."

"Thank you."

"So you were close to your grandfather, to Max?" he asked.

"Yes," Anna said. "Yes. Very close."

"Would you like to take some time to yourself now?" he asked.

"I think so."

He walked her out of the café. She turned back to her hotel, dodging the bicycles and the tourists and the locals with bread under their arms as if they were some sort of haze. Not the real world.

She was in Paris. In that lane. How many times had Max revisited that time? What if Hitler hadn't taken charge of his country and wreaked havoc on the rest of the world, keeping Max from marrying his true love and spending his life on his beloved family property, as he was meant to?

Anna stopped on top of a bridge over the Herengracht canal. Max had been trying to tell her not to avoid things out of fear, not if they were right. But why, if it was so simple, was it also so impossibly hard to face her own feelings, her own fears? What did she really feel about Wil? And what was she going to do now about Siegel?

CHAPTER NINETEEN

Twenty-four hours later, Anna lugged her suitcase into Amsterdam's Schiphol Airport. She stood right inside the glass doors, her suitcase next to her, her passport in her wallet, her ticket home to San Francisco clasped tight in her hand.

She looked at the ticket. Turned it over. It was just something that she would take to a counter, hand to an airline attendant, exchange for a boarding pass. Get on the plane, go back home. Back to routine. The end.

But her heart ached for Max and Isabelle, and when she had walked back to her hotel the night before, every couple she had seen wandering through Amsterdam's narrow streets, holding hands on bridges, had brought her grandfather and the love that he had lost to her mind.

And Max had kept Isabelle, the memory of her, the love he had for the girl from the Paris apartment, entirely to himself. Perhaps there was a beauty in that.

It was time to go home.

Anna started dragging her suitcase across the hard tiles in the airport. She forced herself to focus on looking for the counter that had been

329

designated for her flight to LA. LA, then San Francisco. Home.

No.

Anna stopped and shook her head at her silly thoughts. She was being ridiculous. There was nothing she could do to save Schloss Siegel now. She could not, would not, go back and take on Nadja's daughter.

Anna could imagine the conversation. Ingrid was good at arguing. She was a hard-nosed businesswoman who was used to making tough decisions. Anyone who could leave a charming old estate like Siegel in disrepair for goodness knew what purpose, let alone not care how the villagers were living, was hardly going to view some love story in Paris as good reason to change her approach.

But then Anna stopped again. She was strong too. She had built up her own business just as Ingrid had, albeit on a smaller scale.

Why should she end what she was doing now, when she had hardly begun?

Schloss Siegel was part of Anna's history too. It wasn't only about Ingrid.

Anna looked at the ticket.

Then she walked in the opposite direction of where she had planned, instead heading to the counter where she could buy another ticket.

She was going to buy a ticket to her other home.

"I want to go to Berlin," she said to the operator sitting in front of her.

And the airline attendant did not question this. She simply tapped information into her computer and printed out a ticket.

Late afternoon light threw a golden blanket over Berlin. Anna felt more at home than ever before as the taxi moved through the bustling city. She gazed out at the Brandenburg Gate, standing there resolute in spite of everything that had happened at its feet.

It was, of course, a symbol of hope and freedom, freedom from the past. Freedom from divisiveness and hatred. And that was what Anna wanted to change. If she were honest with herself, she not only wanted to free Max's reputation—she also wanted to help her cousin. She wanted to help Ingrid see that it didn't have to be like this, that she didn't have to leave things rotting, and she did not have to blame or be bitter at all.

The task was not going to be easy, Anna granted herself that. But as she paid the taxi driver outside the hotel near Wil's house—the same one she had stayed in last time—she did not allow doubts to creep into her thoughts.

Once she had checked into the hotel and freshened up in her room, she headed outside. Then she dialed Ingrid's business number, which she had simply looked up on the Net, and walked like any other Berliner—with purpose, past the cafés and the boutiques, her eyes straight ahead, even though she was only going for a walk around the block.

After a few seconds, she was put through to Ingrid's phone.

"Anna," Ingrid said. She sounded matter-of-fact.

Anna would follow suit. "I hope you are well?" Anna asked.

"Yes."

Anna kept moving forward. "I was wondering if we could meet. I have something I need to run by you."

There was a pause before Ingrid spoke. "Anna, I am out at Siegel right now. Where are you?"

"Berlin." Anna paused for a moment.

"I will be out here for most of tomorrow," Ingrid said.

Anna stopped. "Then can I meet you there, at Siegel, tomorrow?"

The other woman waited a beat before she replied. "Very well. Yes. I have business to attend to here. But if you came at nine o'clock that would work."

Anna agreed. This suited her. She could do this. And what was more, she knew she could deal with Ingrid's businesslike approach.

The next morning, she focused on what she was going to say while she rode out to Siegel on the train. After she alighted at the tiny station, Anna began walking straight to the Schloss.

It was a glorious fall morning. She could hear birdsong in the now-amber trees. Anna marched past the empty buildings and put her phone to her ear.

"I am sitting outside on the terrace," Ingrid said. "I will be here when you arrive."

Anna thanked her. What an odd place to meet. Although being inside the house would hardly work, with its dust and lack of anything at all.

When Anna rounded the Schloss, having focused on her thoughts—not allowing herself to be distracted by the sight of the lake in the distance—she stopped dead on the spot.

The scene in front of her seemed surreal.

A round table covered in a red cloth had been placed in the middle of the terrace. Around it sat Ingrid and several men.

You wouldn't dare, Anna thought. Her insides turned hard.

"Anna," Ingrid said, standing up, extending a hand. "I would like you to meet Mr. Wong, Mr. Chen, and Mr. Li."

Anna stood, unmoving.

Ingrid indicated to Anna that she should sit down.

"Ingrid, can I speak to you privately, please?" Anna asked instead, not smiling at the businessmen but looking straight in her cousin's eye.

Ingrid adjusted her dark navy jacket. Her blond hair was swept into its usual bun. Her blue eyes glittered.

Game on, Anna thought.

She didn't move, didn't budge.

"Certainly." Ingrid smiled suddenly. "Gentlemen, I will be a few minutes. I will walk with my cousin down to the lake. I will leave you to chat."

Just then a uniformed waiter appeared, as if by magic, with a tray of coffee and patisseries. Visions of Schloss Beringer shot into Anna's head. Hideous carpets, a cold, formal hotel. Nasty food . . .

And who was going to stop it?

Anna held back the words that were fighting to be said.

Instead, she moved away from the group, toward the lake.

"Ingrid, I've been in Amsterdam."

"Oh?" The other woman walked alongside her. Her question sounded more like "so what?"

So she had no idea then. She didn't know anything about her half brother.

Anna stopped at the edge of the lake. She was staring directly at the tree under which she and Wil had sat and eaten their picnic. Picnics, and life and family and love, these were what this place needed.

Anna turned to her cousin. Ingrid seemed to be looking at the island too.

"What is going on?" she asked the older woman.

"I'm considering selling the Schloss," Ingrid said, her voice low. "I thought you would be pleased. They will develop it. I will get out. It will be saved after all, Anna."

Anna almost laughed, but she reined in the sad chuckle that was rising in her chest and took another tack. "What if they had all lived?" Anna asked, her words coming out soft. "What do you think they would have wanted?"

"Who?" Ingrid snapped. "What?"

"Didi, Jo . . . Isabelle," Anna answered.

"If you are referring to that woman with whom Max had an affair—" Ingrid said.

"It wasn't an affair," Anna said. "She and Max were going to get married. Spend their lives together." Anna didn't alter her tone. She decided that it was best to simply go on. "But Isabelle was shot. Max was ordered to kill her by the Nazis, because they suspected her maid was a spy, but he couldn't do it. He couldn't kill the woman he loved."

Ingrid looked straight at her, her eyes two infernos.

Anna did not take a step back. "Max was forced to join the Nazi party by his parents, by your grandparents. He was trying to do the right thing by his family, the village. Germany. Always. But when he was ordered to kill the girl he loved, he

335

couldn't do it, so someone else did. Someone who, in turn, had always had a duty to protect Max and his family, and the estate, and the village, from the time he worked here at Siegel, to the time he accompanied Max into the war. He was trained to obey and to look after Max at any cost. So, you see—"

"No!"

Anna had been expecting this, but as Ingrid's voice shot out into the clear, fresh air, she turned in alarm to the men sitting on the terrace. They had all turned too and were facing them.

Ingrid was storming back toward the house.

"Wait!" Anna clutched at her cousin, tugged at the woman's arm.

"Why should I listen to you?" Ingrid growled. They were halfway up the lawn. "How dare you."

"Stop," Anna whispered, and she pulled out the tiny box that she had in her pocket.

Ingrid stopped then, stared down at the old velvet. Her eyes, which had blazed with the fire of lost generations a few seconds ago, now flicked around as if looking for solace. If Anna were a betting girl, she would say Ingrid was fighting angry tears.

"This was their engagement ring. Max had hidden it in the Schloss. It was what he asked me to retrieve just before he died. It was the sole reason that he asked me to come back here, and he said that losing Isabelle was the greatest regret of his life. He never talked about it again until he was ninety-four years old."

Ingrid reached out a manicured hand, took the box, pulled out the ring, and turned it over in her fingers.

"Why should I believe you?" Her voice filled with bitterness again. She handed back the ring.

The older woman marched toward the terrace.

Anna followed her until they were just at its edge.

Ingrid was moving back to her businessmen. But just before she reached them, she turned to Anna, her voice like a steel beam. "I have decided. It is best to let go of the past. I will continue my meeting. Thank you. That is all."

"Ingrid—" Anna started.

Ingrid just stared at her, as if challenging her to say one more word.

"I'm sorry about this," Anna said to the men, who had all turned and were staring at her as if she were some mad . . . relative. Well. So be it.

"Ingrid," she said, "you told me that family meant nothing. You told me that there was only work. But you have family."

"Don't be ridiculous."

"No, you have a half brother. Gabriel. In Amsterdam. He is Hans Kramer's son, just as you are his daughter."

Ingrid did not move.

One of the men coughed.

"And you have me," Anna said, keeping her words at a steady pace. "And I have no one else really, either, you know. Now that Max is gone. It's all come down to me too, you know, just as it has to you. But I'm here and I want to . . . know you."

Ingrid turned back to her businessmen again.

One of them stood up.

"Excuse me," he said.

The others followed suit.

But Ingrid turned back to Anna. "You expect me to accept you and my half brother as family? Now?"

"Yes," Anna said simply. "Because that's what we are."

The men slipped out of sight toward a van that was parked on the driveway. Anna hadn't noticed it until now. "I think we will leave you, Frau Hermann," one of the men said.

"I will be done in a minute," Ingrid muttered, but they all walked off.

Anna took a step toward her cousin. "I know this is hard," she said. "You, me, Max, Nadja. Their younger brothers killed. And your father, cast out when he should have been included."

Ingrid still stayed silent.

"But you see, one thing remains," Anna went on. "Schloss Siegel. And you have a choice. You know what I want to do. And I'm prepared to work with you."

The older woman stood there, her body rigid.

Anna did not move an inch. "You have saved it so far. You haven't let it be destroyed. I think you've waited. And that's something, you know. You haven't given up."

Ingrid folded her arms and stared out at the park.

The sun brightened just then, throwing warmth onto the old terrace, sending light onto the lake. And Anna pictured parties, and boat rides, and parasols, and people—a family—having tea outside here in the sun, while children ran down through the old garden to the water. And aunts visited, and cousins played, and people from Amsterdam, or America, or from wherever the family had spread came here too, came at Christmas, and the house by the lake was alive once more.

That was her dream.

"You can do it. And I can do it with you," Anna said.

"But who will live here?" Ingrid asked, her blue eyes hitting Anna's with some indefinable emotion now. Was it the recognition that comes from family, or from love?

"I don't know who'll live here," Anna said. "We have to take chances, restore things to what they are meant to be, and then who knows what will happen."

Ingrid stared out at the water for a moment. A

bird called a long, sharp note through the quiet.

And then the older woman's shoulders dropped. And her face cleared. And she looked beautiful now.

"We would have a big job, you and I," she said, still staring straight ahead. "And you have your life in San Francisco."

"I could renovate a small apartment in the Schloss, stay here, supervise it all. I need a project. My business can take care of itself for a while."

"We would have to work very carefully. It would have to be done with taste."

"Yes."

"Then," Ingrid said, "I think we had better get to work."

CHAPTER TWENTY

Anna stretched on the bed in the hotel room. Automatically, she reached for her phone. It was the first thing she did each morning, checking if there was anything from the café. But this morning, there was a different sort of message.

A message from Ingrid. Having returned to Ingrid's office in the van with the disappointed businessmen, she and her cousin had stayed talking in Ingrid's office like a couple of schoolgirls until late. Making plans, looking at maps of Siegel.

But now, Anna frowned and put the phone on speaker. Ingrid's voice rang through the room. "I can't believe I forgot to tell you. I am sorry, Anna. But the thing is, it's my lawyer. He seemed to be . . . on your side."

Anna sat up in bed. All her senses were on full alert. "You see, the last time we met, Wil Jager arrived with all these letters. From the villagers at Siegel. He had been back there, spoken to them all, and had convinced them to write to me, telling me why their village should be saved. Why I should save the Schloss.

Why I should trust you to handle it all for me."

Anna felt her lips twitch into a smile. A warmth ran through her body.

"I thought I should let you know. You might want to thank him. It did . . . have a bearing on my decision yesterday."

Anna hung up the phone, swept her knees over the side of her bed, and stood up. She walked to the bathroom, but she felt as if she were gliding or flying there instead.

What did that mean? It was typical of Wil, of course it was, to do something like that and not tell her, not take any credit.

She stood under the shower, letting the hot water run over her shoulders and down her back. Dressed, sprayed on some perfume, did her makeup. Went down to breakfast. Once she had eaten and was back in her room, she picked up her phone. Then put it down.

Instead, she opened her bag and pulled out the thing, the thing that she had wanted all along and that she finally had. And she walked out of the room.

It was still so, so early. Surely Wil wouldn't have gone to work just yet. Anna had woken before dawn after only a few hours of dashed, harried sleep. She was too excited to rest at all.

She took a taxi straight to his house. It was only just seven. Surely he would be there.

The newspaper was still on his front lawn, wet with dewdrops that lingered on its clear plastic wrap. Anna picked it up for him.

And rang the bell.

Footsteps sounded inside. Wil opened the door, dressed in his suit trousers and a shirt with the top button undone. "Anna!" he said. "My God. Okay. Of course you're here on my doorstep. Good to see you!" He leaned forward and enveloped her in a hug, but then stood back a little awkwardly.

"Can I come in, just for a moment?" Anna smiled.

"Sure, sure," he said. "Early—Anna."

"I know," Anna said. She followed him through to the kitchen.

"Coffee?" he asked.

"Thank you."

He turned to the machine.

"Shall I get the cups?" Anna asked, suddenly wanting to not just stand there, useless.

"Great," he said. "That cupboard."

Anna moved across to the cupboard, which was high above the bench. She opened it and heard him moving closer toward her. He was standing behind her, his voice soft in her ear. "Those ones," he said, reaching behind her, his hands touching hers, as he showed her which to use.

"Okay," she said, turning. But he hadn't moved, was still there.

He looked down at her, and something kindled in his green eyes. She had seen that before. It relaxed her and excited her and she could hardly breathe. Could she think?

"Why are you back?" he asked, his voice suddenly quiet.

"To say thank you." She smiled, but her voice was only a whisper.

He reached out to stroke her hair.

She reached in her pocket, took the key to the old palace out, and held it between them. "It was what I came to ask you for, but now I want to give it to you instead, because you are welcome to visit me there anytime," she said, her eyes locked with his. She didn't want to turn away. "Ingrid and I, we have come to an agreement, if you can believe it."

Wil looked down at the old key and gently took it out of Anna's hand. He returned his eyes to hers. "I know. Ingrid called me last night. I had to deal with a bevy of disappointed businessmen. It was up to me to entertain them last night."

"Oh." Anna felt herself giggling.

"This key is going to open up all sorts of possibilities," Wil said, bringing her hand up to his lips. "You know, Anna, you've helped me realize that there is something that is more important than everything else in this life."

Anna smiled up at him. She was ready. It was time. He leaned down toward her, his lips touching hers with a first featherlike kiss. She closed her eyes, but she didn't have to dream anymore.

AUTHOR'S NOTE

This book was inspired by two true stories that are woven together to form this fictional story surrounding Isabelle and Max, and Anna and Wil.

As many readers will know, an apartment was abandoned in Paris for seventy years after the owner, a Mme de Florian, fled on the eve of the Nazi invasion. While there was nothing unusual about the fact that the owner left her home in Paris, the legacy she left behind was an extraordinary find and has captivated the world since its discovery in 2010.

Mme de Florian's apartment was a treasure trove. The apartment turned out to have belonged to Mme de Florian's grandmother, the famous 1890s Belle Époque actress and courtesan Marthe de Florian. Marthe had entertained an astonishing list of gentlemen clients in the apartment, including prime ministers of France, powerful businessmen, and members of the English aristocracy.

All of this was revealed in love letters that were found in the apartment by the executors of her estate, one of whom described the experience of walking into Marthe's locked-up apartment as like entering Sleeping Beauty's castle.

The story—along with several haunting images of the rooms—was picked up by international newspapers and bloggers alike, and it went viral.

But perhaps what was most extraordinary was that a painting found on the wall of the apartment turned out to be the work of the most famous portrait painter of Paris's Belle Époque—the Italian artist Giovanni Boldini. The portrait of Marthe sold at auction for a record 2.1 million euros, with several bidders all wanting to pay the price for love.

Apart from these few things that we know about Marthe, all the characters and the story contained in *Paris Time Capsule* and *The House by the Lake* are fictional and entirely a product of my own imagination.

Schloss Siegel is also inspired by a true story. I have a friend who has a photograph on her wall. Every time I walk into her house, I am drawn to it and stand there, drinking in the details of what was clearly a beautiful old palace. But the more I looked at the photograph, the more I noticed that something was not quite right; the walls were pockmarked and the garden was in a state of despair, but there was also beauty—inherent, aching beauty. A mystery, then?

So I read my friend's mother's memoir, *I Close My Eyes and Dream*, in which Isa Mitchell describes with great clarity her childhood memories of growing up in her family Schloss just outside Berlin during the 1930s, before the family was forced to leave their home right before the Soviets came through.

But again, I have to emphasize that the characters in the Berlin part of the story are entirely of my own invention and bear no resemblance to anyone, living or dead. Max's struggles with Nazism were inspired by my own travels to Berlin and have nothing to do with any of the family that lived in Isa's real Schloss until they had to flee in 1945.

ACKNOWLEDGMENTS

I am incredibly fortunate to have wonderful people around me, and without them, this book would not exist. Thanks to Jodi Warshaw, my editor at Lake Union Publishing—I have been lucky to work with you. We share the same creative vision and I appreciate your calm and thoughtful approach—the process is seamless. Thanks to my editor Christina Henry de Tessan. I adore working with you. I was thrilled that you were able to work with me again on *The House by the Lake*. Thanks to Gabriella Dumpit, my wonderful, always-there author relations manager, to my marketing manager, Tyler Stoops for all your support, and to Brent Fattore, my production manager for coordinating the entire process.

My appreciation to Shasti O'Leary-Soudant for designing a beautiful cover that reflects this grand old Schloss to perfection, to Amanda Gibson for such thorough, careful copyediting, and to Ramona Gault for proofreading the novel.

To my agent, Peter Giagni—you are a great mentor, with an innate understanding of story that I admire and respect. To my marketing manager,

Tracy Balsz—I benefit enormously from having you around—you have, quite simply, the best ideas. Thank you to Nas Dean for your ongoing virtual assistance and for organizing things for me.

Thanks to my friend Denita Mitchell for allowing me to read the memoir of her late mother, Isa Mitchell, about her childhood in Germany during the 1930s. Denita, your mother's story resonated with me so very much—and as for the images of your old family Schloss, they move me every time I see them. I simply had to write this book.

I cannot thank several of my closest friends enough for their support over the past year, and I cannot say how much it means to have had you around—Kelli Jones, Melanie Milburne, and Fiona Calvert. Thanks to my friend Miriam Connor for reading my work before it is sent off—I appreciate you so much. Thank you to all my other friends—you know who you are. Particular thanks to Alison Imbriotis, Jo Carnaby, and Tracey Walls for helping out with my children when I have needed to travel for my work.

Thank you to Harry and Val Stanton for all your support during the past year. Thanks to Jasmin Emerson and Craig Keane—you both go way above and beyond for me. And thank you to Frances di Giovanni for your excellent advice.

Thanks to the bloggers who have reviewed *Paris Time Capsule*, to the lovely readers, each and every one of you, with particular thanks to the lovely Helen Sibritt. Thanks in particular to those readers who have contacted me, often telling me their own personal stories. I read all your messages, even if it takes me a while to reply. I love hearing all your thoughts.

Thank you to Margie Lawson. Catching up with you was a treat. I look forward to working with you again in the future.

To my sister, Jane—you are an inspiration. Thank you.

Most importantly, huge thanks to Ben and Sophie, for allowing me the time and space to write—it's all for you. It always will be.

ABOUT THE AUTHOR

Ella Carey is a writer and Francophile who claims Paris as her second home. Her first book is *Paris Time Capsule*, and her work has been published in the *Review of Australian Fiction*. She lives in Australia with her two children and two Italian greyhounds.

Center Point Large Print
600 Brooks Road / PO Box 1
Thorndike, ME 04986-0001 USA

(207) 568-3717

US & Canada:
1 800 929-9108
www.centerpointlargeprint.com